Gospel of the Feathered Serpent

By

Stanley Struble

Feathered Serpent Press

ISBN: 978-1-7345949-1-1

PUBLISHED BY Feathered Serpent Press

Printed in the United States of America

Gospel of the Feathered Serpent is printed in Palatino Linotype

With Great Appreciation

Like all my stories, "Gospel" would not have been completed without the advice and assistance of many people. Foremost among these is Valerie, my wife of 32 years. Her intellect, encouragement, and ideas have always sustained me when I doubted myself. She labored tirelessly on this book to ensure that each sentence and idea followed in logical sequence. Fellow mensan, Jim Bunstock, proofed the original manuscript and designed the book cover. Harriet Ottenheimer, Professor Emeritus of Anthropology at Kansas State University read a first draft and offered very helpful assistance.

Thanks, Thanks!

The Gonzalez - Corso family of Guadalajara, Mexico are very special people. I want to thank them for their friendship and hospitality over the years, and for politely suffering my "gringo" ways and wretched Spanish on so many occasions. Your friendship is a treasure.

Thanks Especially

To those readers of mine who enjoy the unusual story set in exotic places and who have read one or more of my three early novels – thank you for your time and interest. All writers want to be read. Finding people that enjoy the uncommon story in very different settings is always a blessing.

Praise for Gospel of the Feathered Serpent

"Struble does it again with unexpected new twists on a classic theme. Archaeology and ancient religion are intertwined with corruption and contemporary politics in this compelling page-turner."
— **Dr. Harriet Ottenheimer**, Professor of Anthropology, Kansas State University

"It's here…another Struble mystery! **Gospel of the Feathered Serpent** *is a whirlwind of excitement and an enticing mystery for those who don't like mysteries and religion. When Christianity's long lost, sacred objects appear unexpectedly in the ruins of a Catholic church in southern Mexico, the great religions of the world contest to own them. Struble's page-turner and prose and plotting will keep you reading late into the night."*
—**Dr. Lew Hunter**, Chair Emeritus, UCLA Screenwriting School

"Full of fascinating historical details, vivid descriptions and enough plot twists to keep everyone satisfied, Stan Struble's new book, **Gospel of the Feathered Serpent** *is a welcome addition to the niche of archaeological thrillers that Struble has carved out for himself."*
—**Hugh Reilly**, Director UNO School of Communication and author of *Bound to Have Blood.*

Quotes

On May 16, 2013, Pope Francis reminded new ambassadors at the Vatican that he: *"loves everyone, rich and poor alike, but the Pope has the duty, in Christ's name, to remind the rich to help the poor, to respect them, to promote them."*
—Pope Francis

"Being unwanted, unloved, uncared for, forgotten by everybody, I think that is a much greater hunger, a much greater poverty than the person who has nothing to eat."
—Mother Teresa

"Wars of nations are fought to change maps. But wars of poverty are fought to map change."
—Muhammad Ali

Gospel of the Feathered Serpent

by

Stanley Struble

PROLOGUE

Far below the cliff on which the bearded man stood, foaming Mediterranean waves dashed against barnacle-covered boulders. The girl at his side, delighting in the play of the waters, cried out when splashed by salt spray.

Joseph of Arimathea—gray-robed, sandaled, and large of stature—smiled at his charge. "Careful not to fall."

She crept closer to the edge, daring the waves to chase her away.

"There." He pointed. "You can see it now."

"Is it a Roman ship?" She peered toward the horizon where her uncle gestured.

"No. See the sails and prow? It's from the East, Tyre most likely, maybe even Carthage."

"Egypt?" she asked thoughtfully. She'd heard many stories of pagan Egypt, of enormous temples called pyramids, a huge god called the Sphinx that was part lion and part human, and odd tales of fertility rites beyond her preadolescent understanding.

Her face and arms shone tawny brown. She had white, straight teeth, and her long, dark hair was tied back in the custom of southern Gaul. Brown eyes under black eyebrows peered into the distance.

As Joseph watched, she crossed her arms and struck a serious reflective pose. When she pursed her lips, her expression was contemplative and inward-looking. That look and her posture were familiar, reminding him of the man he felt certain was the child's father. She sensed change, and, like all children, didn't like it.

Ever since her infancy, a steady stream of travelers, mysterious to the girl, came and went from the home in the foothills of the Pyrenees. They told of events in distant places she'd never seen. The name Jesus of Nazareth came from their lips in a language she barely spoke. She heard that name repeatedly, always uttered with awe.

Joseph observed the child while the guests talked late into the night. Although fascinated, she didn't understand the strangers' stories. How could she? None of them had anything to do with her or how she and her family lived. She didn't know that before leaving Palestine, Joseph turned his considerable holdings into cash.

She was born in Gaul, in their large country village in the foothills that her "uncle" purchased. She always lived within walking distance of a town that held her mother, Mary Magdalene, in high esteem, and expressed curiosity about the reclusive Uncle Joseph, who spent much time praying and very little time working.

"The ship will dock soon," he said. "Return to the inn and tell Mary that the Doubter will arrive soon. I'll bring him along shortly."

"The who?"

"Er…Thomas. Tell her that Thomas has arrived. Pray to God he's healthy. Off with you, Child."

She backed away two steps, then asked rapidly, "Is he Jewish like us? Will he tell me about my father?"

"Oh, well, yes. He's a bit strange, but, yes, he'll talk to you. Maybe he knows something, maybe not. Get on with you now. I mean it." He shooed her away.

Stealing a last glance at the turquoise sea, she turned and shuffled down the rocky path toward the seaside village.

Joseph watched her lithe figure glide around the bend. *Walks like her father, looks like her mother,* he thought.

The old man scratched his beard absently, sighed, and turned to watch the ship reef its sails as it neared. The child bothered him. The woman from Magdalene disturbed him even more. Nowadays, she spent all her time praying and meditating in a nearby cave. Why she chose that spot to find solace and seek a spiritual connection with Jesus was beyond his understanding.

When Joseph attempted to talk with her about her motivation for praying in the cave, she shut him out. He wondered about her special relationship with Jesus, and such speculation left him desperate to understand it. Who was the child's father? Why wouldn't she say? What would become of them?

Strange stories were the norm after Jesus' death. The yoke of Rome lay heavily on Jerusalem's neck, and Palestine was no longer a safe place to live, but was any place safe? The southern coast of Gaul, surprisingly, offered the best combination of stability with its distance from the chaos of Jewish zealotry and Roman imperialism.

As he promised, Joseph sold his home and businesses and spirited Mary Magdalene away to safety, but now what? Thirteen years passed, and the second coming of the true Christ hadn't occurred as everyone believed. He promised to return, but how much longer would He delay before redeeming His followers? That He would, Joseph didn't doubt, but when?

Lately, Joseph heard tales he knew were fictitious—fantastic renditions of Jesus' feats. New miracles and stories were attributed to Him, which Joseph had never heard before, though they were discussed as if witnessed by all. Places, events, and things Jesus allegedly said and did were spun into a cloth He never would have recognized and probably would have refused to wear.

There was even a man named Paul, whom Joseph never met, who traveled the world claiming to know Christ's mind, Jesus' nature. The man said he preached what the Lord said and meant. It was incredible. How could he know? How could anyone remember it all? And the man had never seen Jesus!

Joseph's flight from Judea and search of anonymity in Gaul lasted only a few years. How had anyone found them in such a large world? Who revealed his whereabouts? Was it a slip of the tongue, or had someone deliberately betrayed them? If so, why?

His mouth set in a tight line. The old question didn't seem important any longer. What was done was done. It must be part of a divine plan. As Jesus repeatedly said, "Only the pursuit of the Kingdom of God here on earth remains important."

As he turned away from the sea, inchoate excitement stirred within. Thomas thought unlike the others. He was the disciple with the inquiring mind—bold, educated, curious, and always posing questions. Thomas' relationship with Jesus was always problematic. The man operated with a reluctant compass in his head.

Doubter was a misnomer, though. Joseph remembered Thomas was always very doubtful, though he always asked questions and was anxious to learn all their Lord could teach.

Teach Jesus had. He led them away from the tyranny of thousand-year-old scriptures to the essential truths gleaned from the Essene community in the desert. Their "Teacher of Righteousness," their founder, was a brilliant man. Jesus studied his writings and teachings with His blessed insight into all things and without the hidebound approach of the Jewish priests obsessed with ritual, bathing purification, and dogma. Jesus gleaned simple, uncomplicated truths from the scriptures, and, with God's guidance, reinterpreted and presented them to anyone in Palestine who would listen. Many had, knowing the truth when they heard it, but truth was sometimes uncomfortable. It ultimately destroyed Him when the elders and priests in the temple turned on Him.

The old man's mind brimmed with curiosity as it returned to the imminent arrival of his old friend. What had Thomas seen and done these last thirteen years? What countries had he traveled? What news did he bring from Jerusalem? Had Judea revolted?

Deep in thought, Joseph carefully navigated the well-worn, stony path. Although he fulfilled his promises, many decisions remained unresolved. He hoped Thomas would help. Joseph could use him as a sounding board for his ideas. Thomas would have his own opinion on what to do with the cup, the girl, and Mary Magdalene. He would help Joseph sort it out and perhaps affirm his decision to leave Gaul.

Joseph slowed his pace, content to pause and consider the issues. Half an hour later, he reached the valley floor and began his trek to the small harbor. A large smile graced his face. A very special friend had come from the old country to visit. It was a joy, a wonderful gift God brought that day.

Thank You, Lord, he prayed. *Thank You for Your many gifts.*

* * *

The pungent odor of burning whale oil permeated the gloom. An oil lamp on the table and two candles provided the room's only light.

"Off to bed, Child," Joseph said. "Is there no end to your questions?"

"Let her stay, Joseph," Thomas urged. "She's nearly a grown woman."

"Nay. We have much to discuss she has no need to hear." He turned to the child. "Thank your Uncle Thomas for the gift, then go with your mother and say your prayers."

"But I want to…."

"No buts, Child. Embrace us before you leave. You can begin your questions anew tomorrow."

Pained by the dismissal, she hugged both men and thanked her new uncle for the string toy he brought all the way from

Syria. With flickering shadows dancing like wraiths on the wall, Mary and her daughter disappeared into the back of the spacious home.

"The child does not yet know her father?" Thomas asked.

"None of us do, really. Mary won't say," Joseph replied guardedly.

"Did she prostitute herself?"

Joseph's eyebrows arched, then he frowned. "You know better than that. That's jealousy speaking."

Thomas' head dipped momentarily. "I never knew what He saw in her. She was always a little too self-assured for me, a little too smart for a woman."

Joseph of Arimathea extended a wine flask to his friend. "She's definitely her own person. She's quite devout, actually. I envy her and wonder what truths Jesus shared with her.

Certainly, they had…a special relationship."

"So the child is actually…?"

"Leave it, Thomas," he said quickly, pouring wine into the younger man's goblet. "Your speculations are of no value. If she

is as you think, it's part of a divine plan."

"But this child might be…."

"It's of no benefit to the child to know at this point. Mary will tell her if and when she's ready."

Thomas, staring into the lamp's flame as if searching for answers, shook his head ruefully. "Jesus taught us so much and left us knowing so little."

Thomas stood and walked to the room's only shelf, briefly touching a basket, a ceramic cup, and a plate. "These were our Lord's."

"You won't return to India." Joseph changed the subject.

"No. I'm going west."

"West? Where?" Joseph scratched his beard. "There's little west but Iberia and the Great Water."

"Atlantis."

"Eh? Where?"

"Atlantis. West of the peninsula. It's there, Joseph. Homer, the Greek historian, wrote of it, and so did…."

"Greeks are sodomites, and Homer was a liar! Glorifying their history as if they invented everything. Fools and liars. You must have a death wish to pursue such a ridiculous plan. You'll fall off the end of the world. Why not stay with us? I have the cup, and you have your writings, your history of our time with Jesus. You walked the same path He traveled as a young man. You're the most learned of us and the best writer. We could spread His message together, maybe start a church and begin converting the heathens. Maybe we should go to Britain."

"Not likely. Rome is everywhere. The new emperor, Claudius, will soon be in Britain. I want to go where Rome is but a myth and people are ripe for Christ's word."

"But why Atlantis, even if it exists?"

"It exists. I believe it was settled by the tribe of Benjamin. They're outcasts like us and will recognize the truth when they hear it."

"You have evidence of this?" Joseph scoffed. Two thousand years earlier, after engaging the other tribes of Israel in war, the tribe of Benjamin was defeated, exiled, and scattered to unknown places.

"I've prayed long and studied much these thirteen years." He gestured toward his sack of belongings. "I wrote a short narrative of my travels through Persia and India. I believe I traveled the same path He did. I visited every town, lake, site, and holy man He did, and I wrote my impressions of Jesus during my time with Him in Palestine."

"You'll die at sea," Joseph said without emotion. "Your plan is crazy."

"What of your plan, Old Friend? Why stay here with Mary Magdalene and not return to Jerusalem?"

"She refuses." He raised his hands palms-up in resignation. "She won't say why, just that she believes God wants her to stay and raise her daughter where no one knows who she is. She feels safe here after the craziness of Israel."

Joseph, staring at the flickering candle, collected his thoughts. "I, too, have prayed for guidance. I have the cup. People are starting to come, to ask for it. I had to put distance between myself and Judea."

"Bury it."

"Out of the question."

"Why?"

"It seems wrong somehow. I can't explain it. I must keep it safe until…." His voice trailed off.

"Until what?"

"I don't know, Thomas. I know only that it's special.

Someday, others can sort it out if Jesus doesn't return soon. Until then, it's my charge, and I'll do everything I can to protect it."

"Send it with me." Thomas picked up the cup.

"I can't give it to you."

"You should. As soon as you become too noticeable in Gaul, Rome will end your work here as they did in Judea. They'll take the cup and kill you. You know this, Joseph."

Joseph of Arimathea met Thomas' gaze, holding it for a long time before looking away and burying his head in his hands.

"Please," Thomas asked, "won't your share our Lord's blood and break bread with me one last time?"

"You talk as if you'll never return."

"I leave in two days. The ship's captain is from Tyre, and his family is descended from Phoenicians. He's a brave man who listens to my stories of Jesus. My heart and prayers have always led me on paths apart from others, Joseph. You know that. Unlike you, I don't believe our Lord is returning soon. There's much work to do, and I believe He wants us to spread his message of love and brotherhood, so I must make this journey. I feel it strongly."

They broke bread and shared the cup.

The man from Arimathea looked long at his friend. In the dim light, they joined hands across the table, smiling in a moment of friendship and sadness, succumbing to the melancholy of memory.

Thomas, reaching into his satchel, extracted a scroll. "Here, my friend. I made a copy of my journey and my impressions of Jesus' teachings." He placed it into Joseph's hands, as his tears fell onto the scroll.

The old man cradled it against his breast. "This is a great treasure."

They conversed long into the night, talking of the insurrection in Palestine and the temple's destruction. Finally, as the cock heralded the new day, and the conversation reduced to a trickle, Joseph led his guest toward a bedroom in the back of the house.

Halfway there, they paused and looked outside at the soft light leaking over the hilly, eastern horizon.

After a companionable silence, Joseph turned to Thomas. "Wait here, old friend. I changed my mind. I have some special things for you. They will give you much to think about during your long journey."

CHAPTER ONE

Professor David Wolf, an archeologist on sabbatical from Mexico's National University, UNAM, sat at the desk in his bedroom. Mesoamerican archaeology was his passion, and he was a leader in his field. A small lamp cast a beam of light across a desk strewn with a myriad of papers, maps, drawings, books, magazines, and a half-empty bottle of Fundador brandy and two glasses.

Alexandra, his wife, slept restlessly in their bed near the window. A low moan escaped her lips, and she jerked. Turning to make sure she was all right, he wondered what she dreamed. It was June in Chiapas State in southern Mexico, and the light of a full moon cast a ghostly, pale glow through the window and across the bed, revealing her bare shoulders, neck, and tousled hair. It was a warm night, and her sleepwear was light and revealing. She slept fitfully, as if worry was her bed companion, though she tried to ignore it.

He sighed, leaned back into the overstuffed chair, and placed his arms on the arm rests. Yawning, he frowned and glanced at his wristwatch. It was nearly two o'clock, yet he had accomplished little. The project wasn't coming together. In the last thirty-five years, he participated in or led more excavations than he could count. The others were easy, but the present one was difficult all the way.

Fatigued, he glanced at the bed, tempted to join Alexandra, to feel cozy, comfortable, and his mind at ease. Instead, he obsessed over small details of the excavation that kept distracting him from the big picture. He couldn't shake the feeling he was missing something very important, and he should know what it was.

The team acquired volumes of raw data, but no one could place it into a framework to determine or infer a chronology. It wasn't telling a coherent story. So much appeared unrelated or pointed enticingly in other directions, especially the caves or pseudocaves. Those manmade holes were everywhere in the hills and mountainsides up and down the floor and walls of Council Valley. The more the team looked, the more they found.

What did they mean? How did they fit into the cultural/religious fabric of that proto-Mayan culture? The main cave, Xibalba, was definitely the site's centerpiece. It alone would require years of painstaking labor to excavate and even longer to interpret the data. They found fascinating objects from several distinct cultural groups, all dating within the same time span of 1,000 years. Were the dates anomalies, or had the cave been inhabited at least three different times for periods of several hundred years?

The enormous challenges the evidence presented would require slowing down to perform good detective work and creative thinking. He vacillated, agonizing over which direction to move the project. The situation created friction with his excavation leader, Karen Dumas, a young archeologist from the United States, who was totally focused on completing the work.

Karen proved to be determined and very capable, but David was beginning to wonder if she had the imagination or creativity to step outside the working frame of reference and approach the data from another perspective. That damned Zapatista, Marcos, hovered around, distracting her. That was no help at all.

He chastised himself for being so critical. In all fairness, Karen did what David asked. Her duties included making sure the excavation was carried out and completed by the book, supervising the native Indian workers, and overseeing the myriad functions of an archeological excavation. It was a big job, but professionalism and accuracy were paramount.

Meanwhile, David, who supervised the work of many excavations around the country, was perhaps too busy. He needed to spend more time with Karen to place their preliminary data in a neat, orderly form for publication. Blowing into town for a few days sometimes created more problems than it solved. When he arrived two days earlier, her reception was almost frosty, interspersed with occasional sarcasm. He let it pass, knowing from experience that working in the tropics for months at a time without the civilized accoutrements of running water, sewage disposal, and home cooked food could make people behave in unusual ways.

"David," Alexandra called from the bed.

Turning, he saw her sitting up, her nightgown top off one shoulder, exposing her breast. She ran a hand through dark hair streaked with gray, yawned, and gave him a sleepy smile. She blinked and rubbed her eyes, while he marveled at how ageless she appeared. Except for the gray, she didn't look a day over thirty-five. How did she do it?

"Turn out that light and come to be, *Querido*. I can't sleep with you rattling your papers and clunking your glass on the desk. You didn't drink too much brandy again, did you?"

"You know I don't drink too much, Ale. I was just looking over some data from the dig, and…."

"Shhh." Her finger went to her mouth, and she smiled, pulling her flimsy nightgown over her head. "It's hot in here, and I'm having trouble sleeping."

"I can help with that."

Moonlit shadows on her bare torso made him catch his breath. Standing abruptly, he walked to the bathroom.

"Let me brush my teeth, and I'll be back in a jiffy. I think a good back rub would help you sleep, Ale." "You think so?" she murmured.

"I'm sure of it. First, I'll rub your back, then your front, then…."

"I'm wide awake now. Maybe I should just go sort laundry."

"That's what the maid's for. Just relax. I'm almost there."

He hurried into the bathroom, brushed his teeth, and undressed. Donning a robe, he turned off the light and left the room for the bedroom.

She lay quietly with her eyes closed, the moon casting a beam of translucent light over the bed and her bare shoulders and dark curly hair. He leaned down to stroke her cheek.

"Ale, are you…?"

When she reached for him, the covers fell away. "Come to bed, Old Man. I can't wait forever for you to say good night to me."

"I'm not here to say good night, Ale." He slid in beside her as she made room. "I'm here to ensure you don't have nightmares and don't dream of younger men."

She laughed. "Young men are dumb." She rolled over and exposed her back. "Think you can help me sleep, huh?"

"I'm sure of it." He savored the languid curves of her body, and a familiar sense of urgency rippled through him. He rose and straddled her, rubbing her back in the way he knew she wanted. At first she tensed, then she relaxed and finally surrendered until she felt like warm clay in his hands.

Finally, she sighed and whispered, "That was wonderful. Does it get any better?"

He chuckled and helped her roll onto her back. "Ale, I don't know how, but it always seems to get better."

"Yes, it does, doesn't it?" She pulled him to her.

CHAPTER TWO

David shifted his weight and held the receiver against his ear, his brown eyes twinkling with interest. Smile lines tugged at his mouth as he voiced affirmatives to encourage the speaker while using the sleeve of his free arm to wipe sweat from his brow and silvered sideburns. Growing impatient, he shifted his weight to the other foot. The floor, sticky from spilled soda, tugged at his soles. The booth stank of stale cigarette smoke, and scrawled phone numbers covered the walls. Small bits of paper and candy wrappers littered the floor.

Much to do and too little time, he thought, glancing at his watch.

He drove from San Cristobal de las Casas, Chiapas, early that morning to meet in less than an hour with Father Salvador Lopez, a former student and now a Catholic priest. Meanwhile, he was on the phone with Karen Dumas, who had journeyed from a remote cave in the Lacandon Jungle. He would return to San Cristobal later that evening to look at her data and discuss unresolved issues affecting the excavation—in particular, the encroachment of the federal army and the area's troublesome, homegrown Zapatista movement. Even with the rebel's pledges not to interfere, their constant feints, ploys, and belligerence left

Karen nervous. Her Zapatista boyfriend complicated everything. David knew from experience that, though fun and memorable, science and love affairs were a bad mix. The result was always that neither was done well.

They nearly lost their lives in the continuing Zapatista Rebellion. After searching for and finally finding the Xibalba cave, David was stabbed in the gut for his trouble. Marcos suffered a broken leg at the collapsed cave entrance, and Karen was kidnapped and nearly beaten and raped.

After his recovery, David sought Karen in Omaha, Nebraska, and convinced her to return and assist with the new excavation. After all, it was her idea, with her Smithsonian stele and its promise of lost Mayan books. The cave remained as mysterious and incredible as the day they first entered its labyrinthine passages and began to ferret out its amazing story.

He wouldn't have blamed her if she declined his offer to lead the excavation and make history. She nearly lost her life in the Lacandon Jungle. Dragging Marcos, with his unrequited love, to Omaha, sealed the deal for her return.

Although Karen agreed to undertake the excavation in the remote Lacandon cave and make day-to-day decisions, she insisted David take overall responsibility and be onsite when needed. His thirty years in Mesoamerican archeology made him a very valuable resource. He was familiar with Chiapas, and his political friends made the dig possible and would keep the researchers out of harm's way. Her sometime lover, Marcos, was an influential voice among the rebels, and they gave assurance through their leader, Balaam Reyes, not to interfere with the excavation.

"Soon, I promise," David said. "Maybe tonight. I don't know. I told a friend I'd look at a burial." "What kind of burial?" she asked.

"I don't know. Sally's being coy about the whole thing. It seems the locals have an old man's body they drag out every fifty-two years for ceremonial purposes. The family responsible for its care has completely died out, and…."

"How interesting. Of course, that's not possible without very advanced mummification techniques. Where do they keep it?"

"What?"

"The body, David. Where do they keep it until they bring it out every fifty-two years?"

"In a crypt under an abandoned church…ruin, I should say. It's part of an old Jesuit mission destroyed in an earthquake."

"Any idea how long you'll be?"

"This afternoon, I think. Evening at the latest."

"I'll hold you to that. Alexandra says you aren't to be trusted when it comes to time and schedules."

David frowned. "Look, I gotta go. Tell Alexandra she's wrong. I'll take you both to dinner tonight, OK?"

He looked at his watch, muttered more assurances, and finally extricated himself from the phone booth. Now he could get moving. Sally was waiting. Ten years earlier, the priest was one of David's best students at UNAM. Even then, Salvador, or Sally to his friends, seriously considered a vocation. After eight years as an ordained priest, the past four spent studying in Vatican City, he returned to Mexico to his first parish.

David didn't have time for the excursion, but it was unthinkable to deny a former favorite student's request. Plus, Sally's description of the body and ruins intrigued him. Supposedly the ancient corpse interred there long ago was taken out every fifty-two years, the same number of years in the Mesoamerican life cycle, at which time the world ended and began anew.

David witnessed many unusual ceremonies in his lifetime, many pre-Christian in origin. He watched parades celebrating the birth of Jesus in Indian villages all across Mexico and observed vestigial rites involving the donning of jaguar pelts that were performed in conjunction with various Christian rituals. He saw shamans perform in churches, witches prognosticate the future, and *curanderos* heal the sick.

However, he never heard of a sacred ritual where a body was presented for viewing every fifty-two years. It wasn't that he didn't believe it. Sally was certainly reliable. Despite its entrenched conservatism and obsession with dogma, the historical record clearly showed the Catholic Church erected churches on locations deemed holy by the Indians and allowed their pagan beliefs to blend with Christian theology. Most small Indian villages still incorporated pre-Columbian rituals and beliefs in their Catholicism to make it more palatable.

David would take a look, ask a few questions, and get the priest's version of the events before leaving for San Cristobal.

There, he would meet with Karen and Alexandra—maybe even Marcos if the Zapatista troublemaker was tagging along—and take them all to dinner. Maybe he could sort out some of the key issues at the Lacandon cave excavation that bothered Karen. Sensing her impatience with him, he believed she thought he was neglecting her and the project.

He needed to set the situation right and provide reassurance. He must give the project the attention it deserved, if indeed it deserved any. He climbed into his new, green Ford Explorer, a gift from his wife, and carefully pulled out onto the cobblestone street.

Within a few meters, he braked to avoid a boy of twelve slowly pedaling a bicycle with large metal milk containers strapped to each side of the frame. David sighed, leaned against the steering wheel, and looked around. An impenetrable wall of white stucco lined either side of the street. Each was dirty and worn, with cracked, falling plaster at its base. He supposed that area of town held homes at least 200 years old. They sat firmly above high curbs and wide sidewalks, lining up and following a steep rise before trailing downhill toward the center of town.

A preadolescent girl in pigtails and a brightly colored smocked blouse held a broom handle and briskly pushed dust and mango peels from the sidewalk into the street. Loiterers more interested in gossip than buying groceries crowded the corner *abaceria*, grocery store. A yellow dog, its ribs skeletal and tongue lolling sideways, walked with lowered head, glancing warily at the group in case of thrown sticks or stones.

The boy and bicycle gone, David drove two blocks and turned at the police station. Four blocks later, he was at the village *zocalo*, a traditional park with gazebos, benches, and aging trees that served as the spiritual core of all Latin American towns. Father Salvador sat on the church steps, looking up as he talked to two old Indian women. He saw David's green Explorer and stood to point in his direction, attempting to excuse himself from the ladies. Motioning his old mentor to stay put, he bowed slightly to the matrons, said a few words, and left, striding purposefully to the car. He opened the door and got into the passenger seat.

"Gracious!" he said. "Nice car, David." He gave an impish smile. "Have you begun selling pre-Columbian artifacts?"

David snorted at the jest. "A gift from Alexandra, Sally. It's the first new car I ever owned."

"You look good, Professor."

"As you do. Where are we going?"

"Ah. Excuse me. Straight to business, eh? Out of town." He gestured south. "About 100 kilometers south on the highway, just north of Tapachula, near the Guatemalan border. I'll show you where to turn. It's good you have this." He patted the dashboard. "It's an hour on asphalt, then an unpaved road, more of a goat trail, for several kilometers into the foothills."

"So far? I'm not sure I have enough time. I thought you said we were going to investigate a burial under a local church."

"We are, but not at the church here. It's an old Franciscan mission that was destroyed in an earthquake 250 years ago. It was never rebuilt. The government seized the property after the Revolution. A scattered settlement of Indians lived around the ruins for many years. Most of them don't speak Spanish."

David looked at his wristwatch, then at his former student. *How typical. The best laid plans....* He smiled, resigning himself to the loss of half a day's work.

Once Sally fastened his seat belt, David started the engine. He had a lot of questions, but he would begin slowly, wanting to reacquaint himself with Sally. He wanted to know all about Rome, Salvador's studies, and his family, and whether he was satisfied with his vocation.

Having bested a low layer of gray thunderheads, the sun god moved resolutely toward its zenith, and David lowered the sun visor. Mild gusts of wind carried the tannic smell of diesel and raw sewage through the barrios of adobe and stucco houses, staining and peeling the paint. His nose wrinkled in protest, but he paid no mind to the familiar odor.

He drove past several school playgrounds devoid of grass but populated with joyful, active children who chased a soccer ball and scurried over and around well-used, sometimes broken, playground equipment. Full of greetings and avid conversation, women everywhere swept their stoops and sidewalks. Merchants hosed refuse and trash from their landings and walks, spraying it over the edge of the curb into the street.

David navigated his Explorer to the edge of town and onto the black ribbon heading south. He and Sally slid easily into conversation about the previous ten years, letting the other's words simmer in their minds. David did most of the talking, but he grew quiet every five or ten kilometers as he slowed to a crawl, nearly having to stop completely to avoid falling into a crater in the pavement. Still, the kilometers flew by with neither man noticing the countryside.

The poor and ragged, some coming, some returning, toted baskets and bags burgeoning with goods. They were uniformly black-haired, short, and swarthy, and they herded small children or cared for infants as they patiently awaited buses. Many were going into town from the highlands, transporting handmade goods from cottage industries to sell in the markets of San Cristobal, Tapachula, and Tuxtla Gutierrez—woven blankets, sandals, puppets, purses, hand-carved chess sets, and exquisitely smocked and embroidered blouses with colors and native motifs that jarred the vision.

Others headed home along the winding, rugged dirt roads up into Indian villages that lay a world apart from the cities in their religion, culture, and societal norms. Change came slowly or not at all among the native Maya of southern Chiapas and Guatemala.

A companionable but not-quite-comfortable silence developed as David drove slowly down the highway. He glanced at Salvador. Tall with broad shoulders, he gained a little weight. David supposed he was good-looking and didn't appear even slightly effeminate like many priests did. He remembered that Sally had been a first-class soccer player and won a national championship in swimming for Mexico while still in high school. That boy grew into a man who acquired a brooding sense of presence. Gone was the self-assuredness and quick smile that were his trademarks. Instead, Salvador developed an edge, an unappealing, mocking aggression and hint of sarcasm in his conversation.

Perhaps his robe and vocation weighed heavily on his mind, or maybe the years spent at some of the finest schools in Rome led to his viewing the world differently. David knew that a good education destroyed more than one thinking person's reality. A career chosen with naïveté could become a lifelong burden. Some reacted with bitterness, anger, or defeat. Had that happened to Sally? Would the two men be able to resume their former relationship?

Salvador, turning, gave his former teacher a rueful smile. "I lied to you about the body thing, David."

"Eh? You lied? About what?" His foot lifted from the accelerator.

"Keep going. We're close." He studied the surroundings for landmarks, then settled back into his seat. "I mean, I didn't tell you everything." He clasped his hands together as if he were hesitant to begin. "It's all a bit unsettling. There's more to it—lots more."

Salvador, pausing, lifted his eyebrows. "I called the bishop in Tuxtla Gutierrez this morning. He's calling others, I'm sure. I think we might have a papal inquisitor on site in a couple days."

"A papal inquisitor? In Chiapas? Why, Sally? What's up? Are you getting me involved in a mess with the Church? You know what I think of those hidebound, pompous morons with their self-serving opinions on archeology. The last time I spoke with a bishop, I wanted to use the rosary on his belt to strangle him.

He said that the Church had no opinion...."

"David, can you still read Hebrew?"

"Not so good. No, not really, Sally. I mean, Father Salvador."

"Sally's fine when it's just us. We go too far back for pretensions."

"I'm out of practice. You were the whiz kid student of Hebrew and religion at UNAM. I just dabbled with Aramaic and Greek early in grad school. Aramaic was the language of the lower and middle classes during Jesus' time. Hebrew was spoken and written by the upper classes and priests. I know the script and can read a few words, but my Latin-American studies distracted me. There's so much of it, and Mayan writing is challenging and interesting."

"I remember stacks of manila folders full of articles and notes at your house. You seemed very taken with all things Roman and Greek before settling on Mexican prehistory. You even had a nice collection of Greek and Republican Roman coins."

"When I was in grad school, I became fascinated with the 300-year period after Christ's crucifixion, but you can't do it all. You have to focus your studies, and I settled into Mexican prehistory. It was the right decision."

"That's kind of why I called, Professor. This will be out of my hands soon. I thought it might be important for a civilian, an archeologist who knew something about ancient burials, to see it first."

David, catching Sally's eyes, knew he wasn't telling him everything. "Are you going to get into trouble for this?"

"It's doesn't matter, does it? I'm already on probation of sorts."

"What? That surprises me. Anything you feel like sharing?"

Sally hesitated, then casually waved the topic aside and sat back. "Not now. Maybe later." He crossed his legs with difficulty, banging his knee against the dashboard.

"The last couple years have been kind of rough," he said. "You know, when I returned from Rome. Anyway, the bishop wasn't too happy when I told him you were on the way." He smiled, showing all his teeth.

"Judging by his voice," he added, "I'd say he's mad as hell."

"Why? What's going on? What's so special about this burial?"

"Slow down. There." He pointed. "Turn there. The road's awful. Careful with the ruts, or you might high-center the car."

David obediently turned onto the trail and slowly navigated the winding, pocked path for three minutes, passing ramshackle adobe huts, groves of banana and avocado, and a trio of grazing donkeys until a jumble of fallen stone, weed-covered mounds, and broken, decaying walls came into view. Rounded, dusky red mountains lined the southern sky before disappearing into trees and scrub that grew thick and wild. Unexpectedly, two people emerged from the tall grass to walk on the trail.

"Mormons," Sally said in disapproval, noting the approaching young men in black slacks, white shirts, and dark neckties. Both carried backpacks. "Damned Mormons are everywhere these days."

David cast a furtive look at his friend. *Damned Mormons?*

As they drove slowly past the duo, David raised his hand in greeting. Neither young man responded, though both watched intently as the Explorer passed.

Sally turned in his seat, studying them carefully as the vehicle's tires wallowed in and out of ruts. David peered at them in the rear-view mirror. In their early twenties, they didn't seem very friendly for religious people. One red-faced youth talked and gestured as he walked. The other, deep in thought, wasn't listening to his animated companion.

They stopped and watched the Explorer move away along the trail. Something about their expressions caused David concern. What was that all about?

"Can't stand Mormons," Sally muttered. "I wonder if they found the body."

"What? They know about it?"

"Over there." Sally pointed. "Follow those wheel tracks around back. See those Indian huts?"

David slowly circled the ruins, which still resembled the shape of a cross though they were just a jumble of fallen rock, and stopped before two adobe huts with faded, yellow-brown palm-leaf roofs. The homes had been recently occupied, and the fetid odor of pigs and chickens remained. Feathers and feces littered the ground from the unpenned animals.

"Anyone home?" David asked.

"Not anymore. I buried Miguel Reyes last Tuesday. He was the last caretaker of *El Hombre Sagrado.*"

"A sacred man? Is that the burial you told me about? Come on. What's this about?"

Again, Sally ignored him and got out of the car. "Bring a lantern?"

"Of course."

"Grab your pack and come along, then." He walked between the two huts toward a dark opening at the base of the old stone structure's foundation. Looking over his shoulder, he stopped to wait for David, who followed with a satchel and lighted propane lantern.

"Here." David offered the lantern. "You know the way." Sally, accepting the lamp, held it out to illuminate the path. They entered a stone-lined passage. The tunnel was nearly six meters across, and the roof had been built for shorter people, forcing the two men to stoop to avoid hitting their heads.

"Where are we going?" David asked.

"To a crypt beneath the sacristy." His voice was tight and weak, no longer sounding sure and decisive.

Bending low, they shuffled forward cautiously. David glanced right and left, noting their surroundings. The cloying odor of mold made his nose itch as he looked around in the wavering light. Dull, golden reflections came from the walls, making his heart skip a beat.

Entering tombs and caves came with a jolt of adrenalin and always gave David a thrill. He spent his adulthood reconstructing lives and events from dirt and ruins and caves. The dead were frequently buried with secrets. Sometimes, those mysteries were easily ferreted out. Other times, they were unwilling to divulge their stories. Sometimes, the tale was revealed as a tangle of lies.

The crypt, like the passage, was relatively clean and well-ordered. Whatever lay within was very dear to someone. Statues of saints, all distinctly Indian in appearance, were carved from mahogany tree trunks and placed as silent sentinels around the room. Brightly colored frescoes were dulled by age, flaking and peeling from the humidity. The crypt seemed much older than the structure above, and the walls resembled other Mayan constructions David excavated. The decayed mission was obviously very old, but it couldn't have been built before the Conquest. The Spanish and the

Catholic Church were notorious for building churches over Indian holy sites, which he assumed was the case here, too. How old was the crypt? Was it even listed on the church records?

His interest piqued, David realized the trip wasn't a waste of time after all. The aggravation of the detour from his planned activities no longer mattered. The trip was worth the annoyance. "There." The priest raised the lantern high.

David stepped toward the box on the stone pedestal. When Sally stayed behind, David turned toward him. "You aren't coming?"

He raised a hand to shield his eyes. "I…I've seen it already. Him, I mean. It bothers me to…."

"Here. Hand me the lantern." David took it from the young man's trembling hand and noticed sweat covered Sally's face, and his eyes were wide with…fear?

David moved the lantern away to reduce the glare. He briefly wondered if he should crack a joke to lighten the situation, then decided against it. He was momentarily uncomfortable. Archaeologists encountered dead people and cultures as part of their work, but the uninitiated sometimes reacted oddly to burials and relics. Still, he was surprised to see Sally almost cower in the darkness.

Ignoring his guide, David turned his attention to the sarcophagus. The lid lay ajar, nearly ready to fall to the floor.

That's rather poor, he thought. *Did Sally leave it off?*

He looked into the box and saw a man, his hands at his sides. He moved the lantern closer to the head, searching for details.

David turned toward Sally. "Who left the top off the sarcophagus?"

"The lid's off? I'm sure I replaced it before leaving the other day." He seemed nonplussed. "Must be those Mormon vermin. We've got problems if they've been messing around in here." *Mormon vermin?* David looked askance at his former student. *Why are the Mormons a problem? They're often a nuisance but never a big deal. Sally's a nervous wreck for some reason.*

David edged to the side of the burial box and peered in, seeing a bearded man with a skull cap. The face appeared, well.... He wasn't Indian and had a beard, so maybe he was a Spaniard. Actually, he looked Middle Eastern.

Damn this light, he thought. *I can't see that well.*

Against the oppressive darkness, his lantern emitted translucent light, poorly illuminating the area. He bent forward for a closer look. The man seemed almost....

Good Lord! His breath caught. *Except for the clothes, he looks as if he's been dead for only a few hours!*

David's excitement quickly turned to disappointment. He stood. "Sally, I expected better of you. This is a piss-poor joke." He glared at his former student.

"It's no joke, Professor," he whispered. "Look closer." Turning abruptly, he moved toward the hall and the distant glow of the entrance. His hands extended to touch the wall for balance, he shuffled away from the crypt.

"Salvador! Where? What?" David stomped his foot in disgust. *Chicken shit. What's wrong with that boy? He's a nervous wreck. Another good mind ruined by the Church.*

He thought of following the priest to express concern, but he decided to investigate what affected his friend so profoundly. Why would Sally call him after so many years and involve him in such nonsense? He'd been a good student and showed promise as an academic, especially in primitive and modern religions, but....

David turned back to the box, determined to take a good look now that his concern over disturbing an ancient burial fled with the priest.

The coffin was made of wood, probably mahogany, polished to maintain its luster. He wondered if the recently deceased caretaker polished and maintained it that way.

The pictures on the box showed Quetzalcoatl, the feathered serpent of Mexican lore, on both sides, the red-and-blue feathered snake showing in stark contrast to the wood.

What's this? He leaned closer. *Bars and dots? There's a lot of them. Ah, those are Mayan dates. Fascinating.*

The serpent represented Kulkulkan, the Mayan version of the Toltec myth of Quetzalcoatl, but what was a well-known pagan image doing on the side of a coffin in a Christian church with Mayan dates on the burial container?

Has this box ever been in the ground? he wondered. *That's not unusual. The ancients didn't bury their dead like the Europeans. Sometimes they were placed in the ground or interred in tombs, some lined with stone and ceremonial and spiritual artifacts to assist them in the afterlife.*

He retrieved the lantern and circled the casket again. The box appeared very old, and, if genuine, was a rare find. The burial itself raised a host of questions, including why a recently deceased, strangely dressed man lay in such an old, ornate box. The serpent and Mayan dates were incongruous. The whole thing looked contrived, obviously the work of an amateur fraud, but why?

He raised the lamp higher. A final, closer inspection was needed before he joined Sally to berate him for religious hysteria. Frowning, he set down the lamp. Lifting and moving bones and artifacts was one thing, but touching the skin and clothing of someone recently deceased was completely foreign. He shivered. Maybe he should just call the police. He decided to take a quick glance at the clothing.

He grasped the hem of the corpse's robe to inspect the material. It was wool of a familiar weave—or was it? He strained to see better in the light. Wool was unknown in Mexico before the conquest, so why did the cloth seem familiar? He wished he could see the gown in its entirety.

Light reflected from metal, and he glanced at the body's left hand, which held an ornament, perhaps a necklace. He brought the lantern closer. It was a gold Star of David, a crudely wrought fish, and what appeared to be a cup or chalice hanging from a delicate chain. That was unusual. Wasn't the fish the early symbol of the church before the shepherd's crook, which was finally supplanted by the cross? The chalice never caught on. What was the story behind that?

Feeling bolder, he touched the necklace, and the hand released it. In horror, David dropped it to touch gently the skin of the hand. It was supple and cool.

His stomach flipped, and his flesh crawled. Something wasn't right. Judging by the corpse's life-like skin, the man died very recently. How long had it lain in the casket? Unless the body was only a few hours old, it should be locked in rigor mortis. Any longer than that, and the corpse would be bloated with gas. Why wasn't it stinking to high heaven? Had the body been professionally embalmed?

It was so eerie it was frightening. He inhaled deeply, but he caught no odor of decaying flesh, nor the sweet tannic smell of embalming preservatives.

Placing his palm against the corpse's stomach, he pressed.

The body sprung back immediately, spongy and resilient.

What the hell? he wondered.

Inspecting the feet, he gasped when he saw ancient sandals, perhaps Greek, Roman, or Middle Eastern. They appeared heavily worn and had been repaired a few times. The lantern grew heavy in his hand, and shadows danced on the wall as his hand shook.

He paused to steady himself, taking several deep breaths until his head cleared. Why was he so upset? The poor lighting was frustrating, and none of what he saw made sense. He should confront Salvador to find out the real reason why the priest wanted him to see the body. Maybe he should carry the coffin outside so the sun would reveal all and explain the mystery.

He saw several wood cylinders at the foot of the casket. Stepping back, he appraised it and saw the body lay too shallow in the deep box. Peering in again, he saw the body lay on a cracked plank that broke just below the feet. Perhaps the cylinders rolled down to the coffin's base. Something was supporting the plank and the body.

He tapped the box with his knuckles and heard a hollow tone. What else lay under the box's subfloor? Was the space empty, or were other items hidden from view?

He looked at the cylinders and felt a chill. With total disregard to archeological protocol and oblivious to any possible ramifications, he lifted out one of the tubes and held it closer to the lantern to examine. It was about ten centimeters long and three wide. Setting down the lantern on the flagstones, he knelt and grasped the cylinder with both hands to better inspect it.

The tube was light, probably made of wood, and had been tooled to store something. Turning it end over end, he finally held it in the center and scraped at the wax seal that protected the thin lid. Wax crumbled and fell to the floor.

Holding the tube steady, he pulled off the lid and hunkered down to let light from the lantern shine inside. Placing two fingers inside, he pulled gently.

What appeared to be a leaf of paper slid out easily, and he held it up to the light. It wasn't paper. It was papyrus, but that was impossible. Papyrus was unknown in the New World. It was very Old World, invented in Egypt.

With trembling hands, he carefully extracted the remaining sheets and touched them delicately, fearing they would crumble at any moment. When they didn't, he slowly unrolled five or six pages.

The supple paper must have been treated with resin to preserve it, or it would have fallen to pieces.

I should stop now, he told himself. *This isn't how one handles ancient documents.*

He groaned inwardly. He was being stupid and negligent, acting like an amateur, but compulsion and curiosity pushed him onward, and he carefully unrolled the scroll.

It was in Aramaic, written by a clear hand in the language he once attempted to learn. A lump formed in his throat, making it hard to swallow. The enormity of the find was overwhelming. Either someone created an elaborate hoax, or Sally's behavior was suddenly understandable.

It appeared they had a 2,000-year-old, uncorrupted body, but that wasn't possible or reasonable. It was insane, an elaborate fiction.

He carefully returned the papyrus scroll to its cylinder and placed it in his satchel, telling himself it would be irresponsible to leave it unattended. Lifting the lantern high, he gazed intently at the body and surrounding environment. With such poor lighting, it would be easy to miss something important. He had to examine everything with care, including the papyrus pages. Many would see his taking them as theft. So be it. He wouldn't leave important documents lying around to be lost or misappropriated by others.

He ran his hand under the corpse's legs and feet, then rolled the head aside to see what else might be hidden. Satisfied nothing lay under the body, he quickly removed the other wooden cylinders, telling himself it was for safe-keeping. After all, he might not return. No doubt others would become involved in the affair soon.

He stood, overcome by an eerie feeling he never felt before. There was something unreal about the body and its presentation. The whole situation was out of context. His legs felt rubbery, his arms weak. He needed to get out of there, clear his head, and plan.

He understood how Sally felt. Confusion gripped him, and panic touched the border of his thoughts. Hefting the satchel and lantern, he retraced his steps down the stone-lined passageway.

Panic receded as he emerged into the outside world and took several bracing breaths. Gone was his intention to berate Sally for a juvenile hoax. He needed answers. If the priest told the truth—and he had no reason to believe he hadn't—it was a very bizarre find.

In the light of day, David was troubled not only by the body of the bearded man with a skull cap but also by the images from the casket: Kulkulkan, a chalice, and a six-pointed star. It wasn't likely to be a Star of David. A star was a star, a symbol, very common in art and archeology worldwide. The casket, necklace, and other artifacts were mixed themes, motifs, and time frames.

The easiest explanation was a stupid, sophomoric hoax, but what about the pliable, lifelike corpse? The papyrus? The obvious age of the crypt?

As he walked to the Explorer, he wanted to run back and take everything out into the light of day for a better look.

He turned back, but an electric tingle went through him like the rush of being struck by a cold, salty wave. Suddenly, he couldn't wait to get in his car and leave.

CHAPTER THREE

The priest inhaled deeply from his Baronet cigarette. Smoking wasn't healthy, but his friends in Rome assured him it was important to have personal flaws. Only one man had ever been perfect, and that got him killed. He gazed through the valley into the distance, north toward the state capitol of Tuxtla Gutierrez. Red earthen patches and terraced fields competed for space with exuberant plants and trees on the high-altitude, forested, round mountains of Chiapas on that cloudy, gray day. Light, smoggy haze of automobile exhaust and small factories hovered above the distant city.

Closer to him, among the red agave cactus, sage grass, and purple-flowering datura, the light breeze had gone quiet, but the air felt crisp and dry. As foothills gradually rolled into the highlands, vegetation grew more abundant and more varied than a few kilometers to the south. Far up into the hills, near the foot of the mountains, barely visible, ant-like Indians threaded a narrow, rocky path among pines, mahogany, and acacia trees to a village of adobe huts clinging tenuously to the mountainside.

Father Salvador waited impatiently, smoking, chewing his lower lip, and fumbling nervously with the rosary at his belt. Guilt hung over his shoulders like a wet blanket. He should have called the bishop first, not David. Why had he done that? Was it yet another reflection of his personal dilemma, his crisis of faith? Didn't he trust the Church to conduct an impartial inquiry? Was it the nagging, constant concern that truth would be sacrificed for expediency and appearance?

"Sally," David called.

Father Salvador, taking a deep breath, turned to meet his former mentor. The archeologist had the startled expression of a deer caught in the headlights as he walked up carrying his pack and lantern.

"Here." He handed the lantern to Sally. "Give me a hand." Walking to the back of the Explorer, he placed the pack on the tailgate. Salvador followed without speaking, waiting for the professor to speak first.

David opened the backpack and carefully placed the wood cylinders on the car's carpeted rear floor.

"What do you think, David?" Salvador asked.

"What do I think? Has all that Church doctrine left you completely addled? Salvador, this is the craziest damn thing I've ever seen."

"The body is ancient but totally preserved."

"That's not possible."

"I agree, but it is. It's genuine, isn't it?"

"It can't be. It would have to be a…."

"Miracle. The body, clothes, everything can be dated with Carbon-14 dating. The truth will be borne out. You'll see."

David gave him a sour look. "Salvador, when do the bishop and his people arrive?"

"I don't know. Soon. Maybe tomorrow or the next day." He shook another cigarette from his pack of Baronets and struck a match with a trembling hand.

"Are you in trouble?" David tried to act casual as he perused the items he took from the coffin. When Sally didn't answer, David turned to ask again only to stop at seeing his friend's distressed expression.

"Trouble?" Sally repeated slowly, inhaling from his cigarette. "Yes. No. Probably. David…I've been thinking for some time that I need to get away, to get my head together."

He studied his former student and quietly asked, "Is this a faith problem, Sally?"

"Yes." He looked into David's eyes with a grim smile before his chin drooped again.

David nervously rolled the cylinder back and forth on the SUV's floor, then replaced it in the backpack. An uncomfortable silence ensued, as Sally smoked.

Finally, David asked, "What do you want to do?"

"I don't know, David. Leave, I think."

"Leave where? Here? The Church? What are we talking about?"

"I don't know. I've been thinking of taking a break from all this for a while."

"From the Church and being a priest?"

"Yes."

"Wow. That's a little…."

"Unexpected? Dramatic? I guess it would be for most people. It certainly will be for my family. Priests don't take breaks from their vows. It renders them meaningless."

"Have you told them yet?"

"Are you crazy? My mother would die." His expression dissolved into a mask of pain. He inhaled from the cigarette and exhaled through his nose.

David saw the young man's agony was tearing him apart and felt obliged to offer assistance. "What's your plan, Sally? How can I help?" He placed the backpack into the Explorer and closed the tailgate. "Do you need a place to stay for a few days?"

The priest paused, staring at the ground, then dropped the cigarette and stamped on it before looking up. "What do you suggest?"

"No pressure. You're welcome to stay with Alexandra and me at my place for a few days until you decide what you want to do."

"No pressure, eh?"

"None intended or implied."

"Your wife won't be alarmed?"

"Alexandra's a good Catholic, but she's an enlightened soul and very open-minded. Come on." Walking to the passenger door, he opened it. "We can talk while we drive." He went to the driver's side and got in before starting the engine.

As Salvador got into the passenger seat, David asked, "Want to run by the rectory and pick up some things?"

"No. That's the last place I want to go. Are you heading to San Cristobal?"

David glanced at his wristwatch. "That's the plan."

"I'm in. Let's go."

"You won't be missed?"

"I will. I'm scheduled for seven-o'clock mass tonight. Father Sanchez will want me around if and when the Papal Inquisitor and bishop arrive. He'll need someone to excoriate and blame.

"No. I'm outta here. As far as they're concerned, I've really messed things up, but you know what? I don't feel too bad about it. If you've got a second, I'll tell you about my new passion."

"You haven't been sucked into this Catholic Liberation Theology stuff, have you?"

"Of course not." Salvador settled into his seat. When he spoke again, his voice was tinged with irony. "I went into it willingly, my eyes open and mind focused on making a difference. It's the future of Latin America, Professor, the only way to fix a half century of injustice and endemic poverty.

You know our legacy—our political systems are corrupt and ensure poverty through subjugating millions of poor Indians. Surely you're aware of…."

"Sally." He held up his hand, smiling and shaking his head. "This sounds like a replay of something I got involved in a few years back. Maybe you'd better start at the beginning."

Sally looked at his mentor. How much did he trust the man? Shaking his head, he stared out the windshield again. Maybe it was time. He needed to tell the story to someone.

"It's a long story, David."

"It's a two-hour ride to San Cristobal. I'm listening."

Sally began talking. In the beginning, Rome was everything and more than he expected. However, the six years before he was ordained were built on many years of studying anthropology, history, and biology, which brought festering doubts to the forefront of his mind. His unquestioning faith slowly evaporated with each page he read. Unlike many of his fellow seminarians, he became an empiricist. The credulity and overconfident passion of his youthful belief that everything was explained in proverbs written 2,000 years earlier was replaced by a desire to see the world through the crisp, vivid lens of cause and effect.

It was basic epistemology—how do we know what we know? Do people rely on a complacent paradigm of nebulous truths and philosophical inconsistencies, or do they recognize the world and relationships as nothing more than the laws of physics plus the expression of human frailties like passion, poverty, greed, and ignorance?

His transformation from devout believer into radical liberation idealist began one night when he walked a few blocks off the Via Andrea Doria in Rome. He encountered a group of priests, one of whom was an old schoolmate who completed his studies and was dispatched home to Nicaragua three years earlier. Although his friend was wary at seeing him, Salvador was invited over and introduced. He quickly surmised that all the priests were in disfavor with the Vatican hierarchy and were summoned home from Central and South America for meditation, reflection, and reeducation.

In the eyes of the church, those priests were troublemakers. None of them seemed happy. Malcontents all, to a man they were imbued with the vision of changing their world through Catholic Liberation Theology, an approach to Catholic missionary work that fell out of favor in recent years.

Poverty and misery, already 500-year-old realities in the New World, became even more entrenched as the rich and powerful became richer and more grasping, while the world moved toward a global economy, leaving millions of the disenfranchised behind. Those young priests, storm troopers for Christ, succumbed to the liberal, leftist ideology of change from Marx's legacy. All told stories of heartbreak, gripping poverty, incredible injustice, and friends beaten and murdered because of their work among the poor.

Salvador initially remained aloof and distant, because that new vision of reality challenged his neatly packaged, middleclass upbringing. Although poverty in the midst of plenty was easily visible in Mexico, his childhood had been remarkably insulated. He knew a series of nice homes, private schools, many friends, and success in athletics.

After listening to the priests' stories for many nights, he was startled from his complacent reverie and gripped by new awareness. Along with his new comrades, he acquired a sense of conviction and urgency. He wanted to make a difference, to return home and help the poor overcome the tyranny of the system.

The Church didn't share his enthusiasm. With three months of schooling yet to go, Salvador was suddenly sent home to Mexico.

He was assigned to a backwater parish in the small towns surrounding the foothills of Tuxtla Gutierrez, under a bishop jealous of Salvador's Vatican education. Unlike the famous Bishop Samuel Ruiz Allis of nearby San Cristobal diocese, who was very sympathetic to the Indians and their tribulations, the bishop in Tuxtla wasn't. He went out of his way to point out to Sally that the Church condemned such teachings as Marxist, and Marx denied the existence of God.

Salvador followed his heart. He ignored his bishop's admonitions and sought every opportunity to spend time with the poor Indians in their poverty-stricken hovels, even when it kept him from his daily duties of parish priest in and around the neighboring diocese of San Cristobal, high in the Sierra Madres.

He maintained contact with his friends-in-revolution in Rome. His work with the Indians allowed him to view himself as a purveyor of liberation theology on the front lines in Latin America. With his new mind set, he became embarrassed not by his family's prosperity but by his own ignorance of the world and chosen path of achieving status and rank within the Church. He was in crisis. He knew with certainty that the world wasn't set up the way he was taught.

Becoming a priest was easy compared to remaining one. Despite the training, education, prayer, seminars, counseling sessions, and late-night intimate conversations with colleagues, it was impossible to prepare any novice for the realities of priesthood. It wasn't that Sally hadn't been forewarned. It was a common problem for many. Ten years earlier, he never would have imagined himself in such a predicament.

He couldn't recall the single event that planted the virus in his mind that resulted in a disease that ate his soul. If faith was the engine of Christianity and prayer its fuel, Sally's engine stalled to the point where all the prayers in the world couldn't fuel it again. He was marking time, and he knew it. At the age of thirty-two, he felt frustrated, limp, and washed up. Nagging guilt gnawed at him, insipid yet insistent, his soul dark with stain and festering with doubt as he tried to deny that his life was a fraud.

His work with the Indians helped a bit. His commitment to liberation theology changed nothing. Years of prayer made no difference. He searched his soul for proof of his calling but found it spent. The firm paradigm of his world view, his faith, had crumbled. Unshakable faith no longer bridged his search for knowledge and hunger for God.

Belief, he realized, was the manna of the ignorant. Ideology was the foundation of an aged, corrupt, self-serving male fraternity. The realities of the universe they tried to deny became, for him, impossible to ignore. Everywhere he looked, the vast abyss separating the ideal and real worlds stood as mocking testimony to man's ways. The strange discovery of the uncorrupted body in its anachronistic casket shook him to his core.

Salvador discovered the old, ruined mission and its remnant population five months earlier. He became good friends with those people, a dying group of illiterate Indians, long disconnected from their original tribe. Fascinated by their simplicity and dedication to tradition, he found them welcoming and generous in a way that was at odds with their economic reality.

The head man, Miguel, told him that an earthquake a few years earlier brought hard times. The church's largesse disappeared, as did the group's viability. Only Miguel's family and extended family maintained their ancestral commitment to the old mission and *El Hombre Sagrado.* Salvador found their dedication confusing. He came to know the family well, but what purpose was served in remaining at the long-abandoned mission for so many centuries?

Even after hearing Miguel's deathbed confession, Salvador didn't understand. He assumed the story was created by dementia and stroke. The old fellow was obsessed with dates and some nonsense about the end of the world. He rambled incoherently, speaking of the Maya and repeating the word *baktun.*

Sally knew from anthropology classes that a *baktun* was a 500-year dating cycle the Mayans used. There were several such cycles, including *katuns, baktuns*, and others. It was all esoteric academic arcana he couldn't recall.

The average person, especially the Mexican peasants, didn't know anything about Mayan glyphs and dating. Delirium and death were ugly no matter how often one witnessed them. Still, Miguel's rant left Salvador with a very unspiritual uneasiness.

Sally assumed he had misheard the man. Then he visited the wood coffin and saw the strange man for whom Miguel's family had provided care for so many years. The box was odd with its winding snake body and image of Kulkulkan and Mayan glyphs interspersed randomly on the sides. Finding the body perfectly preserved was even more unsettling. Seeing it, Sally suspected that his crisis of faith was about to get worse.

The remains contradicted every scrap of knowledge he gained throughout all his years of study. He suspected the body was ancient, and the implications terrified him. He worried the Catholic Church would hide such a discovery. Even if the powers-that-be knew nothing yet, Salvador feared the body's existence, if it wasn't a fraud, could threaten the complicated ecclesiastical world. His life would never be the same.

He had to make the best of a bad situation. Though it seemed logical at the time, calling David first instead of the bishop appeared to be another stupid mistake in a string of bad decisions. The more errors in judgment he committed, though, the less it seemed to matter. All reflected his growing indifference to Church authority.

He seriously considered leaving the priesthood and becoming a civilian. Though his parents would be horrified and ashamed of his failure, he couldn't live a lie anymore. Even if the body wasn't what he feared or hoped, his life was about to change.

Exhausted from his story, Salvador slumped in his seat.

David drove for a mile and said casually, "I'm not trying to get rid of you, but I have a dinner date this evening at my place in San Cristobal with Alexandra and an archeologist who's working with me. Alexandra is preparing Spanish *paella* with all the trimmings."

He swerved to avoid a tope, a speed bump.

"You're welcome to come. I'm sure Karen and Alexandra would enjoy your company."

"Karen?"

"My archeologist friend. You remember the story I told you about the mess I was in last year with the Zapatistas?"

"This is the same woman?"

"The same."

Sally chewed his lower lip. "Interesting. Sure. Why not?"

"She's bringing her friend, Marcos."

"You know Marcos, the leader of the Zapatistas?"

"Well, yes. Actually, he's another former student of mine."

"And Karen knows him, too?"

"Only too well, actually."

The priest sat quietly, considering the implications. He glanced at David, trying to intuit his meaning. "You always know the most-interesting people. Will you introduce me to your Zapatista friends?"

David sighed, smiled wryly, and asked, "How can I help it? Be careful what you wish for, Sally. Your life might get a little *too* interesting around these people. They don't just ruminate on philosophy and theology like armchair academics. They're all doers. You could end up in a shit storm like your priest friend from El Salvador."

CHAPTER FOUR

John Wilson, an elder and member of the elite First Presidency at Brigham Young University, sat anxiously awaiting a return call from one of his missionaries in southern Mexico. What the young man described the previous day was too good to be true, but it might translate into a huge benefit to John's career. After thirty years of steady progress in the Church of Jesus Christ of Latter Day Saints, his career had stagnated at BYU and within the LDS hierarchy. He knew he had no chance of reaching the inner sanctum of absolute power unless something extraordinary happened, along the lines of a miracle, similar to the intervention of LDS founder Joseph Smith's magic stones and golden tables.

There were several Mormon Temples in Mexico, including a very large one in Tuxtla Gutierrez, the capitol of Chiapas, and John administered the largest video network in the world, capable of interfacing with any cable system in North and Central America. He also controlled a $10-million budget for the church's missions and its thousands of young missionaries throughout the world. If money were equated with power, he certainly had the means, but it took more than money to ascend into the LDS' upper echelons.

The three-man presidency that controlled the LDS was almost certainly out of reach, but the Quorum of Twelve Apostles might be attainable, especially if John were invited to join the secret Council of Fifty established 150 years earlier by Joseph Smith. Even that possibility seemed remote without divine intervention. Based on what he witnessed so far in his life, that wasn't likely.

To move to the next level of power, John had to take matters into his own hands. How that could be done, he didn't know, but the call from the young missionary in southern Mexico ensured John a restless night's sleep.

He waited for the return call, which was due soon, judging by the wall clock. After ruminating over the conversation, John returned home realizing he hadn't asked enough questions, certainly not the critical ones he focused on afterward.

The young missionary, though inexperienced, was no fool. He did the right thing by immediately calling John after inadvertently stumbling on something that could validate many of Joseph Smith's early teachings regarding the lost tribes of Israel. It would catapult John into the upper hierarchy of the LDS and ensure he remained a household name until the end of times, when God called them all home and gave John his own planet for eternity.

He saw his secretary's main line light up. A moment later, the phone rang as the call was transferred to John's office.

Taking a deep breath, he lifted the receiver.

"Hello. John Wilson here."

"Yes, Elder Wilson, this is Evan. I called yesterday about the, ah, the strange-looking body in a coffin down here in Chiapas, Mexico."

"Of course, Evan. I've been waiting for your call," he replied smoothly. "I've given some thought to the situation you described. I don't know if I should involve myself in the matter.

Do you have a second to answer a few questions?"

"Yes, Sir. Absolutely."

"Actually, I have a meeting in five minutes, so I'll start with a couple that you can give a quick yes or no to. Is that OK?"

"Yes, Sir."

"Good. Did you return to view the body as I asked?"

"Yes, Sir."

"Does it appear to be in the same physical condition as two days ago?"

"Yes, Sir."

"You're sure? The body hasn't been embalmed?"

"I don't believe so. I mean, I moved its shirt aside and didn't see any incisions that would indicate organs were removed."

"Were you able to retrieve any of the items in the casket?"

"Yes…and no."

"Yes and no?"

"Well, no." The young man hesitated. "I wanted to, but Jacob freaked out." He paused. "He's thinking about quitting and going home."

"And Jacob is…?"

"One of the missionaries I supervise, Sir. He's eighteen and just learning his way around. He's the one who told me about the strange group of Indians living near the old church. He refuses to go back to the ruin."

"Yes. He shouldn't go with you anymore, Evan. I don't want him bothered with this affair, understand? Let's see about sending him home, OK? You're a mature young man and seem to have good judgment. This can be handled just between the two of us."

"Yes, Sir."

"Tell me again about the things in the casket."

"There's a necklace that has what looks like a shepherd's staff, a star kind of like a Star of David the Jews have, and what looks like a drinking cup or glass. Maybe it's a vase or jar. The cylinders I told you about are missing."

"You're sure one or more of them are missing?"

"Yes, Sir. I looked really good."

"That's really, really unfortunate. Does anyone else know about the unusual situation with this church ruin?"

"Just that nosy Catholic priest who keeps coming around. I would have taken the cylinders for you, but Jacob heard their car coming down the road and went nuts. I had to get him out of there to calm him down."

"And did you?"

"Did I what, Sir?"

"Calm him down?"

"Mostly, but he acted all stressed out again when the priest and another guy drove past us on the road."

"The priest saw the body after you left?"

"I guess. It was the priest and another guy in a Ford Explorer. The priest gave us a dirty look as they went by."

"I can imagine," he replied in a droll tone. "Listen, Evan, this is very important. I want you to return to the site today and retrieve everything that's left, the cylinders, the jewelry on the body, his clothes…."

"His clothes?"

"Absolutely. Now listen very closely. I want a lock of hair from the body."

A long pause followed.

"Are you still there, Evan?"

"Well, yeah. Let me get this straight. If I can speak frankly, Sir, it sounds like you're asking me to strip the body for you."

John suppressed a sigh. This would take work. He had to know quickly if he could count on the mission coordinator.

"Yes, I guess it does, doesn't it? Evan, I hope you understand I wouldn't ask unless it was absolutely, terribly important that you do this. We aren't grave robbers, but it could be wrong to leave the body unattended and in the hands of someone like the Catholics. This might be the remains of someone who was never baptized. I'm sure you understand the implications of that. It's our duty in Christ's eyes to baptize him and ensure his soul's salvation.

"There's more, Evan. There's something I can't put my finger on. I suspect the corpse is someone very important to our church's history. Do you follow me? I want you to return to the ruin today and remove everything you can from the body and anything else in the coffin or box."

Evan paused, then said, "I guess I can do that. This is important church business, isn't it, Brother John?"

"I can't think of anything more important right now. I think God played a hand by placing you, of all people, in this situation to help our church and promote our mission in Mexico. I feel very strongly the Lord has presented you with this opportunity, because He sees in you a strong, visible leadership role."

"I'm sure I don't deserve…."

"Others will decide that, Evan. Please do as I ask. Return to the ruin today. Can you do that for us, Young Man?"

"I'm on it, Sir. Let me run by and talk to Jacob, then I'll be off."

"Will you walk?"

"I ride a bicycle most of the time, but the roads down here are really crummy."

"Use a credit card and rent a car. Charge it to the mission budget."

"Rent a car? You're sure?"

"Yes. Call me as soon as you've retrieved all that stuff. Get all of it, remember? And get a lock of his hair. You have my cell number?"

"Yes, Sir, but I don't want to bother you with…."

"It's no bother. I insist. Call me tonight. I'll have more instructions when you return. Got it?"

"Got it."

"Good. Off with you now. I'm late for a meeting. A couple more things, Evan. Don't tell anyone at our temple in Tuxtla of our business, and be very careful about our misguided Catholic brethren."

"I see…sort of. That means…."

"That means that the temple personnel in Tuxtle have nothing to do with decision-making regarding our international mission, and I don't want the Catholic Church nosing around or having any more to do with this than can be avoided. They'll deliberately mess this up and will steal or hide anything in the coffin. If there's time, let's bury the body. If not, get in and get out. Try not to be seen."

"Yes, Sir."

"Good man. I'll be waiting." Hanging up the receiver, he looked at his watch. It was nearly time for his appointment. A little blonde freshman with nice tits should be arriving about now. Her behavior was a little too visible. At a place like BYU, it was scandalous. Brother John received reports she'd been behaving in a very un-Mormon-like fashion; drinking alcohol, dressing risqué, flirting with boys, maybe having sex. She would obviously benefit from his special guidance, or he'd be forced to report her to her parents, by all accounts a nice family living in Ogden.

He might even have to expel her from Brigham Young if she didn't see the error of her ways and offer to make amends. He should probably reserve a hotel room right now in case she required being told what to do if she wanted to stay enrolled at BYU. He could visit the room an hour early and take his university-supplied laptop to check out the newest girls on his favorite porn sites.

He was doing her a favor. The little slut was on the fast track to perdition if she was drinking and having sex as a freshman.

His telephone buzzed, and he picked up the receiver. "Yes?"

"A student, Miss Petersen, is here for her meeting, John."

Feeling his cock stir, he reached down to massage it. "Send her back, Marilyn, and please clear my calendar for the rest of the afternoon."

"The rest of the afternoon?" He waited without speaking.

"Yes," she said finally. "Of course, John."

"Thank you, Marilyn. You know how I hate to be bothered on Friday afternoons. You can reach me on my cell in case of an emergency." He took a deep breath and eased the crotch of his pants before smoothing back his hair and practicing his friendliest smile.

When he heard a light tap on the door, he called, "Come in, please."

A wide-eyed, petite girl stepped into the room, wearing a conservative skirt and blouse with high collar. Her breasts, however, bulged against her shirt, showing a first-class chest.

"Come in, Miss Petersen." He pointed at the chair before his desk. "I've received some alarming reports about your behavior at BYU." He tossed a manila folder onto his desk. "This is all very sad. I see you're the recipient of a full scholarship from BYU." He paused, ready to launch into his prepared talk about how disappointed he was for her and her parents.

She sat in the proffered chair, squirmed, and tugged down her skirt hem. Looking directly at him with a pale, fearful gaze, she asked, "Am I really in that much trouble, Sir?"

"I'd be lying if I said otherwise, Young Lady. Mother Wilson at your dormitory is certain you're engaging in morally questionable behavior that will likely mean rescinding your scholarship and expelling you from BYU. You know that drinking alcohol is absolutely forbidden, and I hear that might be the least of your sins.

"I'm also told you've engaged in sexual play and probably sexual intercourse with boys. Such behavior isn't tolerated by BYU or your parents. It's embarrassing and sinful. It will damn you for eternity. At a bare minimum, it's a violation of the scholarship behavioral contract you signed before enrolling at BYU, wouldn't you agree? I feel really sorry for your parents, but this is one of the bad parts of my job, telling parents that their dollars and daughters are destined for the sewer."

With a stricken look, she slumped in the chair. "I haven't hurt anyone," she said, her voice trembling, "and…and I study hard, and I…."

"I'm actually very busy this afternoon." He glanced at his wristwatch. "I have a late meeting downtown. I was prepared to expel you and call your parents, Young Lady. I don't have time to listen to your excuses, because I completely trust Mother Wilson's judgment."

He gave her a sad smile, shaking his head in disapproval. "I don't know if there's any way out of this, Miss Petersen. I try to be fair."

When she finally looked up at him, he offered the bait. "Maybe we can work something out. If you really want to present your case to me, after you've had time to think about what's at stake, I suppose I could visit with you downtown after my meeting and listen to what you have to say. What do you think? Should we pick up the phone and call your parents, or do you want to meet me later?"

She looked overwhelmed. "Meet you? Where? But I haven't done anything really bad. There are other girls...."

He raised his hand to stop her. "Please. I'm a reasonable man. Think about it. Let's see if there's a solution to your problem that will satisfy both of us."

He wrote down the phone number of the Comfort Motel and handed it to her. "Take this number and call the front desk if you decide to meet me. I'll be free around four o'clock this afternoon."

Confused and almost speechless, she accepted the note. After she stared at the number, she glanced quickly at him but didn't want to meet his eyes.

"Miss Petersen.... I believe your name is Melissa?" She nodded.

"You should come alone if you decide to meet me. This is a private matter, and I don't want to involve your friends or any staff at BYU. It's to protect your privacy, you understand?" She looked at him, her eyes wide and questioning.

He looked at his watch again. "OK. Off with you. I'll be late for my meeting." He pointed at the door. "Remember, I'll be free around four o'clock."

After she rose from her chair, he walked her to the door. "I really hope we don't have to rescind your scholarship and call your parents, Melissa, but we'll see how it goes. Later today, maybe?"

She searched his face and attempted a half-hearted smile. She hesitated as if wanting to say something, but turned and left the office with her head down, as if deep in thought.

Brother John watched her tight bottom sway under her skirt, then called to his secretary, "Marilyn, I'm running downtown for a quick meeting. You can reach me on my cell if there's an emergency."

He closed the office door and went to retrieve the laptop.

Melissa was a well-built little piece who would look great in a Fredericks of Hollywood outfit. He wondered what her cup size was. She had great tits and legs all the way up to her ass.

He hoped she called and came to see him. He could save her. He could really help her and do her family a favor if she cooperated. If she didn't show, he would have a few hours to peruse his erotic web sites. There was no sense subscribing to online porn unless he took time to enjoy it occasionally. He certainly couldn't do that at home with his wife around all the time.

CHAPTER FIVE

Julio, exhausted, stood with hands on hips in the scant shadow cast by the hut in an attempt to escape the early morning heat. He glanced at his young colleague, Evan, who plopped onto the ground by the tunnel entrance, where shade quickly became darkness. Julio, stretching and walking slowly away from the empty shacks, wondered where the Indians were. The area looked as if the inhabitants abandoned it quickly, leaving behind items poor people would normally have taken.

Moving the body and coffin from the crypt through the dark underground corridor took longer than expected. He glanced at his wristwatch and saw it was 2:39 PM. His sweat-soaked shirt clung to his body, and his nose wrinkled as his body odor mixed with the cloying smell of spoiled milk, rotten meat, and dog shit. Perhaps, knowing they were leaving soon, the villagers became careless and began tossing garbage closer to home.

His dirty hands acquired various scratches and a broken index fingernail. It was time to get moving. Being stopped in Mexico with a dead body that didn't belong to him was a very bad idea.

His two years in Mexico working for the CIA had so far been spent tracking firearms, drugs, and cartel leaders. The current job came as a complete surprise. What was a corpse doing out here were no one lived, with no friends or relatives? Why didn't they just bury the damned body and be done with it? The few times he worked with bodies was to bury them after he or someone else killed them, but Control insisted he take everything, including the body, clothes, coffin, and anything in the room. He took lots of photos, too, of the walls and anything else that had the strange designs and paintings.

The orders were to clean it up and get out. If he had a can of gasoline and a match, he'd show them how to leave a site clean. It was a weird assignment. The body didn't stink, which was odd. He raised a grimy, sweat-soaked sleeve to wipe his forehead.

Cabron! he thought. *Such crazy work I do these days, and sometimes it makes no sense.*

The new kid, as Julio expected, showed up on his bicycle, ready to help and knowing how to get there. Julio rented a van and found the off-road backwater. It was much easier for two to carry a body than one.

"Time to go, Big Guy," Julio said. "You can catch your breath in the truck. Let's move before people we don't want to know show up."

Evan looked up. "Where will we bury the body?"

"We won't. I'll drop you off, then take it to San Carlos on the Pacific coast. I'm handing it off to someone named Jackson at a warehouse near the wharf. What happens next is up to him."

"Oh." Evan seemed troubled for a moment, then his face smoothed into neutrality.

The quick change of expression raised Julio's hackles. *What's the kid hiding? There are hundreds of agents in Mexico. Some are LDS personnel from the ten or eleven Mormon Temples, including one in Tuxtla.*

Evan's cover was as a supervisor for the LDS missionaries. Maybe the kid was trying to serve two masters. Julio had to talk to him to see if he could sense the problem. If the kid had another boss and was a double agent, the Firm needed to know.

Julio felt all Mormons were a little nutty. Joseph Smith with his golden tablets and an angel called Moroni were pretty strange stuff. If Smith were alive currently, someone would medicate him and put him in a padded cell. Julio saw a lot of Mormons in Arizona when he grew up. They lived in their own small communities of mobile homes, were rumored to have lots of wives and kids, and behaved like they were holier than anyone else.

Most of the guys Julio grew up with thought it was a way some men used religion to keep lots of young pussy around. Most of the Mormon boys or young men were encouraged to leave or were forced from the group to fend for themselves soon after adolescence, leaving more females for the older guys.

Julio jerked his head toward the van. *"Vamonos!"*

"You can drop me off at the *zocalo."* Evan, pushing himself upright, grabbed his bag as he walked toward the van.

"I'm not going into Tuxtla. You'll have to take the bus from the highway. I don't want to take chances."

The kid frowned. "Fine. Let's go. I'm tired." He tossed his bag onto the floorboards and slid into the passenger seat.

Julio looked around one last time before getting in. He set his camera on the glove box, started the engine, and put the transmission into gear before making a sharp U-turn and heading down the dirt road.

After a quick glance in his rearview mirror, he asked, "Been working for the Firm for a while?"

"Yeah. A bit, I guess."

"Who's your control?"

"Don't know. Never met him." He stared straight ahead.

"I see. Just making conversation." Two could play that game. Irritated, Julio reached for his sunglasses, slipped them on, and focused on the black, patched asphalt road ahead. Cumulus clouds built in the west, moving toward the highlands. The sunglasses turned the world drab and gray, mirroring his mood.

Suddenly, a white van moving too fast rounded a curve, swerving to miss them and skidding on the loose gravel. Julio jerked the wheel to the right to avoid a collision.

"*Chingada!*" he cursed.

Evan's head turned to follow the van, and Julio watched it in his rearview mirror. The van's brake lights came on as the van slowed, then it took the dirt road leading to the ruins they just left.

"Jesus H. Christ." Julio's foot touched the brake pedal.

"No. Federales. Don't slow. Keep going."

"How'd they know we were there?"

"They probably don't, but the word's out. Keep moving."

"What word?" Julio was alarmed. "What do you know about this thing, anyway? What's so special about the dead guy?"

Evan turned sideways in the seat to watch the white van disappear up the old road. "Nothing, really." He shrugged. "It's got some sort of religious significance."

"Yeah?" He took his eyes from the road to glance at Evan.

"This a priest who just died?"

"Don't know. I suspect there's more to it than that."
"Weird." He shook his head.

The kid pivoted back to face front. After a few moments, he frowned and pointed. "Pull over at that little *tienda* just past the
Pemex. I need a pack of smokes."

Julio glanced at him. "This is hardly the time for a break."

61

"I need a smoke. It'll just take a second. There." He waved his hand. "Beside the sign that reads *Refrescos Frias.*"

"Shit. What the…? Just for a second, Kid. I have to call control and pick up some cash so I can take this cadaver to San Carlos." He glanced again in the mirror and slowed to pull of the highway onto the gravelly, rutted apron in front of the small store. "You'll get ptomaine buying shit from these places."

"Could you pull around back? I don't want anyone to see our license plate." He motioned with his hand.

"Who gives a fuck?" Julio frowned. He didn't know Mormons smoked. Maybe the kid wasn't a Mormon after all. "The dead guy doesn't care who knows."

"Humor me. There. Back under those shade trees." He pointed. "It's safe. I'll just be a sec." He reached for his backpack as the van slowed.

Julio grunted in frustration. *Who does this kid think he is to give me orders?* He gripped the wheel and stopped, shaking his head in disgust. "Just hurry."

"I will," the kid said in an odd voice.

Julio turned and stared down the barrel of a Walther PPK with silencer. "Look, Kid…."

"The body isn't going to Oaxaca. It's going in the ground."
"What? Why, you stupid, fuckin'…. He reached for the door handle.

Evan fired twice. The sunglasses flew off Julio's head as it whipped back. He slumped, and two bloody holes leaked syrupy, red-tinged gray ooze down his face.

* * *

Evan glanced toward the small red brick *tienda.* Seeing no one, he pulled his dead colleague onto the floorboard between the seats. He removed a rag from his knapsack and wiped blood off the vinyl seat and steering wheel before dropping it on the body. Opening the door, he climbed out, grabbed a blanket from behind the seat, and covered Julio. He looked around, but no one was moving around the *tienda*. Business was slow.

After walking around the back of the van, he checked the back doors and got behind the wheel before driving back down the highway the way they came. He glanced in the rearview mirror to make sure the coffin hadn't shifted before glancing at Julio's shape on the floor. Taking a calming breath, he checked the speedometer to make sure he was under the limit.

"It's all good," he told himself.

He had to focus on the task at hand. He barely glanced at the trail entrance to the old church ruin. There was no sign of the white panel truck that entered just as they left.

He drove for an hour, moving easily over the blacktop, frequently checking his mirrors until he left he turned off on the road that skirted Tuxtla Gutierrez, rising into the highlands on the old highway to San Cristobal de las Casas. Winding, narrow, and treacherous, the asphalt snake required careful navigation as it climbed higher and higher toward the pine-forested highlands of Chiapas State. Evan took his eyes off the road momentarily to peek at the lump on the floor.

He had two bodies to bury, and Elder John wanted the body in the coffin stripped first, which was easier said than done. If the Federals or the military stopped him, he was in big trouble.

How could anyone ever get accustomed to all the roadblocks? It was a crazy damn country. At any given time, every major highway could be blocked to search for smuggled drugs and guns. That was a big problem for someone in his line of work, made worse because Mexico still operated under Napoleonic Law—suspects were guilty until proven innocent. Even though he was an American citizen, he could end up in a shitty Mexican prison taking it in the ass or giving blow jobs to narco kingpins until someone in DC or the LDS in Salt Lake decided he merited retrieval and paid the bribe or used their connections to free him.

Evan's palms grew sweaty. He wiped them on his pant leg and finally saw what he was looking for midway up the mountain—a road that was barely more than a path, with tire tracks heading away from the highway into a thicket. He followed the trail, praying he wouldn't meet anyone coming in the opposite direction.

The road was deeply rutted, and the van's struts creaked as it dipped and wallowed in the red earth. It was slow going. After checking his rearview mirror, he stopped about 100 meters in. He jumped out, pulled Julio from the van, and dragged him into the brush, thinking, *Good riddance.*

His breath came in gasps, and his heart beat rapidly as he ran back to the road and listened to see if anyone was following. He returned to the van, opened the back doors, slid out the wood box, and let it drop to the bumper before hitting the ground.

He removed the lid and quickly stripped the body, taking necklace, sandals, shirt, and pants. He pulled the corpse out and let it slump to the ground. Taking a camera from his backpack, he circled the box and snapped photos of the odd Indian-priest character design and its snake-like legs and Mayan writing. Without the body, it didn't really look like a coffin.

As he put away the camera, leaves rustled, and a twig snapped.

Shit! he thought, slowly scanning the perimeter, trying to see through the brush. His breath came more rapidly, and he had a creepy feeling he was being watched.

I can't be caught in the Mexican bush with two dead men. Damn.

He needed to investigate. Retrieving his gun from the van floor, he walked down the path, calling, "Who's there? Anybody there?"

Pausing, he heard nothing. He circled back through the brush and checked Julio's body. He was still dead.

Shit. I'm turning into a weak-kneed pussy, hearing things and nearly pissing my pants. It was probably a limb falling from a tree or an animal in the brush.

He shoved the gun into his waistband and returned to work.

Taking a pocketknife from his pants pocket, he cut a lock of hair from the stripped corpse and shoved it into his pocket. He stuffed the dead guy's items into a plastic bag, tossed it in through the open van window, and gripped one leg with both hands to pull the corpse farther into the brush than Julio.

His lower back ached, and his arms trembled from exertion. He paused to catch his breath. Once more, the prickly feeling of being watched struck.

Is someone walking down the trail right now? he wondered, looking around again.

The area seemed more open and visible than he originally thought. Realizing he didn't have a shovel, he began gasping with fear, unable to calm himself.

There was no time for burials. Elder John would be disappointed, but he would be even more disappointed if Evan ended up in a Mexican jail. He needed to get out of there fast. Without brushing himself, he ran toward the van.

* * *

The Bone Man, a Maya Indian whose real name was Balaam Reyes, stood unnoticed in the shade and dense overgrowth beside a dirt road near the highway heading toward San

Cristobal de las Casas. Small in stature and slightly stooped with age, he wore dirty white cotton pants and a worn blue flannel shirt with breast pocket.

When the van first arrived, he ignored it and the occupant, concentrating instead on the colorful visions and unsure reality in which he was immersed.

Balaam Reyes was a shaman and *curandero* who frequently wandered the wooded mountains in the area when he took medicine to boost his soul into the spirit world. Four hours earlier, after performing curing rituals and enjoying a few minutes with one of his wives, Balaam wandered away from the highland Indian village of Chamula, walking slowly past small, terraced fields of corn and coffee orchards. Away from the intrusive presence of others, he could relax and rejuvenate his spirit.

He ate two psilocybin mushrooms to launch his soul, soaring unfettered into the spirit world, free of earthly concerns while his mind navigated the spiritual ether of the Real Universe. He breathed slowly and calmly as he walked, quietly engrossed in his vision, allowing whatever he might encounter to come freely. Eventually, he began to fall from his path as the medicine left his body, and the ether of the other universe slowly dissipated.

As earthly perception returned, the tired reality of *now* slowly captured his attention, and he saw he wandered far from the village. His mind became anchored in the present as he watched a young man pull a body from a van. The old shaman realized he was witnessing a crime. The body was

66

quickly discarded in the bushes, and the young man wrestled a beautiful, very old wooden box to the ground. The old shaman believed he recognized that box, and that shook him. Maybe it was the mushroom medicine, or maybe he was imagining things.

He blinked and rubbed his eyes, still partially in the other universe. He looked again at the coffin, hoping he was wrong, but no. As a young man fifty years earlier, he saw that box and knew the sinuous, red-enameled Kulkulkan, the feathered serpent of the old ones, a taunting reminder that the ancients had access to nearly infinite knowledge.

The story that all knew was of a great Toltec king who left the world after shaming himself, but he vowed to return someday. Why had the ancient ones departed from the world, leaving their people at the mercy of the foul-smelling bearded ones from across the sea?

He recalled Miguel Carranza telling the story of his family, the keepers of *El Hombre Sagrado,* the holy man who never died and whose body didn't rot and turn to dust. The box was the resting place of the man who resided both in the present and simultaneously in the spirit world. He was an unexplained miracle that many hoped would someday be the returning Kulkulkan.

When the keeper of *El Hombre Sagrado* showed him the burial box and its contents, he felt connected to the ancient man, linked by an unknown fate and a spiritual affinity he couldn't describe.

Balaam lost track of Miguel when civil war broke out in Guatemala, and the great need of his Maya Quiche brethren in the highlands stole his life. The terror and repression of the puppet government in Guatemala City, supported by rich white men from the north, was a constant companion. Perhaps *El Hombre Sagrado* was trying to intervene.

Balaam watched the young man strip the body and dump it on the ground. As the desecrator circled the burial box, Balaam deliberately moved his foot and broke a twig.

The young man stood, rushed to the van, and retrieved a gun. He quickly scoured the area, calling out as he searched. When the desecrator returned, he put away the gun and used his pocketknife to saw off a hank of the holy man's hair.

Balaam's awareness of the universe shifted. He gasped, as his breath seemed stolen from his lungs. The desecrator pulled *El Hombre Sagrado* into the bushes, paused, and ran back to the van. He jumped into the driver's seat, slammed the door, and started the engine, making a sloppy U-turn before driving toward the highway.

The shaman stood quietly, collecting his thoughts and catching his breath. His mind was clearer, but he still must be careful. Had the van and its driver truly left? Balaam's spiritual journey, begun well, went awry shortly after taking his medicine. Normally, his soul's flight into the ether was an uplifting, transcendental experience, but that day's sojourn became aimless. The ether remained murky and formless. Every journey with the medicine was different, and he had to accept whatever dwelled in the other universe he entered, though great sadness still gripped him.

Walking quietly to the red dirt road, he looked toward the highway, listening intently before feeling assured that the transgressor and murderer fled, taking his evil aura with him. Chanting a prayer to protect himself from evil spirits, Balaam ignored the first body and traced the desecrator's steps to where the holy man lay.

Bare flesh showed in the brush. It was *El Hombre Sagrado.* He arranged the holy man's limbs into a more-comfortable position and walked back to the funeral box lying on its side. Kulkulkan, the feathered serpent, was depicted there, a man ornately decorated in Mayan attire, his lower body transformed into the writhing body of a snake that wrapped sinuously around the box.

With the box askew, Kulkulkan seemed to stare at the sky with his mouth open, crying out for help. The shaman circled the box before stooping and testing its weight. It had bulk, but it wasn't overly heavy. Rocking it back and forth, he attempted to turn it upright.

On the second push, the floor inside the box shifted and slid, nearly falling out, and an old ceramic cup rolled out. He stooped to retrieve it, turning the cup over in his hands, though there was nothing remarkable about it. He could always use a cup, even an old one, so he set it aside.

On his hands and knees, he moved the loose board aside and saw a leather pouch, a rectangular bundle wrapped in leather and tied with twine. He also saw wadded cloth or clothing and three wooden cylinders. He assumed they were junk, mementoes of the deceased, but he saw that the cylinders were painted with pictographs, the old ones' writing.

Puzzled, he pursed his lips and reflected on what he might have. The cylinders looked very old. Maybe he would open them later. He placed them in his satchel along with the cup. The stiff and wooly animal hide was worn bare in places, the cloth faded. Maybe he should leave that. There were lots of items from the time of the old ones scattered throughout Mexico. As far as Balaam was concerned, most of it was junk without value. Still, he added it to his satchel to decide later.

Returning to the box, he took a deep breath and rocked it a few times, rolling it from its side onto its back. He went into the brush and grasped the corpse's arms, pulling it into a sitting position. The man was too heavy and floppy to carry, so Balaam gritted his teeth and dragged *El Hombre Sagrado* back to his resting place. The body went into the box with an arm first, then the torso, then the legs.

Panting with effort, Balaam stopped to lean against the box. It was too heavy for him to move. He had to return to Chamula as quickly as possible to get help. Though the box and body weren't his responsibility, he felt compelled to do it. He knew it was important. The body must be restored to a safe hiding place before the priests and *Ladinos* came to defile it. They would study it and find a way to make money from it until they desecrated it. They had no understanding of the old ones aside from what they read in books. They were as arrogant as they were ignorant, and the Bone Man felt confident that was why the mushroom medicine gave him such a disquieting journey, guiding him to that spot and his destiny.

He glanced into the brush where the other body lay, but there was no reason to interfere. He must hurry. The authorities could sort out the issues with the murdered man, but the holy man must be protected. His soldiers, the rebel Zapatistas who were simple villagers and farmers, would help transport the body to safety. He had business that night with his Zapatista brothers, but the box and its body had to be taken care of first.

He looked for a walking stick. Seeing a likely candidate, he retrieved it, measured it with his eye, and broke it over his thigh to the proper length. He walked into the woods, his back bent with age but still strong. With each step, his makeshift cane struck the earth.

He backtracked as he came, chanting medicine, his satchel hanging from his shoulder. It was an arduous day to travel the spirit world, and it was time to find a new home for the holy man.

* * *

Evan glanced in the rearview mirror but saw nothing alarming. *A clean exit from the crime site,* he thought.

He felt better with an empty van. Two dead bodies in it gave him the heebie-jeebies. Even at that high altitude, he perspired, making his shirt stick to his body. It was a crazy job, but he could do it. He had to stay calm.

He chuckled nervously to himself. What were the chances of being sent on the same mission in Mexico by two different masters, the LDS church and the CIA? There weren't any odds. It was impossible. He had no idea how or why something as strange as an old dead body in a ruined church in Mexico would intersect as a concern between two such disparate entities.

As part of his agreement with the Firm, he had to report all his daily activities to his control.

"Everything," the man said, "even how many times a day you take a shit." He laughed. "We collect information, so everything is important."

He would send a text message to his control on his cell phone in four hours when he reached Palenque, then he would motor upriver and hand over the cylinder and clothes to others on the Guatemala side. John called last night and gave him the details of the plan. The Guatemala twist was a surprise, but, after listening, Evan felt it was doable.

Mexico was too hot at the moment. American DEA agents, Mexican Federals, and the Mexican Army were everywhere, fighting the drug cartels. Everyone tried to track everyone else. It would be impossible to send something north via the Pan American Highway.

Guatemala wasn't as hot, and it was nearby. It made sense to move everything out of the country, even if it appeared to be meaningless junk. Evan already accomplished more-difficult tasks than transporting clothes and memorabilia into the hinterlands of Mexican to deliver to someone else.

He would tell his CIA control that Julio ditched him in San Marcos and hadn't explained his plan beyond that point. The body and box were Julio's job. Evan was a bottom-rung soldier. No one shared the big picture with underlings. He was trained to be a good soldier who performed as his control told him. He did his job, didn't ask questions, and kept his mouth shut. His only concern was his small assignment.

With luck, no one would find Julio's body for days or weeks. With really good luck, an animal would eat him and remove the evidence.

The CIA gig presented itself unexpectedly three years earlier, and Evan jumped at the opportunity. Training at Langley lasted ninety days, then he spent three weeks in Guadalajara, showing one of the Firm's agents how field personnel were managed. The money was damned good. People with connections had opportunities and options unavailable to the average person. Without connections, people were nobodies, victims who couldn't control their future, always having to grovel and suck up and depend on the good will and competence of those further up the food chain who may or may not have an interest in those lower down. It was better to play both sides.

After a couple years doing small, clandestine jobs, mostly tracing drugs and the people who trafficked in them, Evan learned his way around the system and bet no one would be able to finger him as the perp. What the guys at Langley might deduce was unknown, but he didn't see how they could tie him to Julio's disappearing or the missing body. He had no motive and nothing to gain by sabotaging a snatch-and-transport.

He didn't understand the fuss over a corpse and its clothes. Elder John was very specific about leaving the cylinder unopened and intact. If John and the CIA both wanted it that meant it had value.

Evan chuckled, recalling how he lied when he called John. He *had* removed a cylinder from the box earlier. Jacob threw a fit, but Evan insisted. It remained in the top drawer of his bedroom chest of drawers at the mission house. It could be his ticket to something big. Did the cylinders really have an unknown religious significance? He doubted it.

He didn't know why John wanted it, but the Mormon elder promised Evan an as-yet-unknown position with a substantial salary at Salt Lake. Having a patron in the LDS hierarchy was a huge benefit. The Latter Day Saints had enormous financial resources, and Evan planned to play Elder John and his assets into a lucrative nest egg that would give him the respect and wealth he deserved back home.

His faith had never been strong. Raised in a devout family with his two sisters, he quickly saw that the Mormon Church was a springboard of opportunity if he did the right things. He feared ending up like his father, a good man but an underachieving, mediocre bureaucrat mired in the magic and hocus-pocus of Mormon faith, living in near poverty in a mobile home outside Provo. Evan would never accept his father's life.

He pushed all doubts and speculations aside. The coffin had been too risky, too much trouble, and he hoped if the clothes and cylinder arrived safely in the States, Elder John would keep his promises.

* * *

Half an hour later, Evan approached the highland colonial town of San Cristobal de las Casas, where traffic thickened. A cool, brisk breeze stroked the trees, rattling their leaves, while thick, dark cumulus clouds rode capricious winds to form rippling carpets against a cobalt sky. Dina trucks laden with mangos and bananas, their wood-slatted ribs straining to near breaking, struggled ponderously along the road. Engines bellowing and black diesel exhaust fogging the highway, they toiled upward into the wooded highlands.

The narrow, serpentine road had no safety rail, making it almost impossible to pass the slower vehicles. Being careless meant driving off the road and falling over 1,000 feet to certain death. He was glad he was going up, not down, where the view into the rocky abyss at the roadside gave him a tingle down his spine.

At the outskirts of San Cristobal, he turned to bypass the town, driving past the new Pemex and dozens of small *tiendas* that sold daily essentials like sugar, tortillas, cigarettes, soda pop, and *Sabritas* chips. Tall pine forests blanketed the mountainsides, and the air felt thinner and smelled cleaner once he was off the main road.

Openings appeared in the woods, trailheads for paths leading up into highland Indian villages. The Maya believed that the higher one went, the closer he was to God or the gods, depending on how someone interpreted their absurd Catholic beliefs. In Evan's capacity as mission director in Chiapas, he tried several times without success to proselytize and gain an inroad into those small, homogenous communities. Some of the poorer Indians in the villagers joined Evangelical sects like the Seventh Day Adventists and the Assembly of God in the 1970s and '80s, but most rejected the new LDS variety of Christianity, maintaining a unanimous xenophobic front toward anyone who invaded their space.

The Mormon faith didn't resonate with the Indians. Initially, only the Indian village of Mayapan had been successfully infiltrated by Pentecostal groups, but that was twenty years earlier. A small faction of those Pentecostal Maya agitated enough to be expelled as troublemakers and were forced to resettle down the mountain near San Cristobal, where they built a new village called Betania, or Bethany. That incident served as a warning to other Mayan villages, so they became even more resolute and intolerant in adhering to their own version of Catholicism mixed with traditional beliefs.

Stay focused, he told himself. *I need to put as much distance as possible between me and those two bodies.*

Avoiding San Cristobal, which was a major tourist trap, was the best plan. Although many Europeans made the difficult journey each year to experience the Old World colonial delights of the town, it was also a nexus of intrigue. Socialist malcontents, communist wannabes, drug traffickers, and thousands of Indians, many of whom were Zapatista sympathizers, moved in and out of the area pursuing personal agendas, while the military and federal police tried to track them.

So did the CIA, which was one reason they hired Evan. Information was power. Without it, no one could make good decisions. He planned to take the old road east into the nearly impassable Sierras, navigating one of the most-spectacular, dangerous roads in the world through the heavily forested highland of the Lacandon Jungle before descending into the lowlands and the town of Palenque, named after the nearby classic Mayan ruin of Palenque.

That wasn't his final destination. He would turn south there, driving past the ruins of Bonampak and Piedras Negras to the Usumacinta River, the border between Mexico and Guatemala. He already called to lease a fourteen-foot river launch, a small, maneuverable aluminum boat used to transport tourists to the Yaxchilan ruin. He would go upriver to the ruin but would dock on the Guatemala side directly opposite, where Elder John supposedly arranged for someone, probably other Mormon missionaries, to receive the items Evan removed from the body. Evan guessed those items would be taken to Utah, though he didn't know how.

He would abandon the van with its keys near a small Indian town within walking distance of Palenque. Brother John insisted that Evan arrange a rental car there. He should return to Tuxtla Gutierrez by late the next evening.

All the villages in the area were Indian communities. Most, if not all, were Zapatistas or sympathizers. They could have the van. He chuckled, thinking of the CIA scrambling to track down a van appropriated by the Zapatistas. Maybe they would be blamed for Julio's murder. They might even be blamed for the box and the weird corpse. It was a sweet idea, and he knew it would work.

He needed to pee, but he didn't see a likely place to pull over. Driving for another thirty minutes, he reviewed his plan for flaws, checking off each stage to ensure contingencies.

Evan jerked in surprise when he remembered the lock of hair in his shirt pocket. He had to include that with the other items.

What do they want it for? he wondered. *To check its DNA? Not likely.*

His lip curled in distaste. It was probably a souvenir for somebody. Elder John was adamant that the lock of hair be sent with the clothing and any other items found with the body, including all the pictures Evan took.

He reached into his pocket to ensure the hair was still there. *Yes!* he thought when he touched it. *Good save.*

His bladder near to bursting, he found an opening at the road's edge and slowed to turn in. It was a trailhead, heavily rutted, with dense, encroaching vegetation. He could drive forward only thirty meters, but that was enough.

He stopped the car out of sight. Taking the plastic bag of items he removed from the burial box and corpse, he shoved the lock of hair into the bag and retrieved his small Canon camera from the glove box, tossing it into the sack before sealing it.

He placed it on the seat, got out of the van, and lowered his zipper.

"Ah," he groaned, as he relieved himself. "One of life's few free pleasures."

A rustle in the underbrush drew his attention. Was something there? He saw movement. It looked like two or more little cats. Staghorn fern, bindweed, and exuberant broad-leafed bushes hid them from view.

Little cats? he wondered. *That can't be good. Time to get out of here.*

Nearly done, he shook his penis a few times and tucked it into his pants before closing the zipper. As he turned toward the vehicle and reached for the door handle, something heavy slammed him against the van.

Teeth and claws ripped into him. Howling in pain, he tried to turn to see his attacker, but his scream ended as the jaguar's fangs tore into throat.

He gagged, attempted mightily to struggle, placing his hands and pushing against the head of the black, sleek cat. Claws and vise-like jaws held on tightly as Evan's body convulsed. A moment later, his limp form fell to the forest floor.

The female jaguar, large and black with faint rosette images in her fur, chewed as she shook the body. Jerking her head up and about, she heard another intruder in the forest. She coughed a warning to her cubs as she crouched low and stared. Growling an admonition, she bent her head and shoulders on short, powerful legs before slinking into the brush. The three cubs followed.

CHAPTER SIX

Elder John, lying in the hotel bed with his back propped against the headboard with pillows, glanced over the edge of his laptop to the TV. The sound was off, but Glenn Beck was weeping again on his talk show. He loved Glenn Beck, but his sobbing and emotional tirades were embarrassing. Even John knew that Beck, though a Mormon, was a charlatan. His silly-assed graphs and conspiracy theories made for good entertainment, though.

The stinking liberals deserved it. Beck wasn't a serious student of religion, either. His admonition for Christians to run from their churches in horror if their pastors spoke of social justice was pure ignorance. Hadn't the man read any books in his life? Had he ever read the Gospels?

John considered his crotch, where his erection failed him again. He couldn't blame Beck for that. The promiscuous little twat he invited to his hotel room to talk about her lost scholarship hadn't shown up, and even worse, John's porn sites weren't doing the job for him, either. Didn't they ever get new material on those filthy sites? There was no imagination. It was all fucking and sucking, with the same tired-looking whores who couldn't fake a smile, let alone an orgasm. He should cancel his subscription and find new sites. At his age, he needed inspiration. Young girls were best, but in a pinch, good porn video should firm him up long enough to climax.

He slammed shut the laptop screen and tossed it to the other side of the bed. He was still distracted by that body in Mexico. It was driving him nuts. He hated not being in control, and here he was, in a low-rent motel room with his dick in his hand waiting for a call from a young missionary supervisor he didn't know.

If the young man's spectacular find panned out, his future was made for eternity. He would ascend to the Quorum of Twelve Apostles, maybe eventually the three-man presidency, with his discovery. The Kingdom of Heaven would commence while he was still on earth.

The Book of Mormon clearly stated that American Indians were the Lamanites, descended from the lost Israeli tribe of Lehi. The Angel Moroni revealed that to Joseph Smith, their founder. Around 600 BC, Lehi's children split into warring factions, the white Nephites and brown Lamanites. By 500 BC, the victorious Lamanites killed all the white Nephites, leaving the brown Lamanites to live on as Native Americans. They could only become *white and delightsome* once they converted to Mormonism.

For too long, the improbable assertion had been an embarrassing story, yet it was a central theme taught to Mormon children. For many years, BYU had been conducting genetic tests of thousands of "volunteers" in Israel and among various members of aboriginal tribes in the Pacific Islands and South America. Although the results of the research hadn't been released, Brother John heard that the data could not yet verify that central and important tenet of Mormon doctrine.

He wasn't a biologist, but he suspected that was because Native American DNA had become degraded by the Spanish or other Europeans to the point where it became unverifiable. The body Evan told him about, if it was as old as he said, would change that. John had an intuition that the dead man in Mexico would turn the ecclesiastic and scientific communities on their heads. The LDS church would no longer be the laughingstock of the Abrahamic religions and would be able to shed the word "cult." The Mormon Church would have instant, permanent credibility, the kind only science brought, which was very rare in the world of religion.

He glanced at his wristwatch. Evan wouldn't call for several hours, and John needed to contact Dean Amos to see if he could put the boy in contact with that key researcher in the

Department of Life Sciences who directed the Lamanite Research Project. When Evan produced a lock of hair from the body, Brother John would celebrate by buying a new suit and finding a young girl to have sex with. He felt certain he was right about the body, and the saints were working through him.

It was time to go to work. He reached for the TV remote. Glenn Beck blubbered on about Nazis and pointed at his chalkboard. That was enough nonsense for the day.

He turned off the TV and stood, pulling up his underwear and slacks before tucking in his shirt and walking toward the bathroom mirror. The little blonde slut was a disappointment, but he would decide what to do with her the following day. If she had a good excuse, he could offer her another opportunity. If not, she would rue her decision not to come and discuss her scholarship and the benefits of becoming one of his special friends.

CHAPTER SEVEN

Brazier coals smoldered and flickered red in an outdoor stove, while night insects ticked and chirped in the foliage. The moon shone like mother of pearl as it drifted through the night sky before a blinking curtain of sparkling gems. Alexandra returned with two colorful *rebozos,* shrouds made by the Indians, handing one to Karen and placing the other around her own shoulders to ward off the chill of the southern Sierra Madres.

David, though, appeared impervious to the cold and had trouble following the conversation. His wife tried to engage him in the present several times, but his mind remained on the photographs of the scrolls he faxed earlier to his colleague, Yusuf Bin Saud, at American University in Lebanon, Beirut. David couldn't translate the documents himself, but he recognized the script and hadn't hesitated to send copies and a personal note to his colleague who specialized in ancient languages on the other side of the world.

The incongruity of Old World scripts in an archeological site in the New World meant it had to be a fraud. It was ridiculous, but the dilemma had to be resolved. The reasonable thing to do was verify or disqualify their credibility.

How long would it take to hear back? It was too bad he didn't have Yusuf's phone number, or he would have called first, but that wasn't possible.

When Alexandra stood and called his name, David realized his mind was thousands of miles away again. She pointed at his plate and the soiled dishes of their guests stacked on the patio table.

David rose and helped her carry them from the veranda into the house and kitchen. Karen and Father Salvador Lopez remained behind, conversing on the patio, each seemingly tuned to the other's channel, connecting as kindred spirits. In the cool, crisp evening, smoke from the brazier wafted upward into the high-altitude forest carpeting the mountains on either side of the *rancho*. The Milky Way lay softly against a dark velvet sky, a dazzling, sequined belt of heavenly, flickering fireflies.

"It's like we aren't even here," David said, chuckling, "and it's our house." He placed a stack of dirty dishes in the sink. "I was worried they wouldn't get along. Boy, was I wrong."

Alexandra smiled. "Your Father Salvador friend seems to like her, David. It's been awhile since I saw a priest pay so much attention to an attractive female, at least *that* kind of attention." Her mouth twitched with disapproval. "It's a little unnerving, actually." She turned to peer over her glasses at him.

"Yeah, well, I don't really know what to say. I'm surprised, too, but then, maybe I'm not. Lots of unexpected things are going on with Sally…I mean, Father Lopez." He glanced out the window over the sink at the couple on the veranda. "Actually, well…. I invited him to stay awhile with us."

"Really? That will be nice, I guess. How long? What kind of unexpected things do you mean, David?" She walked up to him, rested her arms on his shoulders, and tried to catch his eye.

He glanced at her before looking away. With a sigh, he turned to engage her gaze. He almost explained Sally's situation, but he interrupted himself by asking, "Where's Marcos? Do you know why he isn't here?"

"I think she dumped him, but don't change the subject,

Querido."

"No. Really?"

"You sound surprised."

"I was beginning to think they were connected at the pelvis."

"David!" She placed her hands on her hips and gave him a warning smile. "I don't know the details, but he's never around when she wants him to be, and everyone has heard about his skirt-chasing."

"I like Marcos."

"So do the ladies. Everyone likes him except El Presidente, the governor of Chiapas, and the Army. You're avoiding my questions. What's the situation with our new boarder? I didn't see any luggage."

David took a deep breath. "He's thinking of leaving the priesthood. He's having…problems with faith."

"You're kidding, right? Priests don't break their vows in Mexico or anywhere else. Does the bishop know he's here? I thought they sent priests like that to a special place for talk therapy. How'd you get involved in this mess?"

"He's a former student. I don't know what the bishop knows, but I'm pretty sure Sally isn't interested in any therapy administered by the church." He used the index finger of each hand to add emphasis to the word therapy.

"No need for sarcasm, David."

"Sorry. That wasn't my intent. I'm sure he'll be more than happy to talk with you…with us about it at a different time." Glancing through the window, he saw Sally sitting in the chair beside Karen, not the one across from her. She turned toward him, smiling and hanging on his words.

David shook his head before turning back to Alexandra. "It surprised me, too. I knew he had some issues simmering. He related some of what's going on with him today at the ruin, but I wasn't expecting this. If anything is really occurring…. I mean, who knows what's happening out there?" He gestured with his head. "I'm sure it's all very innocent," he muttered, adding, "maybe we should get out there and…."

"No. That's exactly what we aren't going to do."

He looked ready to protest, but she raised her hand.

"Stay out of it," she advised. "Give them some space. They're guests, and they're both adults. They'll come inside when they're done talking." Taking his hand, she led him into the living area and the TV.

"We were supposed to talk about the Xibalba cave excavation tonight," David said. "She said she had lots of things to discuss."

"You're whining, dear. Leave it alone. Can't you give up your work for a few hours occasionally?"

"OK. I made myself available. It's up to her."

Alexandra plopped down on the couch, while David folded himself into the recliner and groaned.

"She wanted to talk about Marcos, David," Alexandra said. "She was practically in tears when she arrived this afternoon. It's been tough on her, with the excavation, her relationship with Marcos, the Zapatistas, and the Federal Army constantly in and out of the area."

"I like Marcos."

"So do a lot of people, many of them young women in Chiapas."

"And therein is the problem?"

"You're so sharp and attuned to women."

"And I'm being sarcastic?"

She blew him a kiss. "If she wants to discuss the excavation, I'm sure she'll bring it up before she leaves." She walked into the kitchen and returned with two half-filled brandy snifters. Smiling, she gave one to David. "Think our guest would like a glass?"

"They looked intoxicated enough the last I saw. Let's try to get caught up." He sipped from his glass, as did Alexandra, who grimaced as the brandy slid down her throat.

He stared into the amber liquid swirling in his glass. "How would you like a back rub tonight?"

"I had one Wednesday night, remember?"

"Am I on rationing?" He smiled, catching her eye.

"Oh, David, don't be silly." She swatted his foot gently. "We have guests, and, well, go easy on the brandy. Let's see if you're even awake later."

He looked up as Sally and Karen entered the living room. Karen smiled, her gaze on the floor. Sally looked decidedly squeamish and uncomfortable.

"Salvador has kindly asked to see me back to the hotel, and I accepted his offer." She didn't look up, though she glanced at David from the corner of her eyes, as coy and mischievous as a young girl.

"Er, yes, well," Salvador began, "I mean, I'll be only half an hour or so. You see, it's not far to town, and, well…. Can I borrow your car for a short time, David?" He glanced at the professor's face to gauge his response, then turned away and looked around the room as if seeking a place to hide.

"Of course," Alexandra said. "The keys are hanging on the rack near the back door."

David, feeling uncomfortable, quickly turned the conversation to business. "I thought you had a list of things you wanted to discuss from the excavation. There's still time tonight. We can cover a few things now and address the rest tomorrow. You weren't planning on being away from the site more than a day or two, were you?'

Karen frowned and raised her head. "Well, actually, I was. I need to talk about some personal issues, and well, maybe this isn't the right time." She glanced quickly at Sally. "Can it wait until tomorrow?"

"Your call, Karen." David raised his hands with the palms out. "I'm available. Just let me know. The earlier in the day, the better."

Alexandra returned from the kitchen. "I have plans for you tomorrow morning, David. Afternoon would be better."

"It would?" he turned to her with a questioning look, but she wouldn't meet his gaze. "I don't recall anything…."

"Here are the keys, Father…Salvador. The door key is this one." She held it up. "If the lights are out when you return, make yourself at home. We're old folks now and go to bed earlier than you youngsters."

Confused, David stood and chewed his lower lip. Perhaps it was one of those moments when he should think before talking.

"That's settled, then," Alexandra said. "I'll get your purse and briefcase, Karen."

David watched her walk toward the bedroom, then he turned to Sally. "Watch out for cattle on the roads, especially the curves. You know how it is."

"Of course. I'll be safe, David. You know me." He smiled wanly.

David looked at him, then at Karen. He recognized her expression, but he wasn't sure he knew Salvador at all after the day's events. "Yeah, well, have fun, you two. Talk to you tomorrow."

Alexandra returned with Karen's purse and briefcase. "We'll talk, OK?" She winked at the younger woman.

David frowned. *Did she just wink at Karen as if they're sharing a secret conspiracy?* His ability to understand women's communication was tenuous at best. At that moment, it failed him completely, so he smiled and didn't speak. Karen thanked them graciously and walked toward the front door, which Salvador helped open for her.

"Back soon, David." Sally attempted a smile.

"Sure, Sally. Whenever." He stood on the patio with Alexandra, watching the Ford Explorer's red tail lights jiggle and wobble down the gravel driveway to the asphalt road fronting his small ranch house.

As the Explorer disappeared from sight, David and Alexandra stood quietly, peering into the majestic calm. The heavily forested hills and distant mountains loomed dark and forbidding. San Cristobal de las Casas, which lay in a bowl at the foot of the mountains, was too distant to cast its dim halo so far into the foothills of the highlands. The Milky Way splashed like a spangled bolt of silk flung across the sky, while the growl of the car engine faded.

Insects cheeped, and fireflies flickered occasionally on tepid, lazy air currents. David squeezed his wife's hand. "How'd I do?"

"You were great, Sweetie." She leaned against his arm, resting her head on his shoulder. "Sometimes you have to remember that not everyone is your age or shares your concerns. Young people will act like young people whether we want them to or not."

"Well, I suppose, Ali," he tried to appear understanding, "but he's a priest, and she has lots of work to do. I think he's a mess. She isn't the answer. As a matter of fact…."

"David, you promised me a massage."

"Eh?"

"You promised me a foot rub and massage." She squeezed his hand in return, looking expectantly at him.

He sighed and gave her a weary smile. "I'm being manipulated, aren't I?"

"No, Dear. You're being rewarded for being a good man. Should I go sort laundry?"

"I can be there in five minutes. Let me brush my teeth and close a few windows. It gets chilly at this time of year."

CHAPTER EIGHT

The Bone Man woke to the sound of a crying child and muffled conversation. It was dark, early morning, the *madrugada,* the time of day he rose every day of his life. His hut, with its dirt floor and walls of pine planks, many desiccated and crumbling with dry rot, allowed flickers of outdoor fires and grills to come through, as well as the delicious aroma of tortillas roasting on barrel lids and makeshift grill covers. Overripe fruit, frying pork, urine, and smoke from the pits of the *charcoleros,* the charcoal makers, saturated the air.

He experienced a powerful vision as he slept that night. Sometimes, one couldn't tell a dream from a vision so soon after taking the mushroom medicine. It sometimes affected a person's sleep for days. The previous night's dream was definitely a gift from the spirit world. He lay in his hammock, considering the dream vision, nursing his aching joints, and recalling the previous day's events.

He was in the village for Mohuichil for two days, nearly all of it spent dispensing folk medicines and remedies and plying his trade as a *curandero* and shaman. Most of his craft dealt with routine illnesses, like earaches, arthritis and joint pain, menstrual cramps, and occasional cases of male impotence. All serious infections were referred to the white man's medicine.

Unlike some of his fellow practitioners, Balaam learned early that there were some things the white man's medicine treated better, such as snake bites and serious infections.

He also treated two cases of soul sickness in the village, a very serious and sometimes lethal matter that couldn't be diagnosed or treated by white medicine. White people were too stupid or too oblivious to believe in soul sickness, so how could they treat something they didn't believe existed?

All traditional Maya believed in a dual soul, one shared by a companion spirit animal, such as a possum, flying squirrel, or deer. Any of God's creatures can harbor the companion soul with whom one is inextricably linked at birth for his entire life. All life on the planet is linked. That was fundamental to understanding God's nature. How one's companion soul fared during its life directly impacted one's health.

If the companion soul was healthy, the person was healthy. If he had poor health, was injured, or chose a path that deviated from his fellow man, that affected the soul of the animal with whom he shared a bond. Spiritual health and physical wellbeing were inseparable to the Maya. Although it was unknown to most white people, it was common sense and widely accepted to the Indians.

The Bone Man's name, Balaam Reyes, meant jaguar. It was no surprise that his spirit animal was the fierce cat that instilled awe and fear into all who ventured into the jungle. The old man groaned and sat up in his hammock, casting his legs over the edge to sit and orient himself.

He remembered the jaguar in his dream, then he recalled the young criminal gringo in the forest. Had the fierce, black jaguar, perhaps his own companion soul, attacked and killed the evil white man who stole *El Hombre Sagrado?* Whether it happened in the real world as well as in his vision, the Bone Man didn't know. Sometimes his visions came true, and he knew that God punished evil to maintain equilibrium in the universe.

In his dream, the Bone Man recalled he plucked the mushroom medicine from piles of bull manure and ate four of them after their stems turned dark purple. Fully immersed in the spirit world, he sat in the bow of a tree in the Lacandon forest.

The suddenness of the jaguar's attack stole his breath and momentarily thrust him into the mind of the sleek, avenging beast as it nearly severed the white man's head from its neck with one bite of its powerful jaws. Then the Bone Man was back in his body as the jaguar turned and sought his gaze. Was it searching for confirmation or recognition of its deed? The mushroom medicine frequently provided unforgettable adventures and insights that were as humbling as they were awe-inspiring. That was why he chose a spiritual life over that of a common worker and everyday family man. He would take the jaguar's gift with him to his grave.

Balaam sighed. He had to find a home for *El Hombre Sagrado* that day, then he must decide what to do with the box and items he found with the body. He remembered he had a sack full of old artifacts he accumulated in recent years as gifts from various villagers. He had no use for them and knew they would be misused or discarded if left lying about.

He planned to leave them at *Ahua* Wolf's house, the archeologist and occasional employer. Balaam trusted very few white people, but the professor was a good man for a white guy. When Balaam occasionally needed money, which was rare for him, the professor gave him temporary work. Their paths crossed at times in the wooded Lacandon or near the Xibalba excavation site.

In the last few years, though, *Ahua* Wolf seemed to avoid him, probably because of his involvement with the Zapatista Army and the knife wound the professor suffered after following that ridiculous female archeologist into the Lacandon jungle.

How could his son, Marcos, have become so enamored with her? What future could his son see with such a woman? Other than long legs and big breasts, she had nothing to offer. Balaam found her to be willful like a child, disobedient when it pleased her, and having no interest in having a child at her breast. She probably didn't even cook. If she were one of his wives, he would take a switch to her legs and backside, then bed her.

Groaning, he scooted over the edge of the hammock onto the floor. He'd been wandering the jungles and isolated villages of Guatemala and Chiapas for so long, some people assumed he was ageless. Until a few years earlier, he maintained uncommon vitality and a schedule that would have exhausted a younger man. He didn't know why he enjoyed such remarkable vigor for his entire life, but he did.

As in the old tradition, he married and maintained several wives in various villages throughout Chiapas and Guatemala and had already buried several of them. By his own reckoning, he was ninety-four-years old. However, in the last two years, aches and pains that had never been part of his life came to stay, and none of his folk remedies alleviated them.

He stretched a bit, passed wind, and grunted with satisfaction. Stooping, he strapped worn sandals on his calloused, scarred feet. The widow Ortega promised him a breakfast of beans, tortillas, and hot chicken soup, and his mouth watered at the thought. There was much to do, but he could accomplish only one thing at a time. A full belly cleared a man's mind for important decisions.

He would deal with *Ahua* Wolf and his own ragtag Zapatista army later in the day. The council of elders made a very big decision that would affect the lives of all for a long time. The Zapatistas must make a serious statement again, lest the world forget the unconscionable poverty of the poor in Chiapas and other Indian communities in Mexico, who remained outcasts condemned to destitution and neglect.

* * *

Elder John sat at his office desk, the telephone receiver pressed against his ear. When he called the Mission House that morning, a boy named Jacob, who Evan mentioned the previous day, answered and said, "I haven't seen the Mission Father since noon two days ago, when we were at the ruined church. Now there are suspicious-looking people keeping an eye on the Mission House. One is sitting in a pickup truck across the street and doesn't try to hide the fact that he's watching everyone who comes and goes.

"What should I do?" Jacob asked nervously. "Should I call the police? Should I ask the guy in the pickup what he's doing?" "Neither," John said. "How many missionaries do we have on-site in Tuxtla?"

"I'm pretty sure there were seven of us, Sir."

"I want everyone to refrain from going outside or otherwise circulating in the area for now. No mission activities— understood?"

"You want us to stay inside?"

"Exactly. I want Evan to call me immediately when he returns. Understood?"

"Yes, Sir." Jacob paused. "Is it OK to call my mom and dad?"

"Absolutely not, at least for a day or two. Everything will be fine. Let's let Evan sort things out when he returns, OK? You can call your parents soon."

An uncomfortable silence followed. Clearly Jacob didn't like his instructions.

"Look, Jacob, if Evan hasn't returned by evening, call me back. You have the number. You can call your parents then. I just want you to touch base with me first so I know what's going on. Agreed?"

"Agreed," Jacob said glumly.

John, cursing silently, slammed down the receiver. *What the hell's going on down there? The mission director is missing, strangers are skulking around the Mission House, and no one's in charge.*

Nothing had gone right. Evan failed to meet and deliver the goods to John's contact on the Guatemala side of the Usumacinta near the Yaxchilan ruin. He hadn't called the previous night to say he completed the task. What happened to the body, the hair sample, the cylinders, and Evan? Had he drowned in the Usumacinta? Was he arrested by Federals?

There was way too much at stake.

John had to plan and act quickly if Evan didn't call by evening. He might have to visit Chiapas himself to regain control of the situation. His future in the hierarchy of the LDS was at risk, resting in the hands of inexperienced youths who might be fools.

Why were people watching the Mission House? Was Jacob just being paranoid? What should John do?

Pondering briefly, he decided. He had resources—money, personnel, and power. It was time to flex his muscles. He pulled the BYU phone directory from a drawer and dialed the number for Professor Jackson in the Department of Life Sciences. John needed answers from the director of the Lamanite DNA research project before he stuck out his neck any further.

CHAPTER NINE

Father Sean Gregory, fatigued but relaxed, sat in a large overstuffed chair that was the mate to the equally plush couch on his right. Various pictures and paintings with religious themes hung throughout the parlor of the rectory at Tuxtla Gutierrez. Beautiful, colorful curtains woven with Indian themes hung over a set of louvered windows on the east wall. Straight ahead, a large, sliding-glass door opened onto a marble-floored patio replete with central fountain and potted lime and avocado trees. A carnival of red and purple bougainvillea, erupting from a balcony above the patio, cascaded to the floor. The sun shone brightly earlier, but it descended into the western sky, leaving the patio and surrounding red-tiled roof in the shade of towering mahogany trees.

Filled with embarrassment, the bishop had fled to his office and telephone after delivering his regrets. He sternly ordered Father Sanchez to accompany him, no doubt to express his unhappiness, while planning somehow to salvage the debacle he believed this afternoon would be. Father Gregory, however, wasn't so certain the day's activities were a disaster. Although he was disappointed that young Father Lopez hadn't made himself available, Father Gregory left the site very intrigued and more than a little curious.

"Thank you." He smiled and accepted a glass of cold, white *horchata* from the housekeeper. He drank deeply, draining nearly half the glass, which made her smile and offer more, but he declined.

Father Gregory was a priest attached to the Congregation for the Protection of the Faith, formerly known as the Holy

Inquisition. His official tile was Papal Inquisitor, but he thought that sounded overly intimidating and did little to reflect his real work, which was investigating the odd circumstances of natural phenomena and easily explained miracles for the Catholic Church. It wasn't that he didn't believe in miracles, but he was also an archeologist and trained scientist.

As a Cradle Catholic, he approached his religious education with the same fervor and acceptance as his parents and Kate, his sister. Unlike Kate, whose favorite reading was *Lives of the Saints,* as a child he immersed himself in stories of adventure and mystery before moving on to *National Geographic* and *Nature.* His fascination with life led to a determination to understand the nature of man in the universe. God gave mankind the ability to reason, not just restrict itself to catechisms and entrenched moral theology. Yes, He blessed humankind with intuition and faith, two things science couldn't measure. Those were essential in providing insight and direction when analysis and logic failed, but maudlin, credulous belief without common sense didn't illuminate the complexities of God and His creation.

It was unfortunate that religious belief was associated with ignorance and science with atheism. Father Gregory believed that although they seemed polar opposites, reason and faith existed as a duality, because it wasn't possible to understand anything truly without both. He felt certain that was part of God's plan.

Thus he decided to join the priesthood. It came late in his life, when he was thirty, and he scandalized more than a few of his colleagues at Westerols College, a small, four-year liberalarts institution in southern Iowa. As a heterosexual man, he tried several times to find a serious relationship with a woman. Sex was great stuff, better than archeology most of the time, but he never found his soul mate. A final failed relationship with a faculty member five years his senior in the natural sciences department, led him to take a serious look at the vocation he once considered but rejected. The reasons for his earlier rejection seemed less important, especially the foremost of them —sex.

He began rigorous interviews and a time of deep introspection, which led to his acceptance into the seminary. With a PhD in anthropology and a year of seminary behind him, he was fast-tracked, pulled from school, and sent to Rome. Two years later, he was ordained. After a short visit to his family in Omaha, he was assigned to his present job.

When a religious miracle occurred, an event that promised hope or change for the wretched in the world, the Congregation for the Protection of the Faith was called, and specialists like Father Gregory were dispatched to investigate. Many of the places he'd been sent couldn't be found on any printed map. In the last three months he investigated a weeping Madonna portrait in the Peruvian Andes, a bleeding statue of Jesus in an unpronounceable hamlet 600 miles up the Amazon, and a mysterious source of music that always occurred around 3:00 AM in a small village chapel 150 miles southwest of Porto Belo, Brazil.

In the last four years, he'd been hospitalized with bone break fever and malaria and twice with infestations of intestinal parasites. He was spat on by Islamic extremists in Luxor, Egypt, his life was threatened in the small African country of Benin, and he was solicited by a gaggle of prostitutes near the Palatine Hill in Old Rome. Life had never been that interesting in Omaha or on the Westerols campus in southern Iowa.

All of God's works were fraught with difficulties, but some more than others. Patience, he learned, was the first trait he must acquire to perform his job. His famous ancestor, Murphy, was right when he said, "Anything that can go wrong, will go wrong." The present case was a good example.

His Eminence Bishop Alvarez of the Tuxtla Gutierrez Diocese of Chiapas requested an investigation two weeks earlier into a strange story about a body that supposedly refused to putrefy and was associated with possible ancient writing. Father Gregory came to Chiapas and found his eminence functioning with barely maintained fury after discovering that the principal focus or witness in the investigation, Father Salvador Lopez, was missing. The errant priest called earlier that morning, leaving a vague message with the housekeeper that he felt a little confused and would be away for some time.

"They should not worry," he told her. "I'll be in contact later when the time is right."

That was bizarre behavior for a Catholic priest. The visibly embarrassed bishop confided that the young priest had always been a challenge to guide and direct, but the current betrayal and neglect of duty and sworn oath was unconscionable. The Holy See sent an inquisitor to his diocese, and a young priest scuttled the whole affair.

Father Gregory reasoned that the bishop saw it as a personal attack from an underling. It would certainly ruin Father Lopez's career if and when he returned.

His Eminence did his best to put on a good face while working desperately behind the scenes to get the investigation moving in the right direction. He located Father Sanchez, a friend of the missing Father Lopez, or Sally as he was called, another priest in whom he confided and who accompanied him once to the mysterious ruin with its body. Father Sanchez agreed to lead them to the ruin's location.

Father Gregory had no expectation of any serious digging or meddling in the area. That would be premature and hasty. After reading the report and request sent by the bishop, he tried without success to locate the name of the ruined mission on the Vatican's register of churches. The bishop told him the reason it wasn't listed was that, prior to the revolution, the Catholic Church owned 50% of all property in Mexico. After the war, the Church refused to swear allegiance to the new government, which resulted in the confiscation of thousands of parcels of church land and buildings that were redistributed to the poor in the 1820s. The former mission was one of many too numerous to mention that were stolen during the rupture from the Church. The bishop felt the ruin could easily be 400 years old, though it was probably destroyed by an earthquake 150 years ago, left in devastation by the federal government due to lack of funds or that it was a mission and chapel only the Indians used.

In Father Gregory's business, he took circumstances as they were presented and did his best. It was likely that Father Lopez would appear to make his excuses soon enough. Meanwhile, using his most-agreeable demeanor, Father Gregory began organizing and preparing to visit the site. No doubt he would find a simple explanation. Most likely, it was just a hoax.

He needed a few basic items, including battery-powered lamps, a skein of polyester rope, plastic sandwich baggies, adhesive tape, a measuring tape, and tote bags in case he decided to move or carry something back for further examination. A year earlier he acquired a new digital camera and was fascinated by its ability and versatility. It could take video and still shots. He also acquired a Macintosh computer on which to process the video. Occasionally, when he had Internet access, he sent photos over the Web to his superiors in Rome.

The ruined church was more intriguing than he predicted. Bodies decomposed unless specially prepared as they were in Egypt or abandoned in very arid, cold, high altitudes like Peru. Chiapas ranged from lowland jungle to the high Sierra Madres, all of it blessed with an abundant rainy season. It was unlikely he'd find bodies over twenty-four hours old that hadn't begun to decompose. Any corpse that wasn't corrupted or decomposed was a sign of holiness and an important aspect in defining sainthood in the Catholic Church. He believed the locals were mistaken, and he expected he would have patiently to walk them through some event caused by natural phenomena or in the discovery of a hoax.

The problem was that they found the burial box, body, and writings the bishop had carefully described all missing. The stone-lined vault under the ruined church was obviously much older than the chapel and mission above it. That lent credence to the idea that the Church deliberately selected and built over an older site that had religious importance to the Indians.

It was also obvious there was recent activity. Something large, perhaps the coffin the bishop and priest described, had been dragged from the burial chamber through a corbelled stone passageway into the open, where several sets of tire tracks led onto the rutted road giving access to the site. Tracks and footprints of various-sized shoes were everywhere.

The bishop explained that the body hadn't been moved to the chancellery at the insistence of Father Lopez, who claimed it was essential to have the body examined without disturbing the circumstances of its entombment. Although that would normally be correct, the body was missing, and all the inquisitor could examine were the seriously smudged, flaking, deteriorating stuccoed walls painted with scenes of Mayans doing unknown things.

Their lanterns revealed what seemed to be an important person in full Mayan religious regalia with a snake-like lower body entwined with the Mayan World Tree, its roots firmly in the underworld and its branches climbing into the heavens. The priest, king, of whoever he was stood and offered a cup to several kneeling, reverent people during a ritual. Father Gregory assumed the cup contained beer, corn, chocolate, or almost anything else. It could easily be something other than a cup, perhaps a symbol of office, a gift, or a weapon.

Although he was trained as an archaeologist and studied Maya in graduate school, he didn't consider himself an expert. Before leaving the vault, he photographed the cracked, faded, stucco walls and paintings, then took several shots of the ruin from the outside. If he needed a Mayan expert, there were many available.

He wondered what happened to the body, box, and contents. Their absence was odd, even suspicious. If he hoped for a quick investigation and resolution that would allow him a few days to enjoy the fabled beauty of Chiapas, his hopes were dashed. He had to find the missing items, especially the body. Without a corpse, there was no evidence of anything. The purported Jewish and Christian symbols were gone, too.

As a priest and scientist, he wouldn't be able to write a report and submit it to his superiors in Rome without observing the artifacts and body and performing tests. He had to stay until he reached a resolution that satisfied all involved—himself, Bishop Alvarez, Father Lopez, and his superiors in the Vatican.

Father Gregory sipped his *horchata*. Who would want the body? Did it have some value? If so, what could it be? Bishop Alvarez was on the phone to the federal police and anyone else who might be able to aid them in locating the body and learning the reason for its disappearance. He called several people with whom Father Lopez was friends without success.

He also called Bishop Ruiz in San Cristobal, but he was out visiting Indians in their villages again, something that greatly disconcerted Bishop Alvarez. Bishop Ruiz was much-loved by several hundred thousand Mayan villagers in his diocese in the highlands around San Cristobal. He spoke two or three of their dialects and showed his support for the Zapatista uprising that began in 1994.

Father Gregory knew most bishops rarely ventured far from the official trappings and ceremonies of the Church, but Bishop Samuel Ruiz' name was well-known in Rome for his leftist leanings and sympathy for the poor Indians of Chiapas. Although it was extremely unlikely that Bishop Ruiz was involved in the body's disappearance, it was conceivable he might have information who the bishop of Tuxtla could contact for assistance.

If the issue of the missing body didn't resolve itself by noon of the following day, Father Gregory would be forced to call Rome for assistance. That was his last choice, because he didn't want to offend his host, but he couldn't sit around waiting for someone to show up and provide answers. He must be proactive. Events were in motion that must be understood and controlled by the Catholic Church. It was their duty and responsibility.

If there was anything the Eternal City was known for, it was its connections to powerful, important people worldwide. If the bishop of Tuxtla Gutierrez couldn't make things happen, many in Rome could. That was the nature of Rome and the Church in Mexico and any other Catholic country.

CHAPTER TEN

Two Days Later

Father Lopez reclined in a wicker lounge chair on Karen's balcony while she showered. The fragrant odor of baking tortillas from a nearby *tortilleria* contested with the tannic smell of car exhaust and stink of curbside rubbish. The view east into the Lacandon highlands began with a mosaic of a thousand rooftops, some with red tiles, others multicolored with sagging clotheslines, flapping banners, rusted water tanks, broken TV antennas, and an array of miscellaneous junk, toys, and broken furniture. Flat roofs sometimes served as patios or extra rooms for the poor, especially if they had children and nowhere for them to play.

Reddish-brown foothills with impressive rocky outcroppings gave way to heavily terraced fields of bananas, corn, and beans. Finally, the manicured fields blended into pine and hardwood forests densely choked with fern, bindweed, wildflowers, and every imaginable tropical plant, some of which hadn't yet been cataloged.

It was twelve years since he was with a woman. It wasn't because he hadn't wanted to or was afraid of the experience, but because he accepted the vows of the priesthood and remembered the lure and wonderful addiction of females, sex, and their God-given mystique. The mystery of Karen had been everything he remembered and better than he hoped. He should feel distraught and should have felt so guilty beforehand that he couldn't have engaged in the act at all, but he didn't. Instead, he felt cloaked with contentment, comfortable with the finality of breaking his vows.

106

What a wonderful mind and personality she has, he thought. *What a beautiful body.*

Her vulnerability was every bit as distracting as her conversation and worldly ways. He knew he was still in the thrall of emotional euphoria, but that didn't make it any less real. Sex was a biological drive, and it wasn't possible to escape the human condition as long as one had a corporeal body.

Before entering the seminary, he knew only two women, and only one was a serious relationship. He suppressed the memory and dedicated himself to cause and belief, but he never forgot.

He wasn't the first or last man to act on his biology.

Was what we shared something singular and noble, wrought with meaning, or was it just base biology? he wondered.

It wasn't his personal dilemma or for those in the Catholic vocations but of all men and women.

Karen tapped on the sliding-glass door before stepping over the threshold and onto the balcony. She handed him one of the two glasses of red wine as she bent to kiss him. The top of her bathrobe fell aside, exposing an ample breast. She straightened and smiled, while he stroked her leg through thick, soft cotton.

"Cheers, Sally." She raised her glass.

"Cheers, Karen." He touched his glass to hers.

"Are we still good?'

"We're still good."

"You're sure? You won't condemn me as a harlot and go slinking back to your confessor to tell him I'm a succubus who should be burned at the stake?"

He smiled at the joke. "You're a beautiful young woman with a great head on your shoulders who also has a healthy sexual appetite. You also apparently like to pick up strays."

"What does that mean?"

"Sit down, please." He smiled. "It was meant in jest. Please don't be offended. I was merely referring to myself as a priest and possibly to your friend Marcos, the revolutionary."

She was currently on the rebound from her relationship with the famous, if not notorious, leader of the Zapatistas. He knew she experienced many men and had been married once for a short time.

She sat heavily onto the adjacent lounge chair. "I just might be offended if I want to," she huffed. "I wasn't expecting that kind of comment. How did Marcos come into this conversation? I was expecting something more like how wonderful I am, how sexy I am, or how…. I don't know. Picking up strays? It sounds like I'm a hooker."

"Karen, please…."

"Please what? Are all priests this dense and clumsy?"

Alarmed, he stood and knelt beside her. "I'm sorry. I meant nothing malicious. It was intended as a bad joke about my being a stray. Please forget it. Yes, I would imagine most priests are clumsy as me or worse. I haven't had much practice at this stuff."

"You sure know how to kill a good mood." Glaring, she closed her robe.

"Karen, I'm an idiot. Please, let's start over." He stroked her arm.

She smiled wanly. "Say some nice things to me like you did an hour ago, Sally, or I'll push you off the balcony."

"Only a woman as beautiful and intelligent as you could be so understanding as to forgive my awkward attempts at humor."

"That's not bad." She pursed her lips and nodded. "It's true, too. Keep going, you silver-tongued devil."

"Your work as an archeologist provides great knowledge and meaning to the world. You are singularly qualified to be working at the Xibalba excavation site, and David Wolf should appreciate your efforts more than he does."

A real smile tugged at her mouth. She moved a stray strand of hair from her face as she looked at him. "You aren't just saying that?"

He held up his hands palms outward. "On my honor. You're the most-special woman I ever met. It's difficult for me to believe others haven't recognized your superior work and that men aren't beating down your door to be with you."

She chuckled with amusement. "You're forgiven." Sipping from her glass, she squeezed her hand. "OK. We're adults, so tell me where this relationship can go. There's a lot to like about you, but you're a priest. Is this just fun and games, a brief occasion of sin for you? I don't feel one iota bad about what we did, but I need to know your intentions before I really let myself move any further in this relationship." She looked into his eyes.

He sat on the edge of the lounger. "My feelings for you go way beyond sex—which was absolutely fabulous, by the way." He caressed her arm. "But I'm having problems. Some are problems of faith, while others are issues with my vocation. You've been kind to listen and talk with me about them. You understand my situation as much as a woman can, and I need to be around people with that understanding."

"I hope that wasn't supposed to sound like a declaration of love."

"I love you very dearly, Karen, but you must understand, if you don't already know, I have no idea what I want. I'm a mess right now."

"So you aren't looking for a permanent relationship?"

"I'm not a dishonest person. The truth is, I consider myself an extremely poor risk for any kind of relationship with a woman or with God."

She sighed and drank some wine. "And men say women are complicated."

He silently looked at the floor, then up at her again. "I'm sorry."

"So that…." She gestured toward the bed inside, "was what? Just passion, just sex?"

"That was love, passion, sex, and sharing like I never experienced." His head lowered for a moment, then rose again to meet her eye.

She smiled despite herself. "You're really good, Sally. Most men can't say things like that without embarrassment."

"I've been thinking…."

"I was just beginning to think you aren't like other men."

He ignored her sarcasm. "I was thinking I'd like to go with you when you return to the excavation in the Lacandon."

"No way," she said flatly. "It's too, well, you're too…."

"It's too hard, and I'm too soft?"

"Sally, you're great. I don't want to hurt your feelings, but I don't think you've had to live like we do on an excavation. We sleep in hammocks or on bedrolls. There's no refrigeration or plumbing—no toilets. You stoop and poop."

'Stoop and poop certainly conjures an image."

"It's reality, my very eager lover. There's lots of hard work. Depending on the season, it's hot and humid during the day, chilly and humid at night. There are more biting insects than you can imagine, with mosquitoes than can drain you in minutes. The locals, the camp laborers, get cranky and split for days at a time without permission to return to their villages. When they return, they want their jobs back.

"There are macho federales who always arrive inconveniently and ask stupid questions. The Protestant militias piss off everyone and aid drug traffickers. Then there are the Zapatistas." She waved her hand as if wondering what to say about them.

"I need to do this, Karen, with you."

"You're nuts, Sally. Why do you think I'm hiding here, away from David Wolf?"

"I think we can help each other."

She sighed. "Just thinking of returning to the site makes me tired."

"Just thinking about it makes me excited."

"That's because you don't know any better."

"Karen, give me a chance. This is the most-important project you've ever had. This excavation and the publications from it will make your career. It won't last forever."

"It seems like it from here." Her face became grim. "You aren't the only one with a crisis of faith. I'm thirty-five-years old and have no husband, children, or sex life. It looks like our relationship doesn't have the wheels to take me anywhere."

Sally angled his head toward the bedroom. "What was that? Karen, I want to be with you. I want to go to this Xibalba cave and meet the people who work for you, to know more about their lives."

"You're hiding from the bishop. You want to fool around in my bedroll and play social worker with the Indians."

He held up his hands with the palms upward. "Yes, I'd like to share your love and your bed. I'd like to work among the Indians, but I think there's much more for me and for us. I can't explain it. It's like it's right in front of me, crystal clear. I have to do this." He sat on the floor beside her chair, took her hand, and removed the empty wine glass.

"Give me a month at least?" he asked. "Please??" Stroking her hand, he looked up at her.

Karen tucked a lock of hair away from her face, placing it behind her ear. "You beg really well for a man." She caught his eye. "I guess we'll see if we're soul mates. How would you describe our relationship? Very good friends with benefits, or uncommitted lovers immersed in hormonal bliss?" "Probably the latter," he said ruefully.

She paused. "I thought so. I'll give you a week at the cave to see if you're up to the job."

"It's a beginning." He smiled and tugged her arm, urging her to rise and follow him. "Let's go inside and enjoy our benefits."

"OK." She sighed and added, "But it'll take a lot more talking this time."

CHAPTER ELEVEN

"Feel free to go explore San Cristobal, Professor Jackson," Elder John encouraged, setting his fork on the plate beside the remains of his breakfast. The traditional meal of eggs with beans and *chorizo,* sausage, was served in El Hotel Santa Clara by a short Mayan matron sporting a perpetual smile. "It's quite wonderful, very old, and full of nasty Catholic churches and their heathen idols."

John sipped his coffee and carefully centered the cup on the saucer. "I should hear something today from the boys at the Mission House. They're looking everywhere for our missing site director."

"Call me Don, please," replied Mormon Professor Carl Jackson, PhD in DNA technology and a specialist in racial identification. "We've known each other since high school." He looked up from his meal. "I get the distinct impression things aren't as you expected in Mexico." Pushing away from the table, he crossed one leg over the other. "Actually, I'm wondering why you asked me to accompany you. Why *did* you invite me along?"

"Your resumé indicated you speak Spanish, and…. Don, you must have faith. You must understand that I…we…are on the cusp of a big discovery. It's something that could make your career and bring your research to the attention of the Quorum of Twelve, maybe even the Presidency."

"So you say, but I haven't seen much so far, and my Spanish is lousy. You must have known that. When I went to the police yesterday to ask about Evan, a federale came to ask *me* questions. Is it a good idea to go to the police in this country? Everyone knows they're corrupt, and now they're suspicious and probably watching us."

"No doubt, but it had to be done, and I don't speak Spanish."

"I hope you aren't getting us involved in something bad down here. I'm getting a negative feeling about this business. When will I have access to the body you mentioned? I didn't realize we had the kind of connections in Mexico needed for a research project."

John sighed. "Don, I might have used the wrong adjective to describe it. Research project could be a misnomer. What I need you to do is test the tissue samples. The data you produce can't be questioned in scientific journals or by false religions."

Professor Jackson grunted and frowned. "That's not doable without the mysterious body." He disengaged his leg and leaned back in his chair, worrying the scraps on his plate with his fork.

"Yes, I understand. I'll know more this afternoon. I've hired a local talent who speaks English and several of the native languages to see what he can learn for us. The mission boys will check with me later, and we should know something. Those kids are knocking on doors every day. They know every nook and cranny of every alley and pothole in town. Something will turn up.

"There's a traditional marketplace around here somewhere. Go buy your wives in Colorado City something nice to bring home."

The academic frowned. "My personal situation, my *wives*, are nobody's business. I don't think you should be…."

"Don't worry, Professor. I won't interfere with your personal life or blow the whistle on you at Brigham Young, though I'm sure you understand that polygamy is outlawed under civil law and officially frowned upon by the LDS. It's part of our past, not our future. Maintaining a polygamous household is definitely something that could sidetrack or kill one's career."

The old professor looked aghast. "What the hell is this, John? Are you threatening me? I've always done what you asked. I've been honest and straightforward with you. I even helped you out over that mess with a young girl from Ogden. I've always...."

Elder John raised one hand. "Get a grip, Don. I'm just trying to remind you that the stakes are very high. It doesn't matter that you don't know why. Don't worry about that part of it. That's on me." He tapped his chest with one finger. "Just do as I ask, OK? Be part of the solution, not the problem. Go be a tourist and check back with me later this afternoon."

John gave his colleague a tired smile before standing from his chair. Retrieving a wad of pesos from his pocket, he counted several notes and tossed them on the table. With a glance at his wristwatch, he said, "Actually, I have some looking around to do myself." He leered. "I'll check out the local fauna."

CHAPTER TWELVE

Karen stretched and yawned as she sat in the guest chair in David's office. Spending the last few days with Sally and enjoying their friendship and its benefits brought a rare and welcome sense of contentment. She surveyed David's worktable where she deposited the notebooks filled with her transcribed data. They were nearly lost among the old photographs and drawings of glyphs and cave walls.

She knew her translations would be questioned. That was how academics worked. The translations of the glyphs were the result of countless hours at the Xibalba site spent in a tent that was hot during the day and chilly at night. She identified them by lantern light, when possible, because their meanings were known. All too often, though, the glyphs were unknown, so she spent painstaking, frustrating hours and days searching for commonalities in context, hoping to provide understanding and chronology to the site's history. She loved her work and felt compelled to do it. Otherwise, she found herself revisiting unenjoyable aspects of her life.

She and David discussed the excavation for two hours. She had yet to tell him of a new find. They located an adjacent room outside the main area. There, she found an odd picture and accompanying glyphs of a man, probably a priest or noble, holding an item of obvious value, perhaps a cup, aloft above the heads of a line of kneeling acolytes. It tugged at her with a sense of familiarity, but she wasn't able to recall anything similar in works translated by other archeologists at other sites.

To her disappointment, the conversation hadn't gone beyond routine housekeeping chatter. David asked how many workers were still on site, if she needed more, did she have problems with the locals, the Zapatistas, or the Protestant militias, whether she'd seen any suspicious activity that could be narco traffickers.

A few minutes ago, he departed to answer the phone, then he spoke to Sally in the living room. Karen grew impatient for him to return, so she could mention the new room and its glyphs.

Snatches of conversation drifted from the other room.

"Sally, you know spending time with Karen won't help anything."

That prompted her to get up and walk down the hall to the living room. Halfway there, David asked, "You're what? You've got to be kidding."

Karen's throat went dry. She rounded the corner and tried to smile as the professor and her lover looked up at her.

"You never said you intended to take Sally with you," David accused.

"David, I planned to tell you, but…I couldn't find the right time."

"How about now? That would be good, wouldn't it?" His brow furrowed in disgust, as he gestured to the sofa where Sally sat. "Sit down, both of you. Please."

He watched them look at each other before Karen complied. David took the chair facing them. Sally looked him in the eye, but Karen examined what appeared to be a spot on her shoe.

"Look," David began, "I know you two are adults, and I'm not trying to get involved in your relationship, but there's a lot in play right now. Karen, I don't know how much Sally told you, but he found something very odd. It was an uncorrupted body and some burial items. It's all vanished. Now the bishop's office keeps calling me, and there's a papal inquisitor looking for Sally. Add the problem of his vows, and…."

"That isn't something I'll discuss with you, David," Sally interjected. "At least not right now. You and Alexandra have been kind and patient to put up with me and my nonsense. I'll always be grateful, but I'm not ready to submit myself to the papal inquisitor or that overbearing Bishop Alvarez. I need time away from the church and its demands to consider what to do. I have no idea what happened to the body. At this point, I don't care. You have the writings from the cylinders. You can pursue your own ends and see if you want to treat with the church."

"What writings?" Karen asked, looking at David, then Sally. "What are you two talking about? What haven't you told me?"

David waved his hand. "This is your problem, Sally, so you tell her. The bishop and the Vatican won't let you pass on this one. There's too much at stake."

David stood to go, then stopped and turned back. "I'll look over some of Karen's data before you two leave—if you still decide you're going to do this. I still think it's a mistake, Sally."

He looked at Karen. "You're an adult. This wouldn't be any of my concern except that I'm the one who's ultimately responsible for what happens at the excavation."

When Karen stirred and looked to interrupt, he raised one hand. "Probably the worst that could happen is that Sally's accompanying you will be a major distraction and slow down your investigation. It might create other complications. You know who I'm talking about."

Karen bit her bottom lip before turning toward Salvador. Their eyes met, and David saw both of them understood the implication. Alexandra told David that Karen was fed up with Marcos' philandering and intransigence. David also knew it wasn't the couple's first breakup. He wouldn't have cared except that he was genuinely concerned for Karen's welfare, and he was also personally involved in and responsible for the Xibalba site excavation.

As David waited, Karen moved a lock of hair behind her ear. Looking into Sally's eyes, she said, "We'll be fine. If it doesn't work out, we'll do whatever has to be done."

"You can count on it, David," Sally said, before turning toward David. "I have no intention of creating complications for you or your excavation. I just need time to get some resolution and…." He hesitated, his gaze moving back to Karen. "…to see if there's any chance that we want to move our relationship to the next level of commitment." He took her hand.

After a moment, Karen asked, "Why don't you look at the material I left on your table, David? Salvador and I need to get on the road by noon, or we'll have to wait another day."

David thought to offer more advice, but he remembered it might be one of those occasions when he should hold his counsel until someone asked for it.

"Yes. Of course." He walked toward his study. As he walked around the corner, he heard Karen ask, "What writings, Sally? What body? What's he talking about? Why is a papal inquisitor looking for you?"

CHAPTER THIRTEEN

John stood in La Morgue San Cristobal, using a disposable hand towel to cover his nose while studying the remains of his young mission director, apparently mauled by a wild animal somewhere in the Lacandon highlands. The situation was a catastrophe. The body appeared to be Evan's, at least what remained of the face and neck.

The coroner said smaller animals and birds had probably fed on the body for a day or two before it was discovered in a cul-de-sac just off the jungle road. Evan, the van he'd been driving, and its contents were transported back to San Cristobal so the federal *policia* could conduct their investigation. The driver's license and other identification in the wallet revealed the deceased was a gringo who worked out of Tuxtla with the Mormon mission. It was an important case in many respects, especially the Walther PPK pistol, which, like all handguns in Mexico, was strictly prohibited to the general populace. Elder John struggled to remain calm. Over an hour earlier, Inspector Leyeva appeared. Though his accent was atrocious, he spoke passable English, which was good because what little Spanish Elder John understood had deserted him. What followed was the most-unpleasant time of John's life. He stood in a stark, primitive-looking building with dull white walls, fluorescent lights, tile floors, and well-worn, barely functioning equipment with the stench of decomposing bodies, while the inspector questioned him.

Where was the deceased going? When did you last speak with him? Was he conducting business for the Mormon Church before the unseemly accident? If so, what?

Why was the man driving a van that wasn't registered to him? Why did the dead man carry a firearm? Everyone knows firearms, especially pistols, are outlawed in Mexico. Surely, John and the deceased were aware of Mexico's laws before opening a mission there.

The gun appeared to have been fired recently, and there was a very suspicious odor in the vehicle, maybe from blood or tissue splatters. Wouldn't you agree that was suspicious? Why did a Mormon need a gun? Was the deceased involved with drugs? The mission house was in Tuxtla Gutierrez. What were you doing in San Cristobal? Did you come to meet the deceased? If so, what was the nature of the meeting?

The intense questioning, polite denials, shoulder shrugs, and vague statements like, "I simply don't know, Inspector," and "It's a mystery to me, too," went on for an hour. He really didn't know the entire situation, and he certainly couldn't admit what he knew. Evan was given a simple mission to take pictures and transport items from the burial box, along with some hair, to Brother John in the US as part of the Lamanite research project. Evan was probably on his way to meet John's courier on the Guatemala side of the Usumacinta River, so why had he pulled off onto a side road into the highland jungle? According to the inspector, there was no indication of robbery. Why *had* Evan been carrying a gun?

John knew Mexico wasn't always a safe place, especially with the recent incursion of narco traffickers and the crazy situation with the Zapatistas and Protestant militia, who seemed to abound locally.

A gun-packing Mormon missionary? John wondered. *Blood in the van? Whose blood was it?*

He wanted to know the answer to that very much, but the remains on the examining table didn't reveal any more details. There wasn't even much left for an autopsy.

Just when John thought he might buckle under the relentless questions, the inspector was called away for a phone call. John glanced at Evan's remains, then looked away with a grimace. The situation was a mess, and he didn't know what to do.

As far as he could tell, he wasn't complicit or liable except for having to answer for the mission's activities. The discovery of Evan's body, the gun, and blood was a surprise and might damage the LDS' mission in southern Mexico. It was too soon to tell.

John heard voices and a creaking rattle from the hallway. With a bang and a scrape, two people wearing stained white gowns wheeled a gurney holding a dead body into the autopsy room. One spoke a greeting and raised a hand, and John smiled in acknowledgment. They stood momentarily, everyone feeling awkward, and then one motioned to the other with his head, and they left the room rather than engage the gringo in conversation.

As John watched them leave, his eyes fell on a table ten meters away. His heart skipped a beat as he recognized Evan's personal belongings. With a glance at the door, he walked quickly to the table. A quick appraisal assured him they were Evan's, except for a few things that were obviously not his.

They must be from the burial box. He saw a moldy wrap or robe made of coarse animal hair in a heap with a pair of archaic well-worn sandals. Evan's clothing, including jeans, torn bloody shirt, socks, and tennis shoes lay at the opposite end.

John's attention was caught by the items in the middle of the table. A crumpled necklace with what looked like a Star of David and a shepherd's crook hung from a silver chain. He saw a hand gun, probably the one the inspector mentioned, Evan's wallet, two cameras, and a plastic sandwich bag with….

John gasped when he saw a lock of hair in the bag. He reached for it, but his hand jerked back when he heard voices. He quickly glanced at the door, then back at the bag of hair. He should just take it. They'd never miss such a small item. That was what he came for, the thing he needed for the Lamanite Research Project.

Voices outside rang louder and the doors to the autopsy room swung wide as the inspector returned.

He saw where John stood, looking at the evidence. "Please don't touch anything." He waved his hand as if to shoo the Mormon away. "We aren't finished with our investigations." Elder John moved where indicated. "I thought I could take

Evan's clothing and belongings with me. His family in the United States would like to…."

"No. Absolutely not. At least, not yet." The federale beckoned John farther from the table. "It's unfortunate that you have not been able to provide much help in this case, Señor." He retrieved his eyeglasses from the bridge of his nose and polished the lenses while studying John intently.

"We have another body, a person who was shot, probably murdered," he continued, indicating the newly arrived gurney with his glasses. "This is very suspicious. It appears he was shot three or four days ago. The autopsy will tell us. Strange coincidence, don't you think?"

He held the glasses by their stem and put them on, his gaze never leaving the Mormon leader.

"We have lots of bodies, as you can see, and one has a handgun, while the other was shot at close range. Do you believe in coincidences? Look at these things. They're unusual." He pointed at the center of the table. "This clothing is very old, and the necklace certainly isn't from Mexico. At the least, its themes would be out of place here, don't you agree?"

"I wouldn't know," John dissembled. "It seems appropriate to return the young man's remains and belongings to his family."

"It isn't—at least, not until our investigations are complete. Frankly, Señor, I'm sure we'll need to interview you again very soon, perhaps tomorrow. Perhaps your memory will improve, or you'll decide to share something with us you wouldn't tell someone who isn't a…. who isn't a Mormon like yourself." He said the word as if spitting something foul from his mouth.

"One of my men is waiting at the front desk to accompany you to your hotel, where you will turn over your passport to him. You can still wander about the city with your visa, but I wouldn't venture far. It appears there are evil people with bad intentions in my country."

CHAPTER FOURTEEN

Alexandra knocked twice on the professor's office door. "David, you have a call."

He sat at his desk, looking over the pages of Karen's most recent report. The young archeologist did good work. She had a very readable, concise writing style he liked. There was no fluff, just narrative and data presented in a logical format.

She opened the door, making sure he heard. His head swiveled toward her.

"Who is it?" he asked.

"Inspector Leyeva of the *Federale Policia*." Her eyes widened as she cocked her head, implying he needed to share more information with her.

"The *policia?*" He held up a hand as if defending himself. "I have no idea what this is about. It's probably nothing. It might have something to do with Karen's investigations, but I don't know."

It certainly wasn't his first communication from the *policia* or the military. It took numerous calls, letters, and an occasional personal appeal to get the Xibalba excavation going. The area, difficult to find on foot, wasn't accessible at all by vehicle. It lay sixty-five kilometers south of a new military base built after the 1994 rebellion, just west of the huge Parque Natural de Montes Azules and north of several villages that were hotbeds of Zapatista activity. It was an area of few or no roads, populated by Mayan Indian villages so remote they were virtually unaware of the outside world.

The fact that David and Karen were able to work relatively unencumbered so successfully the last three years was a tribute to his relationship with Marcos, the Zapatista leader, as well as the connections of David's brother-in-law, Joaquin, the Honorary Consul of Chiapas. The consul seemed to know everyone in Chiapas and Guatemala, especially those who wished him ill or dead. The occasional intervention of Balaam Reyes, a particularly bothersome shaman, had been particularly critical. David sometimes worried that the influence of that rude, condescending, unreliable man were more important than all the others put together. He preferred to avoid the man, who he found exasperating.

David rose and followed Alexandra to the living room, plopped into his recliner, and accepted the phone she offered.

The conversation lasted only ninety seconds but left the professor shaken. "Since you insist, Inspector, we'll do our best to accommodate important visitors." He hung up and frowned.

"Damn!" he snapped.

"What is it, David?" she asked. "Is this about the burial you saw a few days ago?"

"A papal inquisitor and a couple of federale goons will be here within the hour."

"A papal inquisitor? The Church sent someone? You're kidding, right? What's going on, David?"

He glanced at the phone before looking at her. "The short or long version?"

"Let's start with the short." She sat beside him on the sofa.

"Three or four days ago, Sally took me to an old mission in the foothills that was destroyed by earthquake a couple hundred years ago. It's a property that was seized from the Church to reallocate to the poor after the revolution, but nothing was ever done with it. The soil is rocky with lots of clay, but I don't know much about the place.

"Anyway, Sally found a group of people onsite about a year ago who claim to have been charged with overseeing the burial chamber and body that lay under the ruin. It looks like a holy site for the Indians that the Church deliberately built over to encourage them to adopt Christianity."

"Strange story, David." She tugged at her skirt hem and adjusted the small cloth belt at her waist, before waving her hand at him. "Why would the church get involved in this?"

He spread his hands before placing them on his knees. "OK. Here it is. Sally says the old guy, the last person to be in charge of the body, told him that the corpse didn't decompose. He claimed it was a holy man. They brought out the body every fifty-two years to perform rituals associated with it. They didn't know why. It was what his father, grandfather, and all his ancestors had always done. According to Sally, they couldn't read or write, and they didn't know anything about archeology or Mayan religion."

She smiled. "That's an interesting story, and it's…."

"Impossible. Yes, except that I saw the body. It appeared to be in great shape. The chamber and box in which it was interred was very old and appeared Mayan. There was lots of paintings, glyphs and other fascinating stuff."

She pursed her lips, then studied her nails for a moment. "A crazy story, really." She hesitated for a moment. "What aren't you telling me? Why would the *Federale Policia* and a papal inquisitor be on the way here?"

David took a deep breath. "Well, there were some old writings. You know—books, scrolls, and…."

"Scrolls?"

"Yes, and some other stuff. It appears that it's all missing."

"The scrolls?"

He hesitated. "Yes, and the body, the burial box—everything."

"The body's missing?"

"It seems so."

She groaned. "Who steals an old body? David, why didn't you tell me about this?"

He gestured toward the phone. "I just heard about it."

Her eyebrows rose. "You know what I mean."

He shrugged and spread his hands. "I meant to, really I did. It's just that I got busy, then Karen and Sally took off for the site, and I haven't heard back from Dr. Bin Saud in Lebanon, and…."

"Who? Where?"

"A colleague who's a specialist in ancient languages. I photocopied three of the scrolls and sent them to him in a PDF file. I can read some of it, but it's been too long, and I don't have any reference books here."

Biting her bottom lip, she thought for a moment. "Should I call Joaquin?"

"Please don't." David's back stiffened, and he frowned. The suggestion raised his hackles. He intensely disliked his brotherin-law. Although the diplomat had his uses, David could barely stand to be in his presence, listening to his bald-faced pronouncements on economics, government, and David's chosen profession, which he openly disparaged.

"Just put on some coffee, if you don't mind. I'll handle it. It's just that, well, I wish Sally were here to explain his part in this. He promised to call his bishop in Tuxtla."

The situation didn't look good. There was a missing, uncorrupted corpse and a missing errant priest. Had Sally called his bishop?

David glanced at his watch. Sally and Karen left yesterday morning for Tonina, a Mayan ruin near the city of Ocosingo. From Tonina, they would travel south on wretched dirt roads through many small Indian villages, including Taniperlas, Perla de Acapulco, and finally, Calvario, which was the end of the road and civilization.

From Calvario they would load supplies and equipment onto all-terrain motorcycles and launch themselves into a vast hinterland of jungle and mountains, moving slowly along barely passable, winding cattle trails and footpaths into the Lacandon jungle to the Xibalba excavation. David took the trip many times in recent years, and he recalled the challenging terrain, voracious mosquitoes, and the real fear of bandits lurking in the shadows to prey on unsuspecting travelers.

No one went into that area of the Lacandon jungle, because it was nearly impassable with dense vegetation, sheer mountainsides, and wild animals. There were no roads or villages. It was an area of Chiapas State where civilization never took root. Even the Maya avoided it. If nothing went wrong, and Karen and Sally hadn't lingered, they would arrive at the site within a few hours.

Damn those kids, he thought. *This doesn't look good. Why are the policia suddenly involved in a church matter?*

The sound of the fax machine interrupted his musing. He stood and returned to his office. Lebanon was nine hours ahead of his time zone. Maybe Dr. Bin Saud took the time to examine the file David sent the previous day.

He glanced at his watch. His friend would have been up all night studying the material if he responded at such a late hour. It had to be from someone else.

The fax machine printed a document, but a light winked at him, indicating the paper tray was empty. He took several pages from the bin and saw he had the first couple of pages, a cover page and letter.

My Friend, David,

What have you sent me? We haven't talked in several years, and now you send me this so unexpectedly. Where did you find this? First century Aramaic? So very, very rare.

I hope this is not a joke. I nearly threw it in the trash until I saw it came from you. I'm very agitated and can't sleep, but I sent you what I completed so far. I insist you write back today.

Where did you find this? If it isn't a forgery, it's 200 years older than the Greek version of the Gnostic Gospel of Thomas.

We must talk soon. Better yet, maybe I should come to Mexico?

Send me your telephone number. I will be in touch.

Yusuf Bin Saud, PhD

Dept. Of Middle Eastern History

American University of Lebanon Beirut

Whoa! David thought, feeling the tingle and surge of adrenalin that always accompanied a find. He began reading the translation.

My name is Thomas, and I and others were in the company of Jesus of Nazareth until the Pharisees condemned him and the Romans crucified him. To know Jesus is to know his teachers, and so I have done my best to travel the same roads that Jesus did as a young man.

I lived six months with the Essenes in the desert outside Jerusalem and studied the writings of the Teacher of Righteousness, as did Jesus. I also traveled to Susa in Persia and to Damascus, then through the great expanse of land controlled by the great khans and east over the barren mountains into India, just as Jesus did. Now I know the man Jesus, and I want you to know him also.

David, realizing he stopped breathing, quickly gulped air before rereading the text. Feeling light-headed, he laid it aside and leaned heavily on the edge of his desk.

Oh, my God, he thought. *Oh, my God.*

Alexandra called from the kitchen, "They're here, David! Come and greet them. There are two people. Why do they always travel in pairs?"

Not now, he thought, desperately trying to regain his composure. Answering questions and arguing with the federal police was the last thing he needed at that moment. He glanced at the fax on his desk from Dr. Bin Saud. What had he found? Was it nonsense or an incredible discovery? How had ancient Aramaic come to Mexico?

It had to be a hoax, an amateurish fraud. The burial, he believed, was contrived trickery, but who would do such a thing, and why?

"David?" Alexandra called from the kitchen. "Where are you? You must meet with these people."

He was still immersed in thought when loud knocking resounded throughout the house. Alexandra appeared around the corner, looking concerned. One hand was on her hip, while the knuckles of her other hand were white from gripping a handkerchief.

"David, pay attention and answer the door," she said sternly. "I'm calling Joaquin whether you want me to or not."

CHAPTER FIFTEEN

The *federale* tried to be polite, but David saw that wasn't his nature. He was short and stocky, with creeping baldness in a toilet-seat pattern, and he wore a typical untrimmed Mexican mustache. He was impatient, insinuating, and aggressive, and, David guessed, was also trying to impress the man from the Vatican. The papal inquisitor, however, seemed calm and cerebral, totally in control of his emotions. He was Caucasian, tall and obviously American, all of which David found unusual. He expected a brash, pompous, gesturing Italian.

The inquisitor listened carefully to the *federale's* questions and David's responses. David watched the envoy's eyebrows lift and his mouth set in a grim, fine line. It was clear he was hearing a lot of the discussion for the first time.

Alexandra listened carefully to the *federale* question her husband in the living room, then he excused herself and walked into the kitchen with the pretense of making coffee. David glanced at her as she left, her mouth tight, her hand gripping a handkerchief.

The unexpected questioning continued.

What was your motivation for getting involved in this matter, and why did you think you had the authority to come onto state property to meddle without permission? On what day did you accompany Father Lopez to the mission? How many times did you go to the ruin?

Can you describe the setting in which you found the body in the box? What were the contents of the box? Did you remove any items from the box? You did? Where are they? They must be returned immediately.

Do you know the box and body were missing? Do you know who took them? How many people knew of this mysterious man and this burial box? When did you first see the Mormon missionaries at the ruin, and what were they doing? Do you believe they tampered with the body in the box? Did you speak to the Mormons at the site? If not, why? Where was Father Lopez, and what was the nature of your relationship with him?

David, feeling defensive and at a disadvantage, attempted to be honest and give accurate responses without saying much. He was stunned when he heard the body and box disappeared. What did the Mormons have to do with anything?

As the grilling continued, David felt his focus slipping back to the unsettling fax from Lebanon. His instinct was to cooperate fully with the authorities, but there was the fax to consider. He had only a few moments to read and consider the implications of his friend's translation before dealing with his visitors. He knew there was probably more, because the fax ran out of paper.

Karen and Sally's departure for the Xibalba site irked him, and Sally's failure to provide sufficient information of his plans and personal problems when he called the bishop in Tuxtla was irresponsible and selfish. His immature behavior caused the whole mess. He involved David, then disappeared, and the body and box were gone, too. Was there a connection?

Although David went willingly to the ruined mission with him and decided to take some of the items from the casket for his own investigations, he could never have predicted he would become part of an investigation of theft of religious objects involving the Mormons, the Vatican, and the Federal Police. Theft of antiquities was a serious crime in Mexico.

He viewed his behavior as helpful and innocent, undertaken in the pursuit of nothing more than academic knowledge. He sought no advantage or personal gain. He simply acted on curiosity. He obviously had become a central player in an unwanted, intriguing, and possibly dangerous incident of political and perhaps unprecedented historical and religious importance.

David wished he could will the interrogation to end, but that wasn't going to happen. He must endure the self-important martinet while appearing as honest and gracious as he could.

When the *federale* paused to scribble more notes, the papal inquisitor continued questioning David, exuding calm and intelligence. Within moments, David saw Father Gregory was a serious man who wouldn't settle for nebulous answers devoid of detail. Worse, David had the distinct impression he was being judged, not just on what he said but on what the priest may have deliberately omitted. David suspected he would come to know Father Sean Gregory very well as the situation played itself out.

"Tell me, Professor," Father Gregory said. "You seem to be an honest man. Are you a Christian?" He smiled, showing white, perfect teeth. Seeing David's discomfiture, he added, "I'm an archeologist, too. I understand these things. I know that many in our field are wracked with doubt and indecision regarding faith. How would you describe your beliefs?"

David, surprised by the man's candor and lack of tact, hesitated. The question was very personal, but it would be meaningful to the priest. It would become a filter through which all that David said would be examined for nuance or a hidden, personal agenda.

David's answer would determine the path of events to come. "I don't think my religious beliefs are relevant in any way in this matter, Father Gregory."

The *federal's* head and eyes rose slowly from his notepad. "You aren't a Christian?" A smile of amazement came to his face as he looked at Father Gregory, then at David. "How could a man raised in Mexico not be a Christian, *señor?* You wish to appear smarter than everyone else? You want to go to hell?" He gestured with his pen for emphasis, his eyes wide with incredulity.

"Please, Inspector, let me handle this." The papal inquisitor was no longer smiling. He raised his hand palm outward to calm the *federale.* "I have a few questions that are academic in nature." With a carefully neutral expression, he added,

"Perhaps this would be a good time to look around outside. I have a few questions for the good professor, all boring talk about history and languages. We can begin again once you're through looking around, OK?"

It was more than a suggestion, but it was worded so politely that the *federale* couldn't lose face. He was clearly in thrall to the Vatican representative, and he was also a religious man, what David and others called a Cradle Catholic, who believed and acted without questioning the motives of a representation of the Catholic Church, especially a priest. David knew the *federale* would defer to the papal inquisitor in every case.

"Of course." He smiled. "We'll take a look around and be back in, say, fifteen minutes?" It was a statement more than a question.

Father Gregory smiled in agreement. "Exactly. Thank you, Inspector." He turned toward David. "Do you have an office here, professor?"

"Of course," David replied honestly. "You know I do."

"Could you show me, please?" It wasn't a request. "I'm an academic, too. I enjoy the surroundings of a learned man's office. They tell me many things about him I would not otherwise know."

"This way," David said reluctantly, pointing down the hall. "It's a mess right now."

David turned on the lights and pointed at the chair before his desk, but the priest didn't notice. He surveyed the pictures in the room, the tables strewn with paper, maps, books, and coffee cups, as if by assessing them he could form a mental image of the professor. He stepped behind the desk to peruse a bookshelf, then at the items on the desk.

The tall priest smiled, nudging an open volume on the desk, then turned to David. "You're a pre-Columbian specialist with a specialty in Mayan glyphs."

"Among other things."

"Yes. You're also interested in ancient Greek, and, perhaps, Aramaic." He retrieved the open book on the desk. "I can only assume your interest has been reawakened by the events of the last few days."

David was becoming impatient with the priest's demeanor and penchant for benign, vague accusations. "I don't see what my studies and interests have to do with your investigation, Father Gregory. I've answered honestly everything you asked, all of which I have no knowledge."

"No. You lied through omission, Professor Wolf," the priest replied blandly with a faint smile. "You omitted by not telling all you know. You've provided the least amount of information possible to the inspector's questions." He held up the book, looked at the title on the spine, and returned it to the desk. "You did all that because you're hostile to Christianity."

David frowned, beginning to lose his patient. "You assume too much and know even less. I'm tired of this game and your questions."

"Oh, it's no game, I assure you." He held up one hand, palm outward, to stop David. "Let me share with you what happened. I came to Mexico at the request of the bishop of Tuxtla to investigate what supposedly was a very unusual body, one that reportedly didn't putrefy or decompose. Most would call that a miracle.

"Like you, I am an archeologist and have my doctorate. I taught for fifteen years in the United States before finding my present vocation. I, too, am a scientist, but I don't believe everything can be explained away by science, by accident, or by happenstance. I had a teacher who once told me, 'A miracle is an unnatural event that happened naturally.' That initially put me off as a scientist, but later, it became very meaningful." David tried to speak, but the priest interrupted.

"Humor me, Professor, please." He slowly walked around the room as if collecting his thoughts, glancing at David occasionally to ensure he listened. "There are many things about the early Catholic Church we don't know, such as its history, writings, and events involving the early founders. The Gnostic heresies, the Ebionites, the Marcionites.... You know the history? Everything is a bit confusing for the first 300 years.

There were many different versions of Christianity being practiced around the Mediterranean. It's also true that we possess documents that impart a great deal of knowledge in areas that are very important but aren't commonly known and shared because they are distractions from essential truths."

He paused for effect. "The results of most of my investigations of miracles," he raised his index fingers for emphasis, "are easily explained natural phenomena. Those occurrences in which I can't discern the cause-and-effect relationship, in most cases, are simply not relevant to the central issue, anyway. I forward my findings to others who are more skilled and learned than I am.

"Where am I going with all that? I'm telling you that I trust and have faith."

David was exasperated. "Oh, please. Spare me the sermon, Father. I know you and your brethren in the Vatican are threatened by science and academics like myself. Yes, I'm a scientific agnostic. Is that what you wanted me to say? I'm the worst kind of person on earth, someone who belongs to no organized religion. I...."

"Please let me continue, David." He raised his hand again. "I must say this so you don't mistake my purpose in coming here today with the *Federale Policia.* I'm very serious about this case, and I have the full support of the Mexican government to do whatever I must to investigate and solve this riddle of missing bodies and ancient books that have somehow become misplaced on the wrong side of the world." He pointed a finger at David for emphasis.

"This isn't your business. No, don't interrupt again." He waved his hand in dismissal. "That property, the mission near Tuxtla, belongs to the federal government and before that the Catholic Church. You had no permission, and no, that ridiculous Father Lopez, wherever he is, has no authority to grant you access. You must go through proper channels, but you didn't.

"The body, the scrolls, everything is missing, and you, Professor, seem to be in the middle of it all. Everyone is seemingly fascinated by this miraculous body and its books, but where is it, and where are they? Missing or perhaps stolen? The Catholic Church, which has rights, has been granted authority in this matter, has been ignored and trespassed against. We have an errant priest, a delusional man who thinks he's channeling Jesus to the peasants, but he's violating his oath to God and church and has run away to live in sin with a woman without the benefit of sacred marriage.

"We have a missing miraculous body. We have Mormons suspiciously creeping around. Then we have you, a scientific agnostic who shows no respect or acknowledges the rights of the entity most central in the matter—the Catholic Church."

He turned and paused, pointing at David accusingly. "I know you took those writings, those papyrus scrolls, Dr. Wolf. You can't help yourself. Your type can only substitute knowledge for faith. You took them, and I want to know where they are right now before I request the federal inspector to jail you for your crimes."

David trembled as much from trepidation as from anger. He was accused and rightly so, or so it almost appeared. He removed three documents from the box. Where the sarcophagus, body, and remains went, he had no clue.

"Where are they?" Father Gregory asked. "I see you've been consulting your reference books." He pointed to a thick volume entitled, *Essential Elements of Ancient Greek and Aramaic* that lay on the desktop.

David, fed up with drama and accusations, relented. "OK. I took three of them. They were in the bottom of the box. I don't know how many more there were or if there were any others. I have no idea what happened to that body. I'm as surprised as you to find it missing. Maybe it was the Mormons, but who knows? Anyway, I have them, but I don't think it's right to hand them over to you. They'll be hidden from the public, squirreled away in some Vatican archive to protect," he used his index fingers to add parentheses for emphasis, "the people from the truth of their own senses and reasoning abilities. You're afraid of what they might say. That's why you're threatening me."

"You shared them with others already, haven't you? Who have you told about this? What have you done? Do I need to call the inspector?"

"An acquaintance, in Lebanon. That's all. An academic at the University of Lebanon who specializes in…."

"…ancient Aramaic. Oh, my goodness, Dr. Wolf. Your hubris, pride, and arrogance astound me."

"I find your accusations and threats totally uncalled for, especially from someone who calls himself a Christian."

The envoy's smile vanished. His eyes narrowed to slits, and his white teeth clenched behind drawn lips. The priestly demeanor gone, he looked ready to hit David. "Now, Dr. Wolf," he said with a steely voice, "Where are they?"

"Oh, for Christ's sake," David snapped. "They're in the safe."

"Open it and give them to me, Professor. My patience is at an end." He stood back from the table and leaned against a cabinet near the fax machine. He glanced at it and saw the red light. Recently printed sheets lay in the top bin.

When Father Gregory reached for the document, David froze, knowing the translation would cause a very big problem that wouldn't help his situation.

"That's private."

Father Gregory waved him off and began reading. After finishing the cover sheet, he glanced at David, clearly furious.

"I can explain."

The inquisitor raised his hand for silence and read the next page. When he finished, he looked at David and read the page again. Seeing the red blinking light on the machine, he said, "Your machine is out of paper." He located an open package of paper and quickly inserted them into the fax, which immediately whirred into activity.

"Let's see what else your friend has to tell us, shall we?" He pushed *Start*, and the machine printed six more pages. He glanced at them briefly, stacked and folded them, then placed them in his pants pocket.

He turned to David with an unreadable expression, his engaging demeanor gone. "I need to visit with Inspector Leyeva." He pointed at the safe. "Open that up and return my property. Now, Dr. Wolf."

He strode from the room.

Stricken, David was at a loss for words. He did little to defend himself and was angry he hadn't fought harder. *Damn it all!* he thought. *Damn Catholics! Damn Salvador Lopez! How did I get involved in this? It's not right. Can he just take the translation and leave? I haven't had a chance to read it yet! And now I have to give him the scrolls. Damn it!*

Alexandra appeared at the door. "I contacted Joaquin, David. You need to call him yourself. He doesn't understand. I don't think I explained it clearly enough. He wants to talk to you himself."

"Just a minute, Alexandra. I have to finish with these people first. It's all a mess. I'll be out in a second." He turned and went to one knee to dial the safe's combination. "I hate this," he muttered. "I really hate this."

He removed the three cylinders from the box and carried them outside, looking for the papal inquisitor and the *federale*. It was the biggest find of his life, and it was disappearing. He was about to hand it over willingly to the Catholic Church. If he had a list of the groups or people he most despised working with, they were in the top five.

"Over here," Father Gregory beckoned.

David left the patio, walking through the gate and along a cobblestone pathway toward a small orchard of avocado trees, where a cinderblock tool shed with rusted corrugated roof stood. A slate-gray sky with drooping puffs of white cotton occluded the sun, threatening rain and casting a pall over the terraced fields and forested foothills.

As David approached the priest and *federale,* he became alarmed. The shed door was wide open, and many household and yard-care items were strewn about. The inspector held an unfamiliar cloth sack by its drawstring, but when David looked at the papal inquisitor, he was shocked.

The priest held what looked like a cylinder from the burial box. It was difficult to see clearly, because the priest stood sideways to him, but he seemed to be tinkering with the end of one of the tubes.

Is that a fourth cylinder? Are there more in the sack? David wondered. *Where did they come from?*

The cap loosened. The priest glanced inside, turned briefly to give David a grim glare, and shook the tube several times until the contents slid partially into view.

David realized it was definitely another cylinder, but he didn't know how it came to be in his shed. The priest extracted another cylinder from the cloth sack the *federale* held, giving David a sidelong look.

A sense of foreboding gripped David. He glanced at the cylinders in his own hand, then at the two Father Gregory held. Were there more? Who placed them in his shed? Was it Sally? If so, why did he do it without telling him?

"I'm quite sure you told me you took only three from the burial box, Dr. Wolf." The priest gave him an accusing look.

"I have no idea how those came to be in my tool shed, Father

Gregory. You must believe me. I took only three with me."

"So you say. Let's see. Three plus three is, I believe six. Could there be still more? It's difficult getting a straight story from you. You are not just a man without faith, Dr. Wolf. Your heart is filled with lies and deceit."

The papal inquisitor took the cylinders from David and placed them in the sack the *federale* still held open. Father Gregory stared into David's eyes with the implacable gaze of an enemy who would do anything to achieve his purpose.

"Inspector Leyeva," he said in a cold voice without passion, "this is a very serious matter. It appears this man has lied to us and stolen important religious documents from the Catholic Church."

"What?" David asked. "That's crazy talk. You don't own these any more than I do. It's like you said. The federal government owns that property. They confiscated it and thousands of other hectares of land from the Catholic Church after the revolution. It's been abandoned and undeveloped for years after the earthquake. If anyone has a complaint or authority in this matter, it isn't you or the Vatican."

"I would advise you to arrest this thief and put him in jail where he can be interrogated. Perhaps we can learn more. He might even know something of the dead Mormon or the other victim found in the woods. Perhaps his memory will improve once he's in a jail cell."

"Arrested?" Are you crazy? I'm no criminal."

Inspector Leyeva, a cruel smile on his face, reached inside his jacket and took out a pair of handcuffs. "Turn around and put your hands behind your back, *Señor* Atheist."

"Absolutely not. I have rights. You're wrong. You can't do this."

The *federale* drew his gun. "Now, *Señor* Wolf. I meant it." Waving the gun under David's nose, he glanced at the priest for support.

With his eyes on the gun, David heard a rustle and risked a glance to see Alexandra at the gate, trying to maintain her poise, her eyes fearful as one hand clutched a crumpled handkerchief.

"Go back inside, Alexandra," David said loudly. "Please call your brother again, the Consul of Chiapas in San Cristobal."

He turned slowly and placed his hands behind his back. In a firm, clear voice, he told her, "Tell the consul I've been arrested by fools and religious zealots who want to crucify me."

* * *

Six hours later, Alexandra stood on the patio gazing up into dark, turbulent skies. Thunderheads boiled up into the heavens, and lattice streaks of lightning flickered over the eastern foothills of the mountains, threatening a downpour instead of the sprinkles and light rain of recent weeks.

Joaquin, her younger brother, just left, making little effort to conceal his anger and frustration with David. He never liked David and believed Alexandra married beneath her station and too soon after the premature death of her first husband, but Joaquin was wrong. David was everything she hoped to find in a man—kind and intelligent, a great sense of humor, and considerate in the bedroom. His income was only that of a university professor, but money wasn't an issue. She and her brother traced their family back to the Conquest. The equivalent of bluebloods in Mexico, they were very wealthy.

Joaquin took a very dim view of academics, especially anthropologists, and believed the only suitable occupations for men were business or government. Everything else held little prestige and was soiled by middle-class pretensions.

Still, she knew he would help her. He had no choice. If he didn't, he would face her wrath, no small thing. She was the elder sister, but she also knew he was as outraged and shamed that a member of his family had been arrested and jailed.

The diplomat became furious as he listened to Alexandra's tale of woe, both at David and at the priest and *federale* who committed such folly. The arrest of a family member was so abhorrent that he returned to San Cristobal fuming and humiliated to register his outrage and demand his brother-in-law's release. He promised his sister heads would roll, people would be fired, and reputations would be destroyed over such an offence.

His anger ebbed, though, and he questioned her at length before leaving. The priest wasn't just another priest. He was a papal inquisitor dispatched by the Vatican to investigate a body and some books with which David had become involved. It wasn't common for Joaquin to lock horns with the Vatican or one of its representatives. A typical day's work for a diplomat involved immigration problems, drug cartels, passport and visa issues, and the occasional criminal enterprise that was eventually referred to the federal police. What was a papal inquisitor doing in Chiapas? Why hadn't the bishop contacted the consulate in San Cristobal to inform them of his arrival and purpose, so they could implement the proper protocol and provide the expected amenities for someone of his stature? What exactly did a papal inquisitor do?

* * *

By the time Joaquin reached the Zocalo, the center of San Cristobal and the location of almost all the city's important government offices, his testosterone levels subsided. Although prepared to make demands and threats to see his brother-in-law's release, he first wanted to determine if he would be sticking his own neck in a noose. Preparation was half the battle in a confrontation. His brother-in-law was family, but Joaquin had no love and little respect for him, especially after that ignorant cop friend of David's, Inspector Alvarez from Chihuahua, who visited David several years earlier, somehow implicated Joaquin in a scheme to allow drug traffickers uninhibited passage through areas of Chiapas controlled by Protestant militias.

Those thoughts soured his mood even more. He uncharacteristically coughed and spat phlegm on the sidewalk, a plebian act committed to rid himself of a distasteful memory and humiliation. He should let David rot in a flea- and rat-infested shit hole, but then he would have to answer to Alexandra, something he learned to avoid when he was very young. What could she possible see in him? He was a rock hound and dirt digger who glued clay pots together and wrote boring stories about illiterate, ignorant savages who ate each other.

After driving around the block several times looking for a parking place, he parked and left his 1997 Mercedes S 500 paying little heed to the rugged, 400-year-old cobblestone street that was part of San Cristobal's charm. He pulled up his sleeve to check his Rolex, lingering momentarily in the hope others would see that visible demonstration of his affluence, but there was no one to notice or care besides a dozen colorfully dressed Maya women and their children. Their home-crafted wares were spread over the sidewalk and adjacent hill, including embroidered blouses and purses, earrings, bracelets, cleverly made children's toys, puppets, and cotton blankets with Mayan motifs. The women looked at him expectantly as he passed, but he ignored them with his head held high, fearing they might be brash enough to speak to him.

He would get to the bottom of the mess before word of it spread to Tuxtla Gutierrez or Guadalajara, and he would somehow extract penance from David and his sister for his efforts. He didn't know what that might be, but it would be good. Perhaps it would be an apology. He never once received one from his classless brother-in-law for all his impositions and favors. The archeologist had an excess of pride for a near penniless academic. Joaquin would like to see him beg or grovel, or, just once, acknowledge Joaquin's superior breeding and intelligence.

A slate-gray sky bulging with dark cumulus and nervous lightning moved eastward from the Pacific coast and over the forested sierras. Light sprinkles fell, threatening to keep shoppers away from the outdoor market. Many scurried about in preparation for the inevitable storm.

Pausing, he looked up at the police headquarters, a square concrete building with stained adobe finish. The rag-tag poor and disenfranchised milled about aimlessly, waiting for Mexico's version of Napoleonic law to provide inadequate, unequal justice for their problems.

A gaggle of short Indian women in traditional, full-length black skirts and colorful, smocked blouses approached from the south, toting plastic twine sacks of goods to leave with

147

family members incarcerated within. With bent shoulders and head focused on the ground, a bored janitor in gray khakis shuffled along behind a broad-headed broom, pushing it along a concrete walkway that was already clean from numerous sweepings.

A drunk, rheumy-eyed Indian in filthy, stained cotton pants and torn T-shirt with a picture of the revolutionary Zapata lolled on the ground, his back supported by a statue of one of Mexico's many heroes of the revolution. His leather sandals were caked with mud, their tire treads worn nearly bald from walking to and from his village in the highlands to San Cristobal on endless miles of dirt paths and wretched, rutted roads.

This whole place needs a bath, Joaquin thought grimly, looking neither left nor right as he walked quickly toward the doors.

* * *

Elder John gripped the wooden cylinder tightly and once again touched the pocket containing the lock of hair as he and Professor Jackson left the Mission House and walked two blocks to their parked car. Roiling thunderheads moved like a capricious swirl of gray-black dust devils cavorting in the sky. Wind gusted, and sprinkles threatened to turn into a heavy summer shower.

The late-afternoon sun disappeared behind storm clouds, and shadows hung long and dark over the beautiful white marble Mormon Temple on the corner of Paseo del la Roseta just off the main highway of Chicoasen, a major thoroughfare through the thriving city of Tuxtla Gutierrez. Built of white marble from Torreon, Mexico and newly dedicated in 1999, it boasted two ordinance rooms and two sealing rooms and a total of nearly 11,000 square feet.

John's hired man, a ne'er-do-well named Raul, again proved unusually resourceful. With relatives all over Chiapas, including two employed at the La Morgue San Cristobal, he managed to acquire a sample portion of the bunched lock of hair Elder John saw on the evidence table in the autopsy room. Raul said it was a simple task, and plenty of hair remained.

It was unlikely anyone would know a portion had been removed or even what the lock of hair was for. As if that had been too little to celebrate, a quick search of Evan's bedroom in the Mission House in the San Martin district several blocks south of the temple led to the discovery of what could only be one of the cylinders with a papyrus scroll inside. That was good fortune!

The Mission House had been in disorder and filled with disgruntlement when Dr. Jackson and Elder John arrived. With Evan missing, a leadership vacuum allowed a stew of discontent to simmer. It was obvious the kids had been arguing, and many suffered from acute homesickness. Several visited the temple to ask what was happening and what they should do. That made John very unhappy, because he didn't want the local elders and their staff meddling in his affairs. He didn't want them around at all. It was his mission and discovery, as unprecedented as it was historical, and it could result in his elevation to the next if not top rung of LDS leadership.

He calmed the Tuxtla missionary youth, promising them they could call their parents beginning the following morning, and they could also plan to leave Chiapas if they wished. That brought big smiles to the faces of half the boys in the room. As for the rest, it would probably take two to four weeks to find another mission director, and activities would be scaled back drastically until he arrived.

Elder John told them he would handle everything and would be available to them 24-7 by telephone if they had questions or concerns. They could work if they wanted, visiting their previously assigned neighborhoods, or they could spend their time watching satellite TV in the basement commons. He assured himself it was another crisis handled.

At the Mission House, there was no sign of the police or the stakeout one of the youths reported, which reassured John. When he reached Chicoasen and looked back down the street, he saw two men in suits and one in what appeared to be the robe of a Catholic priest leave their car and walk toward the Mission House. One of the suited men resembled the *federale* who ordered John to stay in San Cristobal.

He thanked God they left the Mission House in time. He didn't mention the men's arrival to Jackson, but he pulled him aside for a quick discussion. Events were moving quickly, and so far, the Mormon academic had been little help. It was time for him to return home and to leave John to his own investigation, regardless what the *federale* said.

The acrid bite of diesel exhaust and rotting refuse captured his attention. Cities in Mexico smelled differently than those in the States. Discarded plastic bottles, ragged, ruined tires, and empty food cans littered the ditches. Torn plastic sacks caught in a web of cyclone fencing flapped helplessly in the wind as the storm approached.

"Donald, I know you're anxious to return to Salt Lake and your research," he said. "I thought there would be more here for you to do, but it hasn't worked out that way."

Don, staring at the dark sky blanketing the beautiful, white Mormon temple across the highway, didn't seem to hear.

"Donald, pay attention, please. Did you hear me say I'm sending you home?"

"Thank God." He turned to face the Mormon elder. "As far as I can tell, this has all been a waste." He glanced at the temple again.

Elder John bit back a retort. He thought to tell that bearded, self-righteous idiot to screw himself, that he was a worthless aide and companion on their mission, but thought better of it. The one thing John needed from Donald was still doable.

A light sprinkle began, and the lightning grew bolder. He extracted the baggie from his pocket. "Here's the hair we came for. I want you to leave tomorrow, take the first plane out, and examine the hair with DNA testing to tell where the body was from or what race he was. You know what I mean. I'm staying awhile. I still have things to finish. Raul is putting together a crew to guide me to that archaeological site that stupid priest and his girlfriend ran away to. I'm positive they know where the body is or at least where the rest of the scrolls are. Raul says he knows guys who can help us. Our mission boys discovered the body first, and I won't let the Catholics or anyone else take credit for our discovery."

Donald frowned. "John, you know as well as I do that some of Joseph Smith's history and revelations are a little peculiar, even embarrassing to defend nowadays. This probably won't amount to anything." He raised the baggie. "There are Jews all around the world now, including Mexico. This hair won't prove anything. What we really need are skin cells. It would be better if we had the whole body and its clothes.

"About the scrolls, why don't you let me take that one?" He pointed at the cylinder John held. "It might be worth something.

It might give us the information we need."

"No way. I might need it."

"For what? You're taking a big chance hanging around down here with that in your possession. You've got the police watching you, and you're talking about running off into that damnable Lacandon Jungle with a bunch of guys who probably have criminal records."

"I have my reasons. I'll be fine. Just do as I ask, OK?"

"Yeah, sure. Whatever." Tucking the baggie into his pants pocket, he glanced up at the sky. "It's going to rain. I'm going to the temple once before I leave. It looks like a nice one. I don't want to come all this way without seeing it." He turned to go, but John stopped him.

"Not a word about what you've been doing here, Don, got it?"

"Don't worry. I'm just a tourist. Your intrigues and secret agent stuff are safe with me. I just want out of this place. The Mexico I like is the one with beaches and resorts. These towns have too many poor people. It's depressing."

He sniffed the air, glanced up at the imminent storm, and joined the hustle of humanity scurrying to find shelter before the deluge. He glanced back at John briefly, nodded, and gave a half smile as he walked toward the pedestrian bridge and Mormon temple to the west.

"Dumb ass," Elder John muttered, watching his colleague's retreating back. *Are all scientists so predictable and unimaginative?*

Frowning, he turned to find his rented Ford F-150 pickup. The silly academic could ogle the facilities across the street.

Brother John abandoned the Holiday Inn the previous day to cover his tracks and checked in at the very nice Camino Real off Boulevard Belisario Dominguez near Canon del Sumidero National Park. There was a great bar called the Club

Palenque, and he met a young waitress named Cuca who was an aspiring singer. She spoke passable English and said she was born on the Gulf coast near Tamaulipas, but she was raised in Laredo, Texas.

John recalled her walking across the room with a tray of drinks—a pretty little thing with short skirt and stunning butt. She perked up and took a liking to him when he gave her a five dollar tip and told her he knew people in Las Vegas. Didn't all waitresses dream of becoming actresses or singers? It would be a shame to visit Mexico and not taste the local product at least once.

He had to take a call from Raul at six o'clock that evening, then he would visit Club Palenque to see what would happen. After the day's good tidings, he felt confident the momentum had changed, and he was on a roll.

Wind gusted even harder, and he stepped into his truck and slammed the door just as rain blew in. He massaged his crotch for a few moments to create a stir, then he turned on the wipers and checked his rearview mirror. He had time for a quick shower and bottle of Corona.

He pulled away from the curb and drove west, deliberately avoiding the Mission House and its unwanted guests. He wondered if Cuca gave good head. She looked awfully young to be working in a bar. Girls who worked clubs in Mexico were known to put out, weren't they? He would find out. Even if she didn't, Raul could surely find someone who could.

CHAPTER SIXTEEN

Karen, Salvador, and their crew of six left the small Maya Indian community of Taniperlas early in the morning. A messenger went ahead the previous night to tell the workers at the excavation site to meet them where the trail was no longer traversable with all-terrain motor bikes. Fatigued after carefully maneuvering 4-wheeled Kawasakis loaded with supplies through rugged jungle paths for nearly four hours, they abandoned the bikes thirty kilometers into the jungle at a shelter that stored gasoline, canned food, spare parts, tents, household and cooking items, and a Honda generator in case the on-site one broke down.

They met five Indians, full-time workers from the Xibalba site, and the party of eleven trekked another three hours along a narrow, rocky path that fought to maintain its existence from the encroaching jungle.

They sometimes drew near but never crossed a stream of clear, percolating water that coursed through the lowlands as it flowed south and east through the wilds of the enormous national reserve called El Parque Natural de Montes Azules. After the river's serpentine journey carried it 100 kilometers through the national park to the broad Usumacinta River, a natural border between Mexico and Guatemala, it flowed north to the lowlands of the Gulf.

Father Lopez began fantasizing about the stream as he walked wearily, sweltering in the rain forest heat under the cruel Chiapas sun. He was careful not to complain, though. Karen warned him of the rigors and discomfort he would experience when he accompanied her into the jungle and highlands of central Chiapas State. He didn't regret coming so far. Being among the poor Indians, seeing how little they had and studying the truly miserable conditions from which they eked out a living in their harsh environment, simply confirmed his ideas and beliefs.

The Mayans were the disenfranchised of the world, those at the bottom of the economic and political food chain with no one to represent them. They'd been dispossessed of their property 400 years earlier during the Conquest and shoved back onto remote, marginal lands on which it was difficult to make a living. He doubted any family among those people made $100 a year. They suffered from diseases, malnutrition, and society's neglect, because they refused to become part of mainstream culture.

The Maya, surprisingly autonomous, preferred to follow the beliefs and customs of their ancestors, living in small, homogenous villages and practicing a way of life that was ancient before the Conquest began at the end of the 15th century. The Indians of Chiapas practiced a type of Catholicism barely recognizable in mainstream churches around the world. Their way of life remained remarkably vital and intact. He admired those resilient people and found them earnest, hardworking, trusting, and devout. He was glad he came, and he planned to see if it was possible to advocate and help empower them to successfully enter an economy of rapacious multinational corporations, corrupt government officials, and a world of advanced technology that left them behind 100 years earlier.

He glanced up to see Karen walking at the front of the line, thirty meters ahead, talking to Rafael Mendez, the Xibalba excavation site's labor boss who hired and supervised the workers. The camp staff was all Mayan Indians from many local villages, most not large enough to merit being placed on a map.

He admired how she interacted with the locals. Their expressions and body movements showed they respected her, even though she was a woman, and they sought her advice and explanations. As the only source of income most of them would see for several years, she was important.

Karen spoke fluent Spanish and appeared to have a basic understanding of the local Maya dialect, which the Indians appreciated. She was a bright woman and also very attractive. He enjoyed their conversations immensely, and her passion and intimacy more than he ever thought possible. None of those helped him resolve the conflicts he felt with issues in his life. His vows as a priest and the path he must follow remained unresolved.

Salvador saw the terrain changing. The narrow trail of the last several hours grew wider, its tightly circumscribed path of dense brush, trees, and occasional sheer cliff sides almost gone, along with green forests filled with thick brush, giant spider webs, and hungry mosquitoes. The chattering howler monkeys that screamed and threatened them while shaking the forest canopy with their fury were gone, too.

The biome had changed. Although it was still hot and humid, they entered a land of visible bare earth, rocky outcroppings, and sparse vegetation, where iguanas basked in the sun atop rocks or in tree boughs. They approached the stream again as it wound on its east-west axis from a copse of trees, and he wondered if they would stop for a break in the shade. Surely they were near the waterfall Karen described. She said it was a walk of two or three hours, and, by his reckoning, they'd been hoofing it at least that long.

He stopped momentarily to shift his backpack, because the straps chafed his shoulders, and when he was ready to start again, he saw Karen standing away from the front line, waiting for him.

"So, how's it going, Sally?" she asked.

He smiled. "No complaints."

"Good. I don't want to send you home with a bad report card." She reached for his hand, but she just gave it a quick squeeze before releasing it. "We're nearly at the falls. I think I can hear them." She cocked her head, listening. "Can you hear it?"

Stopping, he tried to focus. He thought he caught a distant, wispy splash emanating from a very steep foothill speckled with pine trees that rose into the western sky. When his eyes moved left from the point of the forested rocky outcrop, he thought he caught a nearby stream.

"Yes. Over there?" He pointed.

"Yes. You'll love it, Sally. We'll stop to rest before climbing up and over the top and down into the canyon."

At the mention of cool water and rest, he wanted to take her in his arms, but she would be appalled by such a breach of behavior in front of the workers. They didn't know he was a priest or what his role was, but they were unaccustomed to public displays of affection, especially from a female boss.

He and Karen walked forward again. When he looked around, he saw the others weren't in single-file anymore. Crew members moved in twos and threes to talk as they walked. Those who joined them at the way station to help transport supplies back to the site were curious for news from their communities and families. Messages were delivered, along with packages of special foods and items requested from family members to aid them while on the site.

The crash of water soon became audible. On such a hot, fatiguing afternoon, the sound was very enticing. The stream dog-legged west, and the team moved back to single file to follow the meander another fifty meters until it curled into a copse of fir trees and eroded hills that studded a large outcropping of rock.

They moved along a steadily narrowing path, following the stream into a grove of trees backed by a sheer mountain face. Amid the shade and dark shadows, a cool, refreshing mist hung in the air, raising spirits and encouraging laughter and conversation.

The sound grew louder, and the path channeled through a tall, shady canopy of trees into a wide-open area around the falls. Sally saw the others relieving themselves of their packs and copied them.

"You're smiling!" Karen shouted against the roar.

"I'm happy!" he shouted back, helping her with her load.

"Really? You aren't just saying that?"

He glanced upward at the cascade, a tall, gushing spout of water that seemed to split the mountain wall, then his gaze dropped to the surrounding pool and vegetation. The workers joked, and a few removed shoes to soak their feet. Broad-leafed ferns, bushes, and trees dripping with moss and vines rimmed the brink. Water lilies floated along the eastern bank. The overpowering sound of cascading water invigorated Sally.

His fatigue vanished, and he wandered about the ferns, green plants, and damp, grassy bank as a cool, light mist coated his face. At the bank's edge, he watched swirling water eddy and move outward toward the banks and out to the stream. He looked up nearly thirty meters to the crest of the falls. Water leaped from the cliff face to become a diaphanous veil, a sparkling curtain of glass that crashed into the bowl at their feet.

"Wow." Enchanted by the scene, he took deep breaths of the moist, cool air.

Karen walked up beside him, and he reached for her waist to pull her close, but she raised a hand to stop him. Leaning close to his ear, she said, "Later, Lover. This evening after everything is sorted."

He smiled in understanding. "Later is fine."

They rested for nearly an hour. The sun reached the crest of the waterfall, and shade encroached on the crystal pool of refreshment at their feet.

Karen shielded her eyes with one hand and shouted, "Time to go, Sally. It's another hour or so."

He told himself he could do it. As he rose, stretched, and reached for his backpack, he realized it was one of the most interesting days of his life.

Led by Rafael, they climbed high above the cascading water until they were able to pass through the mountain on a narrow trail that hugged the wall far above the stream. After carefully negotiating the corridor, they arrived on a substantial ledge overlooking an immense, jungle-filled canyon. The sound of tumbling water subsided to a whisper.

The oval valley enclosed by sheer cliffs extended nearly three kilometers before narrowing at the southern end. Caves, most with small openings, pocked the valley walls. Karen pointed out the various locations in the basin that were undergoing excavation, as well as the tents and connecting paths that webbed the area.

"We haven't seen the Zapatistas in a while, but a couple of Protestant militants moved hurriedly through. No one knows where they were going or where they came from, but it was likely they wanted to terrorize Indian families who encroached the bio reserve."

Sally knew the militias sometimes worked as guides and scouts for the Mexican Army, unwittingly becoming enablers in the drug trafficking endemic in Chiapas.

While in town, Karen arranged for a helicopter to arrive in a few days to pick up empty fuel barrels and deliver more diesel, which was too heavy or large to transport on foot. They had enough supplies to work on the site for another month before returning to San Cristobal de las Casas.

She looked him in the eye, then turned away. "You can always leave sooner." She hefted her pack and carefully started down the trail built by the Mayans over 1,000 years earlier that ran the length of the valley along the mountain face.

Sally looked at the walls as they traversed the narrow path. He saw pictographic glyphs, obviously Mayan, carved into the walls. Most were worn and faded, but a few were in excellent condition considering their age and weathering. Soon, the party moved even slower, as the trail began a precipitous descent. They slipped and slid down on loose gravel until reaching the valley floor.

When Sally composed himself and regained his breath after the near free-fall down the narrow path, he saw the most amazing cavern opening of his life.

This has to be it, he realized. *It's the big Xibalba cave. I see why they're so enamored of it.*

It was the most-impressive cave he ever saw, with huge, gaping mouth and tumbled edifices on either side. A broad stairway, ruined with age, provided passage from the ground to the cave entrance. Tents, shelters, wheelbarrows, lean-tos, and random piles of rock and trenches spread from the cave's mouth far back into the forested canyon floor. He was awed, and his respect for Karen rose another notch.

He turned to her. "Is it OK if I walk around?"

"Knock yourself out, Lover Boy." She gave him a winning smile before turning to talk with Raul.

Though they conversed quietly, Sally saw the other workers trying to eavesdrop. Raul's head bobbed in agreement as she gave instructions, and Sally heard an occasional, "*Si, señora,*" and "*Por supuesto, señora.*"

Karen turned and walked to where Sally stood on the steps at the cave entrance.

"This is it?" he asked. "This is the place the Maya think they came from?"

She placed her hand on his shoulder but quickly removed it. "Could be. Who knows where the original cave was? If there was one, this is a good candidate. You remember your Mayan cosmology from David's class?"

"It's been fifteen years. I'm a little rusty." He feigned ignorance.

"I'll bet. Let me review it for you."

"Please do. I find this utterly fascinating." He gestured toward the whole area.

She smiled in approval. "The Maya believe their progenitors, their ancestors, came from Xibalba. In a sense, it's their birthplace. It's also a version of hell that's not like ours. We don't really know, because the Spaniards burned all the books that gave explanations for those concepts. Xibalba was a cave, the entrance into the Mayan hell, and it was also the abode of the Nine Lords of Darkness who tried to destroy Hanaphu and Xabalanque, the ancestor Hero Twins. "

She paused briefly. "Are you going inside? We've strung electric cable through much of the cave, but we're nearly out of diesel for the generator. We have lots of hand lamps, and I can take you in for a brief look. It's incredible." She sighed. "We've found lots of fantastic stuff. Some of it's from the pre-classic Mayan era."

"Sure. I guess so. Why not? It's safe, isn't it?" He inhaled deeply, trying to take it all in. Tendrils of vines and roots hung like gossamer curtains. Fern, lichen, moss, and scrub trees obscured the mammoth opening. Below the ruined steps, a stream gurgled from within the bowels of the cave, and a small cenote, a pool of ground water in a limestone cistern commonly found through the Yucatan Peninsula and parts of Chiapas, guarded the entrance.

The cenote, forty meters in diameter, was webbed inside and out with lichen, moss, and weeds. What appeared to be ruined altars of mortared stone covered with glyphs lay tumbled on both sides of the south end of the cenote nearest the steps leading to the cave.

The sun was behind the western canyon walls, and ominous shadows stretched long and deep, cloaking the forested ravine in a blanket of gloom.

"Sure," he said, feeling a reluctance he didn't understand. "Let's do it, but first I need to go to the bathroom or whatever you…."

"Over there." She smiled and pointed toward some tarps fifty meters west along the cliff face. "You'll smell it before you get there."

"Right. I'm sure." He saw several very small structures that appeared to be three wood-frame outhouses and a solar shower with plastic tarps hung for privacy draped over a line strung between two trees. At least ten barrels, some on their sides and others upright, sat ten meters south of the latrine area.

As he walked west toward the camp toilet facilities, he surveyed the distant hillsides and shot glances south into the forested valley. A feeling of foreboding dropped on him like a wet towel. Unquestionably it was one of the most-unusual places he ever visited. He had very little experience with caves. Though he was cautious by nature, he wasn't claustrophobic, but he couldn't account for the feeling of trepidation that caught his mood. Maybe he should wait until morning when there was more daylight, but he realized that was silly. Artificial lighting was needed in the cave all the time.

The odor of the latrine struck his nose, and he frowned as he neared the outhouses. Which one should he use? Did it matter?

They were placed ten feet apart, and he faced the middle one. The odor was rank. He doubted anyone spent much time in the bathroom in the field. Breathing slowly through his mouth, he opened a door, glanced around quickly in the fading light for toilet paper, and went inside.

* * *

Luis Cruz, a discontented sicario (narco trafficker) originally from the northern state of Nuevo Leon, knelt in a pew in the Cathedral of San Marcos. The vaulted ceiling, impressive support pillars, and stained glass with images of saints and Biblical scenes offered familiar comfort. Darting shadows from votive candles flickered on the smoke-stained walls east of the altar. Statues of saints, all with broad foreheads and generous Mayan noses, lined the walls along the outer aisles.

He quit going to church for many years after joining the Zapatistas, but he recently returned, along with many of his brothers in crime. He and his fellow soldiers knew death could come at any moment, most likely when one least expected it. Such was the nature of a fighter in the cartel.

One minute a man was drinking and whoring or spending time with his family. The next he was on the run, hiding, fighting, killing, and sometimes performing barbaric acts against competitors, like decapitating their heads and tossing them onto courthouse lawns.

He became steeled to his work and inured to violence as much as any man could in his profession. Being a cartel soldier certainly paid better than a *campesino*, performing back-breaking labor twelve to fourteen hours a day, earning barely enough to feed his family and put Wal-Mart clothes on their backs.

Still, guilt sometimes stalked him like an avenging demon. He learned to cope with the pressures and dangers, even though they sometimes were unbearable. He needed a little calm at the moment. Sometimes coming to church helped, but just as often it didn't, and this was one of those times. He reached for the little pill bottle in his breast pocket, extracted two yellow Valium, and quickly swallowed. Drug-induced respite from his worries was better than no solace at all.

Ebony-haired Luis was medium height with well-shaped, muscular shoulders and a thick neck. Too many fistfights bent his nose and webbed his large hands with scars. His face was pocked from childhood acne, deeply etched crow's feet extended from each eye, and his forehead was grooved with deep wrinkles. His face was wrought from hard living, constant anxiety, and fear.

Before leaving his car and entering the church, he tied his jacket around his waist by its sleeves to hide the pistol he carried for protection in a rear waistband. Clearly visible on separate forearms were embellished tattoos of the patron saints of narco traffickers, La Santa Muerte, Holy Death, and La Santa Jesus Malverde. He didn't want to take chances, so he prayed to both on behalf of his soul and his life. Who else but the saints of death would understand what he and other cartel soldiers endured every moment to make a living? Who else would provide protection and help them survive battles, murder, and disfigurement?

Luis was dispatched to Chiapas State one year earlier as part of a new vanguard to muscle in on the military's exclusive access to transporting drugs from Guatemala into the United States, where those rich, crazy fuckers apparently couldn't get enough of them. Life was shitty at times, but that was what Luis did, and he did it well. He earned good money and respect from his peers.

Sometimes, family events were harder than killing people. His wife was murdered by the rival La Familia gang two years earlier, leaving him a spoiled, pretty daughter who was sixteen and nearly out of his control. She raised herself that last two years, and it hadn't been easy to have a father like him. She was a good kid. He loved her more than he believed possible. He tried to be a good father and was a good provider, but his lifestyle required he be away for weeks at a time.

Like all teenagers, she wanted her independence. She took his money when she needed it, then threw tantrums and accused him of terrible things which he may or may not have done. She wanted to be a singer, and he thought she sounded fabulous, and not because she was his daughter. She sounded like Selena and even looked a bit like her, though his daughter was prettier. When she smiled at him, which was rare recently, his chest swelled with joy.

Luis just returned from Tapachula at the Guatemala border after meeting with two new drug mules he recruited. He arranged for them to return to Guatemala and pick up a load of meth to transport fifty kilometers northeast across the Usumacinta River. Luis would leave again in the morning for Ocosingo on the other side of the mountains to meet his mules and ensure they didn't run afoul of the military at the new fort built the previous year to intimidate the many Zapatista sympathizers in the small villages throughout the forests and rugged mountains of the Lacandon.

Luis and his money made friends in several small Protestant Indian hamlets in the jungle, which were outside the sphere of political autonomy that was afforded the Zapatistas after their rebellion in 1994. Some of those Protestants joined local militias in opposition to the Catholic Zapatistas, and many were more than willing to take Luis' money to act as guides, provide intelligence, and ensure safe passage for the drug mules across the Usumacinta and through the rugged Lacandon jungle. The money Luis spread around quickly earned their attention and loyalty.

He rolled his shoulders, feeling tension relent as the Valium worked. He considered lighting a votive candle to let the Santa Muerte know he was present but decided against it. That would only draw unwanted attention.

He looked around the church to see if anyone was watching him. People knew who those tattoos on his arms represented, and most priests were opposed to them and the people who displayed them. He hoped no one in the church was stupid enough to comment. He wasn't looking for trouble—just the opposite—but he sure as hell wouldn't run away. He was certain the narco saints protected him. He'd been a soldier in

166

the cartel for almost eight years, and he was still alive. What more proof did he need?

His eyes went to his forearms and the patron saints. He clenched his fists to flex the muscles and animate the tattoos, then he stroked each forearm with the opposite hand for luck, his fingers lingering on the robed, hooded skeleton of La Santa Muerte and her sickle of death before making the sign of the cross and rising to leave. She was his favorite. All narco traffickers knew if they kept their vows to her, she accepted them without judgment no matter what their crimes. Luis' transgressions were many and egregious. He genuflected toward the front of the church and the agonized image of the crucified Christ hanging from the ceiling. Evening mass would begin soon, so he needed to leave.

Luis lived from his suitcase, never staying anywhere too long. Enemies from rival cartels quickly found someone who remained in one place too long. He decided to check in at the Camino Real, a really nice hotel, to see Cuca sing that evening. He hated having his daughter work in a club, even if it was a nice one. In years past, if a girl worked in a bar or club, she was considered a *puta,* a whore, but attitudes toward women, work, and a female's place in society were changing. Still, old customs and values died hard. Her mother would have been angry with Luis for allowing it, but their daughter was almost an adult. She hadn't listened to his counsel in two years, and he knew he didn't have much control over her anymore.

It was time to go outside. He reached behind and inside his light jacket to ensure the 9 mm Browning automatic was securely in place. He stood briefly at the church's broad oak doors before cautiously cracking one open. Peering through the gap with one hand on the pistol butt, he slowly opened the door fully, inspecting the area in front of the church.

He paused to study the street and cars parked up and down the avenue, then he hurriedly descended the worn granite steps and walked toward a black Ford Expedition with tinted windows half a block away. The overcast sky was full of bilious clouds that roiled and tossed overhead. Thunder rumbled in the distance, and lightning flickered through the heavens.

A cool, brisk breeze blew from the west, carrying light rain that threatened to become a downpour. It was good timing that he left the church right before the storm. He quickened his pace.

A child of twelve with a dirty LA Raiders T-shirt and scuffed tennis shoes stood near the car with a proprietary air, making sure no one tampered with Luis' car.

"Todo esta bien." The youth smiled, assuring Luis no one showed undue interest in the car.

"Bueno." Extracting a roll of bills from his pocket, he peeled off two twenty-peso notes for the tawny-skinned youth.

"Gracias, señor." The boy fled with his newfound wealth.

Luis opened the door, started the engine, and wheeled into traffic toward Camino Real. He looked forward to seeing Cuca again. His daughter meant everything to him. She was his only remaining family, and a twinge of heartache flickered in his chest whenever he thought of her.

Life was an emotional rollercoaster when one had a child.

Everything was amplified when working a job like his.

Ah well, he thought, *a couple glasses of brandy and a little Tejano would loosen my mood and set the tone for a relaxing evening at the club.*

He glanced in the rearview mirror to make sure no one was following him, then he turned onto Chicoasen, speeding north on the freeway toward Camino Real.

CHAPTER SEVENTEEN

Alexandra and Joaquin sat at a table in the family visitation room of the San Cristobal jail, waiting for David so they could deliver their bad news. He wasn't going home that day, nor would he be released the next day. Flickering fluorescent bulbs shed poor light on aged, putty-colored walls marred by various scrapes and dents, stained from dirty hands and shoe soles. The room stank of stale cigarettes in the humid, motionless air.

Alexandra, trying to remain composed and maintain her dignity despite the unbelievable turn of events, still grasped a handkerchief to dab her bloodshot eyes. Joaquin, his fancy suit rumpled and hair tousled, slumped in his chair, staring at the tabletop, his face and posture showing he was sullen, humiliated, and angry.

Who would have believed that a member of his family could be arrested and detained? Worse, who would believe that Joaquin couldn't secure his release? The Consul of Chiapas was in unfamiliar territory and circumstances. He fully expected to gain his brother-in-law's release and see the responsible parties chastised, if not punished, for taking outrageous personal liberties in prosecuting a case of no merit against a powerful family like his. At least he got the ridiculous, unsubstantiated murder charge dropped. David lacked the *cojones* for such an action. More importantly, he had a rock-solid alibi for his whereabouts during the purported periods of the crimes.

Joaquin had never been in opposition to the Catholic Church before. He could only assume that the Vatican and its envoy successfully suborned the highest offices in the country to get their way, but why? What was so important? What was really at stake, and what had David really done?

Joaquin glanced at his grim-faced sister. Very disappointed, she avoided his eye, looking stoically at the wall and the clock above the door. She'd been as shocked as he upon hearing Joaquin couldn't affect her husband's release. The Gonzalez Corsos were pedigreed, a powerful, affluent family in Mexico with connections. It was an unimaginable situation.

A red light shone above the door, and David entered, escorted by a hatchet-faced, gun-toting guard in a blue uniform. He wore the same clothes as when arrested, but his hands were cuffed. Though weary and bedraggled, he managed a smile for Alexandra.

"Joaquin," David said with a nod.

"David." He frowned back.

"Why am I still here?" He looked at his wife, then his brother-in-law. "What's going on?"

Joaquin, doing a poor job of hiding his disapproval, looked to his sister.

Alexandra dabbed at her eye and asked the jailer, "Can't we have a few minutes alone?"

"No. I was told to be present throughout this meeting." He glanced at the wall clock. "You have only five minutes. Those are Inspector Leyeva's orders."

"This is an outrage!" Joaquin blustered. "I'll have him cleaning latrines in Tuxtla when this is over!"

"Whatever. You have five minutes," the guard replied calmly. "You're on the clock right now, understand?" He heard many threats in his line of work.

David reached to pull out a chair, but the guard stopped him.

"No sitting. Orders from Inspector Leyeva."

All three glared at the guard, then David said, "OK. We don't have much time. Why can't I get out of here? What am I charged with?"

Alexandra looked to her brother, who frowned and gave David a malevolent stare as if he were a lower form of life.

"You'll be charged with felony theft, David," he said, "for stealing from the Catholic Church." He glanced at his sister, who stared at a crack on the table, before looking back to David. "It would be better if you had murdered someone, my friend. This is shameful. Stealing from a church is the lowest of all crimes."

David laughed. "That's crazy. It's bogus, and you know it. That ruin was abandoned for 150 years. The government wasn't involved and didn't care about it. I was merely retrieving artifacts to investigate. I was there on the request of a priest from the Tuxtla Gutierrez Diocese, Father Salvador Lopez. I don't know where the box and the body are. I don't know what happened to any of that. Maybe Father Salvador knows, but I'm innocent."

Joaquin held up his hand to stop David's protests. "Not so, says the papal inquisitor I have yet to meet, Father Sean Gregory, and also not according to the bishop of the Tuxtla diocese. To him, you're a common thief, like a drug addict who steals to feed his habit."

He paused. "David, I tried, believe me. I don't know how this will turn out, but you're up to your neck in shit, my friend. I'm doing all I can. I don't know what you took or what's involved, but you must cooperate with the Vatican's man, or you'll be in here a long time. I've never seen something like this attract so much attention at the highest levels of our government. For the record, David, this is a very shameful thing in which you have involved my family and my sister." "Joaquin!" Alexandra suddenly leaped to her feet. "Enough!" She glared at him. "You keep trying, you hear me? You keep making calls and doing everything you can, understand?"

"Alexandra, there's nothing more I can do. This is simply scandalous, this thing with David. It's shameful. It's…."

"Shut up, Joaquin," she ordered, angry at his lack of sympathy. "Whose side are you on?"

David held up his cuffed hands and motioned for quiet. Suddenly, he looked very tired, and his shoulders slumped. "Ale, he's right. This is much bigger than anyone could have imagined. They're wrong. I haven't done anything illegal, but I won't get out of here until they have what they want. We need help. We have to get word to Sally and Karen to return to San Cristobal. This is Sally's doing. He started this whole mess. Who knows where that body is? If Sally will meet and talk with

Father Gregory, it will help. It might even get me released."

Alexandra, crying freely, circled the table to embrace him, but the guard held up a warning hand.

"No touching. No hugging or anything else. Inspector's orders."

"You're kidding!" she said.

"Time's up, too."

Alexandra looked at the clock, then at David and her brother. "Give it to him."

"Ale, this isn't necessary," Joaquin protested. "They'll take good care. It's too high-profile a case to treat him like a common criminal. It's too unlikely that it would…."

Her back stiffened, and her mouth became a thin line. "Now, Joaquin."

He groaned and stood from his chair. Turning sideways momentarily, he took something from his pants pocket and walked over to the guard.

"What's your name?" he demanded. "Who's your family?"

The jailer suddenly looked alarmed, though he answered in a surly tone, "Pablo Ramirez, *Señor.*"

"I want you to remember that I am Joaquin Gonzalez-Corso, the consul of Chiapas. I, too, have expectations and orders for you, Ramirez." He palmed the roll of bills he removed from his pants pocket and extended his hand in greeting. "I've already given a gift to Colonel Ramos, the director of this jail, to ensure my brother-in-law's well-being and safety. I expect you to do the same, since you are the one who interacts with him. You'll ensure his safety and see to his needs, whatever they are. I expect him to receive decent food and water and that he is allowed visitors. I'll hold you personally responsible if anything happens to him. Do you understand me?"

The jailer, entirely familiar with the situation, would have been offended if no bribe had been offered. It was expected. If someone wanted proper care, privileges, and humane treatment apart from whatever was normally provided in jail, he paid for it. People in high-income countries wouldn't recognize the legal process in Mexico, because it was based on Napoleonic law. A man was guilty until proven innocent.

The guard eagerly shook Joaquin's hand, removing the bills and sliding them into his pants pocket. *"Si, Señor.* I will do all that I can, but this is…a difficult situation. Many people are watching your brother-in-law. Still, I'll do what I can."

"See that you do." Joaquin's voice held poorly disguised malice. "Inspector Leyeva isn't the only one watching you."

"Si, señor." He tried to appear unconcerned. "It's time to go. Say your good-byes, please."

Defiant, Alexandra embraced David. The guard frowned but didn't comment, clutching the bills in his pocket.

"Get in touch with Sally and Karen," David urged. "It's very important. There's a phone number on the bulletin board in my office to the *Farmacia Reyes* in Ocosingo. Ask for Arturo. He'll do anything I ask of him."

"I will. I still have to go to Tuxtla. It's so busy right now."

He was perplexed. "What's in Tuxtla? Why are you so busy?"

"Oh, I forgot to tell you. Your friend, Dr. Yusuf Bin Saud from Lebanon, arrives tonight. I tried to tell him this was a bad time to visit, but he insisted on coming."

CHAPTER EIGHTEEN

Salvador watched with a bemused expression as Karen spoke to the foreman. He couldn't help noticing the man's surreptitious glances at him. Sally resolved he had to get to know the man soon. No doubt Rafael was the key to understanding all that transpired in the valley and would be pivotal in providing Sally access to the camp workers and their families, something he desired. Remaining apart and disconnected from the villagers and their lives was the last thing he desired. He wanted to find the true path to aiding the poor and miserable of the world. In his estimation, of the seven billion people on the planet, more than five billion lived in endemic poverty, had little or no access to health care, and were subject to repressive political systems that provided little hope of making their lives better. Conviction and commitment weren't the issue. It was how he should implement his beliefs. How did one effectively combine belief with action?

The practices of the Church, though well-meaning, proved of little help in providing either spiritual or economic assistance to those whom Jesus taught while He was on earth—women, the very poor, and the sick. As far as Father Salvador could tell from studying the New Testament, Jesus hadn't said anything that was difficult to understand. It might have been controversial, but it wasn't confusing.

The Son of God had spoken clearly and demonstrated through His actions what He thought of the rich, the powerful, and the money-changers in the Temple of Jerusalem who claimed to control access to God. Jesus had clearly said we must love and help the poor unconditionally, but

Christianity, whether Catholic of Protestant, became subverted by the

Calvinist principles of the Industrial Revolution and the ideology of conservative politics. The poor were not to be pitied or helped. They were despised, examples of God's rejection, and seen as inferior in all respects.

Rather than embrace the promise of science and technology to make the world a better place, the rich and powerful, with the blessing of the world's Christian churches, supported capitalists and their multinational corporations in making wage slaves of the poor in the most-populated regions of the world. It was ideology at its worst, Social Darwinism, and it guaranteed that the helpless and hopeless of the world remained in that condition.

In his opinion, the Catholic Church was as guilty as the Protestants. The Church became an arm of the state and its laws, buttressing and supporting civil law with moral admonitions from the Bible. The relationship became cozy in the extreme and resulted in complacency and orthodoxy in the Church, not the action with purpose based on Jesus' teachings.

Was it possible to serve two masters, the Catholic Church he loved with his heart and soul, and the teachings of Jesus, which he knew were true? Surely a person could work effectively among the poor within the framework of the Church without being hobbled by the politics and errant orthodoxy that cast them all from the same crucible. He felt figuratively and literally lost, looking for reluctant solutions in the middle of the Lacandon jungle, while breaking his sacred vows. How should he spend his life?

He finished his short tour of the campground, arriving back at the cenote and stairs leading to the cave entrance. Karen spoke to Rafael. From all appearances, she gathered equipment needed to explore the cave.

The sun dropped behind the mountain wall, and light quickly fled the valley, leaving a vague ether in which it was difficult to discern detail. Long shadows stretched from the forested mountainsides, and he again felt a twinge of dread at the idea of entering the cave at night.

Karen said all would be fine, and he trusted her.

* * *

Karen noticed Rafael stealing glances at Salvador, eyeing him warily. Sally and Karen had spoken of the matter, and Salvador knew his status at the ruins was still unknown. The foreman, refusing to meet his eyes and focusing on Karen, proved his social ambiguity.

"We won't need assistance, Rafael," Karen said, smiling a greeting to Sally as he returned before turning back to the foreman. "We have lanterns and a canteen. I'll give Salvador a tour of the cave and show him the Room of Inscriptions. We shouldn't be more than an hour. I also have a phone." She pointed to the walkie-talkie at her belt. "I'll call if we need something, but that isn't likely.

"Please see that the gear is sorted and in good shape for tomorrow before anyone eats, OK? Save us a little something for later. Have the guys help clean up. Jose's back is bothering him again. He can cook, but he has trouble lifting and bending when cleaning."

"*Si, señora.* I'll check your tent for snakes and spiders. It's been two weeks since you were here. I don't allow anyone in your tent while you're away."

"Please do. Do the same for the tent beside mine after clearing it out. Put everything in the shed if it will fit, then hang a hammock for Salvador and place a mosquito net around it. He'll be with us for a while."

"*Si, señora.*" The old Mayan eyed Salvador, curious about her new companion. The camp already buzzed with stories and speculation about her relationship with the man.

It appeared on the journey they were more than friends. Even though Karen was a boss and a foreigner, a *gringa* from the other side of the *frontera*, tongues wagged, and a sense of scandal entered the camp. She must keep a tight rein on the men. It was none of their business what she did.

Ahua David and the *gringa* were the bosses—period. They accepted Marcos, and now they had to accept Salvador. What if Marcos arrived? Karen would have to handle that if and when it happened.

* * *

As Salvador watched, Karen bent over, and he couldn't help noticing her shapely figure and long hair as it slid forward. When she straightened, she flipped her head to whisk her hair over her shoulders in an arc. She held two colorful folded cloaks, because it was very chilly at night in the cave complex. She handed him one, wrapped the other around her neck and shoulders, and held out a lantern for him. While she moved a lock of hair aside from her face and eyes, he copied her, tossing the wrap over his shoulder and hefting the lantern to judge its weight.

"Here." She gave him a lantern with fluorescent-tube bulbs. "You turn it on by pushing that rubber-coated switch in the handle. Yes, that one." She smiled again. "Aren't you excited?"

He nodded. He was definitely excited and even a bit shaky with apprehension.

She glanced toward the camp in the valley as she turned on her lantern. Extending her hand, she said, "Come on, Sally. You're going to love this."

He accepted her hand, glanced back over his shoulder, and took a deep breath as she guided him to the cave mouth. For the first time, he noticed that the cave walls contained glyphs and markings. The floor was damp, the air moist and cool, and the big opening split into several tunnels leading in different directions.

Cables connected to diesel generators near the cenote trailed up the steps, into the cave, and on into the passageways. The floor was slick with slime and mud. A faint, moist, cool breath of air raised gooseflesh on his arms. Large piles of fractured rock lay at the sides.

She saw him eyeing the piles. "When we first discovered the cave, there was a big battle between the Zapatistas and government mercenaries. They tried to blow up the entrance. It was a mess. Marcos, the…uh…the Zapatista leader, was hurt but survived. We cleared it all away. It's safe. Trust me. Come on."

She tugged him arm down the left passageway. After twenty meters, it dog-legged to the right. Ten meters farther, and he stood at the entrance to a cavernous room. The two of them held their lanterns high.

"It's like traveling to the moon," he said softly.

Creamy calcite coated the floor, reflecting lantern light throughout the room. Thousands of pearly cones, stalactites of indescribable beauty, dripped from the ceiling. Three small craters, or underground cenotes, were in the center of the room. Thousands of bats grouped in clusters all over the ceiling. They appeared to be tiny, dark cocoons when tightly wrapped in their wings. He could have taken a dozen in one handful if he wished.

As he watched, he heard a soft chirp, and a bat disengaged itself from the ceiling to dart around the room. The scene was eerie and a little unnerving.

"Don't worry about them," she said. "They won't bother you. You get used to it. We've been working here almost five years, and we haven't had any trouble."

"I'm sure. I hear they mostly eat insects or fruit," he said bravely, his gaze focusing on the walls and floor. "It's like being in a creamy glass room," he whispered in awe.

He moved his lantern up and down and from side-to-side.

"Your mouth's hanging open," she joked.

Indeed, he thought. *I must be standing slack-jawed in awe. This is totally unexpected.* "Amazing. It's so…."

"Incredible," she finished for him. "I think they look like teeth, like the canines in a wolf's open mouth. See how pointed they are and how they shine?"

She pointed at the walls. "Glyphs."

Turning, he saw a broad column of calcite with glyphs inscribed on its face. The lantern light revealed figures and stunning pictures on the walls and stalactites throughout the room—nature's treasure trove with Maya art embellishing what God wrought.

He glanced at the floor to ensure his safety, then he held his lantern high to survey the walls. Hundreds of glyphs, some blurred and faded, many still brightly colored, covered an entire wall and parts of others. His eyes went to one in particular that seemed familiar. It was a noble of some type, perhaps a king or priest in full regalia holding what appeared to be a cup or bowl above kneeling supplicants, possibly captives.

The priest's legs disappeared into a serpentine coil that wrapped around the altar behind him. Three unclothed bodies lay to the side, as if they were ill or the focus of the ceremony. When he compared the scene to the glyphs and drawings on either side of the mural, it struck him as incongruent. It seemed out of place. Perhaps it had been painted over an existing mural. It was certainly a stunning marvel.

She grasped his hand firmly, and he let her lead him. "See over there?" She guided him along a well-worn path between the cenotes. "More rooms. That's where we're doing most of our work. David found another room. We don't know how many are in this complex. It could be dozens, but most of the important work is being done in here."

She pointed at a manmade structure near the wall. The path led to a shelf-like structure of milky calcite laid down over thousands of years. Carrying their lanterns aloft, they walked between the cenotes. It felt eerie moving through such a surreal scene. The cave roof and stalactites incandesced with flickering lantern light.

"Watch your step," she said.

The moist, slippery floor offered treacherous footing. The lane widened, and, as they approached their destination, what appeared to be an altar built by the ancients came into view. Skulls, all encased in creamy calcite, sat on the top rack. The heads seemed surreal, alive yet dead, grinning malevolently at the fools who crossed a forbidden portal into their realm — Xibalba, the Mayan hell. He counted nine shiny skulls, all encased in calcite on the top rack.

"My God…." He was speechless.

"Remember your Mayan mythology?"

"Some of it. Is this altar…I mean these skulls…related to the Mayan hero twins?"

"Very good, Sally." Releasing his hand, she put her arm around his waist, genuinely happy that he recalled the story. She felt warm, soft, and very reassuring. He returned her partial embrace while keeping his lantern aloft like hers.

"Look." She pointed with her lantern, casting light onto a creamy pink stalactite with the thickness of a supporting column that extended from the ceiling to the floor in front of the altar of skulls. "Remember the World Tree?"

"Yes. I hadn't noticed. It's beautiful." An ancient artist painted the Maya World Tree on its crystalline exterior. The tree symbolically represented the Maya universe with its roots in the underworld of Xibalba and its branches and leaves in the heavens.

"So this is where those guys, the heroes, were tested by the Lord of Darkness?" he asked.

"Yes. Hanaphu and Xabalanque, the Hero Twins, the ancestors of the Maya. Very good, Sally."

In the dim light, she leaned against him momentarily, moving her arm from his waist to trail a finger down his spine. "Knowledge can be sexy, don't you think?"

All trepidation disappeared, and a tingle of delight traced the path of her fingernail. Incipient passion sparked, and he suddenly felt flush and ardent. The smallest things about her ignited a response in him. He held up his lantern to better see her face. She smiled before burying her face in his chest.

Life is confusing and so wonderful, he thought. Two weeks earlier, he was administering the sacrament to Indians and leading them in saying the rosary. Now he was about to make love in a cave with a beautiful archeologist, in the midst of ancient cenotes where the only sound was the gurgle and hiss of trickling water that fed an underground stream issuing from the cave floor as it flowed into the valley. It was fantasy come true.

They set aside their lanterns, and embraced and kissed, then he succumbed to her warmth and softness. His hand moved to her breast, and he was lost, falling into passion. She did nothing to dissuade him, and they stroked and touched in the dim light, their fluorescent lanterns casting vague shadows and indistinct flickers onto glassy, moist, calcite walls. She seemed enthusiastic and eager.

He reluctantly disengaged from her and placed both their shawls on the floor, one on top of the other before the ancient altar. He turned off one of the lanterns to leave an inadequate light that barely reached twelve feet.

"Are we safe?" he whispered.

"Yes."

"You're sure?"

"No one will bother us, Silly. I promise."

They quickly removed their clothes, helping each other shed their apparel. When they were nearly naked, he pulled her to him, and they quickly knelt on the soft cotton blankets.

"You planned this," he accused gently, breathing deeply with passion.

"Yes." She guided his lips to hers.

They began a long kiss, then he caressed her breast and stroked her hip before moving to the mossy cleft below her belly. She responded to his touch, sighing with contentment. Her thighs parted, and their bodies joined. They began the ancient ritual of passion from which came love and children, family and religion, society and all the terrible and wonderful things of life no one understood.

In the sparkling darkness of a room in which prehistoric and primordial rites of blood sacrifice had renewed the world, the Nine Lords of Darkness waited patiently beneath the World Tree as two lovers consummated the most-important act people could undertake. The skulls grinned capriciously, surreal in their immortality, accepting this gift, this small death, as homage to their eternal vigilance.

CHAPTER NINETEEN

Fickle gusts of wind and lighting-webbed clouds scudded ominously across the western horizon, seeking to hide a full moon that benignly lit the hidden valley of the Xibalba cave. Marcos, commander of the Zapatistas and Karen's occasional lover, arrived with big news. Normally a man who exuded confidence, he was wracked with guilt, and, to his surprise, some jealousy, which was unusual. He heard that Karen and her new friend, a priest if the rumors were true, left San Cristobal two days earlier for Council Valley and the Xibalba cave site.

Although Marcos agreed to meet her in San Cristobal and talk, he took an alternative route, a detour of the heart some would say. First, he stopped to see another lover, a dear friend in Lacanja, an Indian village east across the great Parque Natural de Montes Azules near the ruin of Bonampak. Marcos knew many women. In the last six years since the Zapatista rebellion, he lost count. All were willing, and most seemed eager to bed the charismatic leader of the Mayan rebellion. Though he genuinely cared for Karen, she was just one of many. He realized they were too different psychically, emotionally, and in their backgrounds and values. The sum total of their relationship, he realized was biochemical and sexual, with no enduring love developing after several years of a hit-and-miss relationship.

Rafael, the camp foreman, arrived with a plastic cup of *ponche*, cane alcohol flavored with herbs, sugar, peanuts, and other items. The recipe in every village was different.

Rafael sipped and grimaced, the acrid fumes burning his sinuses. He breathed deeply, pursed his lips, and exhaled in appreciation. Glancing upward, he thanked Rafael and motioned with his cup for the foreman to offer cups to the five men, loyal Zapatista soldiers and sometime farmers, who accompanied him across the nearly impassable mountainous jungle of Montes Azules Park, where he spent the last two weeks in the Lacandon Indian village of Lacanja with Neomi, his new fiancée.

It was time, he decided, and his heart agreed. The Zapatista leader was in his late forties and had no children—at least none who were legitimate—and the Zapatista uprising became entropic and lethargic, losing energy and direction. The Mexican government under Presidente Fox was surprisingly accommodating, granting unprecedented autonomy to the many Mayan villages that peppered the Lacandon forest and mountains of Chiapas. With the conflict in abeyance, at least militarily, Marcos became more sedentary and less needed. Others attended meetings and summits to work out the details of new agreements.

Karen knew he consorted with other women. She never liked it, and he always felt guilty, though never guilty enough to stop. Three years earlier, he met Neomi, a young widow. Their physical relationship deepened, offering longevity. Although they were very different in some ways, with him being educated and worldly, while she was a Lacandon Indian, she was very intelligent and spoke many Indian dialects, as well as excellent Spanish and enough English to get by. Many Mayan women had strong personalities and no qualms about making their opinions known. They took up arms in a moment if asked or given the chance.

When attending area convocations of the Zapatistas, she demonstrated an excellent command of the issues. She showed surprising passion and creativity in bed. Meeting her was unexpected but very welcome. The satisfaction and enjoyment of being with her hadn't abated over the past three years. They planned to marry in a month, and he must tell Karen. As unpleasant as that task might be, it wasn't something he could assign to an underling. He shared too much with her for that. Still, discovering that she had already taken up with another man, a renegade priest if the rumors were true, surprised him.

Rafael, with a curious look and shrug, explained that Karen and her friend went into the Xibalba cave an hour earlier to show him the work she was doing. Two weeks ago, Marcos would have felt his manhood was challenged and charged inside to confront the usurper, but in the present circumstances, he remained where he was. He felt awkward knowing she was alone inside with a former priest, perhaps having sex with him, which conjured unwelcome images. He must not overreact. The priest wasn't the problem. His true discomfort lay in what he must tell Karen.

There was much at stake. His father, Balaam, widely known and respected among the Indians as a *curandero* and leader of the Zapatistas, gave him strict orders to find the priest and talk to him to learn his intentions. It was very confusing. Apparently, the priest friend of Karen's had involved David Wolf in an excavation of some kind that angered the government and the Catholic Church. The professor was in jail in San Cristobal.

That was incredible news. David Wolf was very well connected in southern Mexico, well-liked by the Indians and generally known as a good citizen and learned man. He sympathized with the Zapatista cause and enlisted their help many times to provide security an assistance in the form of good-paying jobs in the Indian community. Professor Wolf was one of the few white men Balaam mentioned favorably.

Laughter rang out around the campfire, as sparks burst from red, pulsing coals, and flames licked high, casting shadows across ruddy faces gone slack from alcohol. Inhibitions lowered, and wits became lively.

As Marcos sat deep in thought, rehearsing how he would tell Karen he was engaged to another, he saw beams of lantern light issue from the cave mouth. The two presumed lovers appeared, lifting their lanterns high to sweep the area ahead and negotiate the ancient steps in the dark.

When Karen called out to Rafael, he answered and told her guests had arrived.

"Guests?" she asked. "Who? What guests?" She was surprised and anxious.

"Your friend Marcos and a few of his men arrived an hour ago," the foreman replied. "They are here, enjoying a glass of *ponche* with us."

Marcos heard the hushed, hurried talk, then an urgent admonition from Karen to wait for her. Her new friend disengaged and descended the stairs in front of the cave. Walking in the center of his lantern light, he approached the workers and campfire as if he belonged.

With his arrival, conversation died, and an awkward, uncomfortable silence reigned. All wondered if Marcos would greet the interloper or kill him for messing with his woman.

Father Salvador surveyed the faces of the men around the fire, looking at them for something, then he asked, "The famous Marcos of the Zapatistas is here? I've always wanted to meet you. Where are you, Sir?"

CHAPTER TWENTY

Dr. Yusuf Bin Saud stood on the sidewalk just outside the airport terminal doors in Tuxtla Gutierrez, breathing deeply of the moist night air. He had a receding hairline since his early twenties, and he was tall and lean with a prominent nose and easy smile. A suit coat hung over one arm, while his other pulled a suitcase. He held a small sign that read *Alexandra Wolf.*

Hopefully, his colleague's wife wouldn't be too late retrieving him from the airport. He was very tired and felt very out of synch in a country of such different odors, dress, customs, and language he didn't understand well.

The sun had long since fled, and the dark, foreboding sky was occluded by fast-moving gray clouds. Rainwater pooled in depressions on the black asphalt, reflecting neon flashes and weak beams of light from overarching light poles lining the road leading to and from the highway. Although a rainstorm blustered through earlier, cleansing the air, the redolence of Mexico still remained strong. It was a very different fragrance from that of Lebanon, except for the diesel. Fuel oil smelled the same everywhere, but the odor of spiced meat, baking tortillas, and the tannic stink of nearby raw sewage alternately intrigued and repulsed.

It was his first visit to Mexico. He read about its wondrous ancient civilizations and many revolutions his entire life. As a Muslim and an academic, he developed great appreciation for and knowledge of world history, languages, and the importance of religion in shaping history. He came to know and visit extensively with David Wolf on two different occasions at universities sponsoring convocations on ancient languages of the Old and New Worlds. In Amsterdam, and later in Chicago, he actually imbibed alcohol with his new friend, something forbidden to all Muslims, as they shared evenings, comparing academic passions and life stories until the early morning hours.

He thanked Allah for the opportunity and his friendship with David Wolf. Yusuf hadn't heard from him in seven years since he married Alexandra. Upon receiving his faxes and queries, Dr. Bin Saud's emotions ranged from mild surprise to rocketing incredulity and disbelief.

Finally, he decided if David's documents were genuine, they were discoveries of incalculable significance, and he wanted to be part of it. He slept only five hours on the plane, his first rest in three days. He felt he might collapse from tension and anxiety from the adrenalin and coffee overdosing caused by David's books, but the brief respite on the plane revived him, allowing him to refocus his attention on the task at hand.

Dr. Bin Saud left his family in disarray, his children crying in sadness at his departure and his wife distressed that he wouldn't tell her why he must go to Mexico. What did Mexico have to do with ancient Greeks and Aramaic and Persian languages? Why couldn't the people or materials be sent to Lebanon? What was the emergency?

He was a lowly professor at the University of Lebanon who made very little money. The journey would cost a substantial portion of their meager savings, but he had to go. Such an opportunity would never come again. It was difficult to believe it at all, that Dr. Wolf had somehow acquired first-century texts from Christianity's early days. Yusuf read them carefully before faxing his translation to David.

The first book, in which the writer claimed to be the Apostle Thomas who traveled the world after the crucifixion to follow the steps he believed Jesus traveled as a young man, was likely a fraud. Although not known for certain, it was believed Thomas died in India ten years after the crucifixion.

The other was a fascinating book that would undoubtedly prove controversial, which he carried in his briefcase. The text was a version of the Gnostic *Gospel of Thomas,* a controversial and famous heresy in the early Christian church. All previously known versions were in Greek. The pages David sent were in ancient Aramaic, the language of Palestine at the time of Jesus. The text could prove to be the oldest ever found, and it contained essential differences from other copies. If so, that book had undergone some very drastic revision.

A third, much shorter parchment, was completely unfamiliar and quite probably a fraud. It might have importance, however, due to its age and subject matter. It was written in the voice of the Apostle Thomas and seemed to be recollections of his visit with Joseph of Arimathea and Mary Magdalene in southern France just before the destruction of Jerusalem in 70 AD. Although a Catholic Church in southern France claimed to retain the bones of Mary Magdalene, there was no written record of her or Joseph of Arimathea after the crucifixion, just legends and apocryphal stories like those of the Knights Templar or of the Holy Grail and the Arthurian Knights of the Round Table in Britain.

Even more intriguing was the mention of a daughter belonging to Mary Magdalene. There was no mention of a father. Was Joseph of Arimathea the father?

All three texts that David faxed were written in Aramaic. That in itself was unprecedented. Where had he acquired such a treasure trove? If they came from Mexico, it was incredible.

The shortest text wasn't as well-written as the others. The writer, seemingly in a hurry, made many grammatical errors. The document appeared to have been penned with several different styluses, too. Yusuf hoped to see the original to determine if the inks were different.

There were many apocryphal stories regarding the demise of the principal players in the Biblical story of Jesus after his death. Many conflicted. Some were odd in the extreme, and only a few were verified in the Bible. The deaths of some, such as John the Baptist, Stephen, and James, John's brother, were chronicled in Acts. Bartholomew was supposedly killed in India, as was Thomas, purportedly meeting his end at spear point.

If that were true, who wrote the texts David sent him? The Apostle Mark came to a bad end when he angered a mob of unsympathetic listeners in Alexandria, and Peter was crucified by Nero, the psychotic Roman emperor. Matthew, a former tax collector, was killed by a halberd ax in Nadabah. James, Jesus' brother and the first bishop of Jerusalem, was beaten to death by Jews in that city. Selling Christianity to Jews had always been problematic.

Yusuf studied all the early Christian and Muslim writings and made them his specialty. The new documents could prove to be first-century books written by early Christians just as the faith was developing. Islam, which is represented in the form of the Koran, Allah's revelation to Muhammad, occurred nearly 700 years after Christ's crucifixion, and much of it wasn't written down initially. Instead, it was memorized and recited for many years after Muhammad's death. The word *Koran* means to recite.

Buses and taxis came and went without any sign of Alexandra Wolf. He craned his neck, peering down the road to the highway entrance ramp. He had their phone number, but it was to their home in another town, San Cristobal de las Casas, and it wasn't much use at the moment. Should he take a taxi and get a hotel room if she didn't arrive within the hour? How long should he wait? Was Mexico like Lebanon, with everyone always late?

He considered going back inside to see if there was a location where people could leave messages. Perhaps he should check ticketing or baggage claim. He sighed, taking a deep breath, reminding himself that patience was a virtue, and he was in a foreign country.

He touched the satchel hanging from his shoulder, reassuring himself that the disk on which his translations and photographs of the ancient texts were still there. A duplicate disk was in his suitcase, while the originals were saved on his office computer in Lebanon.

The fatigue of the last few days caught up with him, and he shifted his weight to the other foot while readjusting the bag's shoulder strap. The airport brimmed with activity. He heard cries of joy as travelers met loved ones. Buses groaned and bellowed black smoke, while vendors hawked everything from rental cars to vacation excursions. It was awkward to stand and hold a sign with someone's name on it. Every minute, he politely declined offers from cabbies and vendors.

Just as he decided to return to the airport, someone asked, "Dr. Bin Saud?"

Turning, he saw a slim, middle-aged woman in a white dress. She glanced at his sign and smiled as she extended her hand.

"Good afternoon. I hope you speak English. I'm Alexandra, David's wife. I'm here to meet you."

He spoke English, of course. It was the language of science. After introducing himself, they chatted briefly, but she seemed distracted, her mind not fully engaged on their meeting.

The moment grew awkward when her shoulders sagged, and her mouth pressed into a thin line below eyes filling with tears.

Oh, Allah, he thought. *What is this about? Where is my friend, David?*

* * *

As Alexandra and Dr. Bin Saud navigated the tortuous asphalt into the highlands and colonial town of San Cristobal de las Casas, she recounted all that transpired over the past two days. The storm and its bluster moved quickly through the area, allowing the twinkling stars and the moon's pearly orb to light the forests and peaks softly.

The Chiapan terrain was rugged, with a road so steep he found himself holding his breath. Lebanon had dusky, rounded mountains, and he was unprepared for the lush bushes and trees that sped past in shades of gray and moving shadows. He imagined how colorful and exuberant it might be in daylight.

Past the edge of the road, a sheer cliff fell several thousand feet to the valley floor. Although Alexandra drove slowly and carefully, there were no protective railings, and he tightly gripped his satchel as he peered across the car and through her window into empty space, occasionally catching a glimmer from a village sprinkled along the highway on the plain below.

Finally, the road leveled off, moving away from the dangerous cliff face into the forest, winding through small villages of ramshackle adobe houses with corrugated roofs.

Such communities had only one municipal light pole casting weak, wavering rays that were quickly swallowed by the dark forest that encroached in each town's perimeter.

He learned David hadn't just been taken in for questioning. He was in jail without cause, according to Alexandra, because he took the manuscripts from a burial box containing a preserved body. The Vatican dispatched a papal inquisitor attached to the Congregation for the Protection of the Faith to investigate the affair. A serious man, he made it clear he intended to return books, body, and all associated with the matter to Rome.

Unfortunately, the box and body were missing. The local priest who initially brought David to the site had disappeared. The Vatican priest, Father Sean Gregory, after successfully acquiring the backing of high government officials for his investigation, apparently thought David was at the heart of the situation. Without boasting, Alexandra indicated that her brother was an important man in Mexico, yet he wasn't able to secure David's release. He remained in jail, and Yusuf wouldn't be able to see him until tomorrow at the earliest, if all went well.

David's predicament disturbed Dr. Bin Saud greatly, but he was even more offended by Father Gregory's actions. Dr. Bin Saud didn't mention this to Alexandra, keeping his own counsel. He was a visitor in Mexico and would be a guest in David's home, but he was outraged by the idea that the discovery might be buried in a Vatican archive along with many other inconvenient facts. He assumed the three manuscripts would be researched, but the data would never be disclosed, because it was too controversial.

There were many proven frauds in history, and it was entirely possible that Yusuf just translated one, but if the documents were determined to be as old as he and David suspected, they could be construed by some as proof that the New Testament was in grave error, incorrectly portraying events in the Bible. He knew there were people who would kill to protect that knowledge.

Alexandra's story wound down, and her fatigue became evident. "So you see, it's very…."

"Complicated. It's also political and very unfortunate. You must feel terrible, Mrs. Wolf. I'm glad I came. There's much to be done, not just for David and the matter at hand, but these books and the body, about which David told me nothing."

"Me, either. He said nothing, then events began happening. We must persuade Father Sally to return. Maybe he can tell the papal inquisitor what he wants to hear, so David will be released."

"Father Sally?"

"Oh, I forgot. Father Lopez is one of David's former students. He discovered the body and the books. He's gotten…. I don't know how to say this, but he's become involved with the woman who's an archeologist working for David. They left several days ago for an archeological site in the middle of the Lacandon jungle. David gave me the phone number of a man who lives in Ocosingo on the other side of the mountains who promised to help. He left today to go to the excavation site, but it takes at least one day to get there."

"It's very difficult to find. There are no roads. It's in the middle of the mountains and forest near El Parque Natural de Montes Azules. He promised to deliver my message to Father Lopez. Sally must return and fix this mess. It's all his fault!" She slammed her hand against the steering wheel before turning to Yusuf. "Now he's off having…doing…I mean…."

"A Catholic priest has gone off into the jungle with a woman? How is this connected to the body and books, Mrs. Wolf? What does this woman…? Why would a priest leave his church and everything to run away into the jungle? I don't understand."

"Oh, Lord," she said in exasperation. "It's so complicated." She glanced at him. "I guess Karen, the woman, doesn't really have anything to do with it. Have you ever heard of something called Catholic Liberation Theology?"

"Actually, I have. It's interesting stuff. It's been around since the sixties and has lots of history in Nicaragua, El Salvador, and places south of here. The pope doesn't much care for it."

"I guess Sally's one of those people. He's grown unhappy with his vocation, with the church and how it works with the poor. I think he planned to leave the priesthood before the affair with the books and body started, but I don't know. I don't know enough about anything." Her voice trailed off.

"I'll bet you're as tired as I am, Mrs. Wolf."

She gave him a wan smile. "Yes. It's been difficult. I'll be honest. I didn't think your coming was a good idea, but I'm glad you're here. Maybe you can help David somehow."

"I'll do everything I can, Alexandra, but I'm a man of little means. Perhaps after I talk with David I can meet the papal inquisitor and try to reason with him. I have concerns of my own I must share."

He was quiet for a moment. "You must remember, Mrs. Wolf, that I'm a Muslim. Sometimes, we are treated poorly by Christians. Hopefully Father Gregory, the Irish priest from Italy, is more enlightened than many of his colleagues. If not, I, too, know many people, some who are influential in my field of study, and they know important people of their own.

All will be very alarmed and unhappy with the Vatican's behavior.

"The documents David discovered belong to everyone. If they are real, they are important history and are the property of Christians, Muslims, Jews, and anyone else who wants to study them. I won't be quiet about this matter, Alexandra. I won't suffer in silence. The Enlightenment happened over 500 years ago. Progress has been slow, but we will never return to the dark days of ignorance."

* * *

Luis rubbed the stubble on his cheek and chin before running his hands through his thick, black hair. It was one o'clock in the morning, and the club at the Camino Real was beginning to close down. Finishing a bottle of Fundador brandy, he felt good. His damned daughter stopped only a few times to talk, and he felt offended, especially when he saw her flirting with an old *gringo* who sat near the stage. She even winked at him once.

What the hell is that about? he wondered. *He looks at least fifty and has more gray than black in his hair. He's wearing a floral-print* guayabara *to hide his substantial belly and probably has more hair on his butt than an alpaca. It's disgusting. What does she see in an old, fat fuck like that? Money?*

The older man tipped her often, finding a way to hang onto the folded bills momentarily to stroke her hand or arm before he released it. She didn't seem to mind, but it pissed Luis off. He was about ready to intervene and take the *gringo* outside to teach him how to respect Mexican women when Cuca took the stage.

She sang two heart-rending tunes by Selena, and he was overcome. Braced with alcohol, his emotions near the surface, he felt tears fill his eyes. He poured two more fingers of Fundador into his empty glass.

Such talent, such a voice, he thought. *She looks so much like her mother. This is the essence of life, with heartbreak and joy fused into one moment.*

Jesus Malverde and La Santa Muerte understood. Life was hard for the poor, and joy was fleeting. Only in precious moments like that was the suffering worth the pain.

The show ended in early morning. An inebriated couple sitting near the bar sang along with almost every song and seemed loathe to say *adios* to the night. Other than the couple, the only patrons left were Luis and the *gringo,* who showed no sign of being drunk.

The sicario decided he didn't like him at all, and he *really* didn't like the way Cuca paid attention to him and not her own father. The band members began packing, rolling up electric cords to the amps and speakers and putting away their instruments. Cuca joked and laughed with them, obviously feeling safe in their company. He raised his arm and called her name, but she ignored him.

Damn it! Enough is enough! I'm her father. What the hell is she doing fawning over that grinning prick?

Angrily finishing his brandy, he thought he should go slap the *gringo* upside the head a few times when he saw the man remove a pen from his pocket and write down a few numbers on a napkin before sliding it to Cuca.

You're shitting me, he thought in shock. *He's giving her his room number, as if my daughter is a puta!*

Cuca smiled at the *gringo* and turned to walk into the kitchen, completely ignoring Luis.

He couldn't take anymore. He quickly followed her into the kitchen. She would listen to him this time, or else…. What?

Bravery and an amoral conscience were his best traits, not clarity of thought. He could rise to any challenge involving gunplay or mayhem, but his daughter's ways left him feeling unsure and unprepared.

"Cuca," he called. *"Esperate un rato. Quiero hablarte de algo.*

Hija! Wait a moment. I want to talk to you about something."

She walked through the kitchen, glanced over her shoulder, and went out the back door. He followed and confronted her where she lit a cigarette near a Dumpster.

"Cuca, why are you playing up to that old *gringo?"*

"Mind your own business, Papa. I'm an adult now. You need to give me my space." She inhaled from the cigarette and gave him a challenging stare, the napkin clutched in her hand.

"Yes, you are, but there are still things you don't know, Cuca. Men like this *gringo* want only one thing." He spread his arms wide, palms up, imploring her to listen.

"He knows people in Las Vegas, Papa. He says I'm very good."

"Yes, you are, Cuca. You're the best, h*ija,* but this isn't how you go to Las Vegas. Why not Cancun or Guadalajara? Maybe I can find something for you. I know people, too, you know?"

"Papa, look, I love you. I know what you do and I know who you know, but they won't help me be anything but the girl of a cartel soldier. I can't do what you do, Papa. I have dreams." She took a final drag off the cigarette and ground the butt under her heel. Glancing at the napkin, she wadded it and tossed it into the Dumpster.

"I don't know what I'm going to do, Papa, but don't worry about it. I'm a big girl now." She stood on tiptoe to kiss his cheek, then she walked back into the hotel kitchen, leaving him confused and angry in an alcoholic haze.

Chingada, he thought. *Children are like unruly cats -disobedient and willful.*

How could he help her? What should he do, have another drink? Should he follow her and argue more? He felt the need to *do* something. Maybe he should beat her and insist she follow his instructions. After all, he was her father.

What good would it do? He glanced up at the full moon. The haze of city lights and smog was like a veil over a bride's face. He didn't even have a hotel room yet. He planned to bunk there that evening, but the idea felt sour.

It was a bit late and dangerous for someone in his profession to be out driving around, looking for a hotel, but then he saw the napkin she tossed and read the number—456. The *gringo* who wanted to fuck his daughter was in that room.

Perhaps he should pay the man a visit before Cuca. Luis hated Americans with their money, arrogance, and superior attitude. He punched more than a few of them in the nose in his life.

Like Cuca, he tossed the napkin down. He needed a drink, perhaps tequila. Was there a half-full bottle of Cuervo Oro in his trunk? He couldn't remember. Maybe he should find it and have a drink or two in his car before leaving the Camino Real.

An image of his beautiful daughter being pawed and petted by the old, wrinkled white guy came to him, and he fumbled for his keys. *Shit*, he thought. *Where's that bottle?*

* * *

Elder John lay in bed, pillows buttressing his back, naked except for an open bathrobe, perusing porn sites. He took another swig from the bottle of Sol beer, something Mormons were forbidden to drink, then returned it to the nightstand cluttered with an ink pen, an unused ashtray, and the scroll he liberated from the drawer of the young Mormon supervisor's bedroom.

The scroll container rolled to the edge of the stand. He should put it where it wouldn't be damaged or lost, but he was in too big a hurry to get downstairs after checking in. Maybe he'd do it in a moment after he logged in to check a couple of sites. He tried to remember if he had a subscription to the site that featured Latino girls. He had a good feeling about this one. He was willing to bet money the cute little singer from the bar would come to his room sometime within the next hour. Her English was heavily accented, but she understood him well enough.

Sure, he knew people in Vegas—Reno, too. They were all Mormons, though, most assuredly not the kind of people who would help Cuca with her career. Maybe he could help her with a few dollars for her efforts, especially if she gave good oral sex.

She wouldn't make much working at a club. What did waitressing and cleaning make? Ten bucks a day? He could easily double her day's earnings if she came to his room.

He opened the menu and perused photographs. One looked a little like Cuca. She was petite, with long hair, a pretty face, and a tight ass begging to be stroked. He turned the volume down to avoid drawing attention, then clicked the icon to start the video. He quickly became so fixated on the cavorting couples he almost missed the soft tap on his door.

"Who's there?"

No one answered. He looked at his computer screen, then heard the knock again. Someone was definitely knocking lightly on his door.

Yes! he thought. *It's the singer, the little puta from the bar.*

He set aside the laptop and stood, adjusting his robe and glancing in the mirror to make sure his hair looked good before walking to the door. He glanced through the peephole, but the hallway was dark. Either a bulb burned out, or someone had turned off the hall light.

He heard another rap.

Welcome to my abode, Chica, he thought, smiling as he opened the door wide.

"Chinga tu madre, Cabron," muttered a malevolent, hulking shadow outside the door. The smell of alcohol was strong on the man's breath, then he lifted his pistol and fired three times, striking John's chest and propelling him back into the room.

The pain was excruciating, and John couldn't breathe. He tried to talk, to beg and protest, as the dark man stepped into the lit room. He looked around once, casually stroking the tattoos on his forearms, then he glanced quickly at the hallway.

There was no sound. Content all was well, he returned to the room and placed the gun barrel against John's forehead.

"Adios, Gringo. Te vere en el infierno. I'll see you in hell." He fired twice more before tucking the automatic into the back of his waistband.

Luis glanced around the room once more and turned to leave, turning out the light before he closed the door and walked slowly down the hallway.

When he reached the elevator, he took the stairs on the left instead, calmly descending three flights before arriving at the first-floor hallway near the elevator on the west wing.

He sauntered down the hall and exited the hotel. The air felt cool and moist from the rain that blew through earlier.

Adrenalin coursed through his blood like molten steel. He took two deep breaths to steady himself.

Sometimes a father had to act in his daughter's best interests even if she didn't want him to. It wasn't easy being a parent, but that sort of thing was what he did best. He felt confident Cuca would thank him someday.

CHAPTER TWENTY-ONE

Marcos decided the odd priest had a good head on his shoulders. Considering the circumstances, he handled a difficult situation with courage and aplomb. There was no need for macho posturing or threats. They were all adults, and, if there was an aggrieved party in this awkward triangle, it was Karen. She followed Father Lopez from the cave mouth, and, while it was difficult to see what she thought in the dark, her tone showed nothing more than curiosity.

After a few moments of small talk, she excused herself and departed to her tent to "put away some things and organize activities for tomorrow."

Marcos didn't respond, knowing she expected him to follow, where they could converse privately. He suspected his news wouldn't be any more of a surprise than hers had been for him, but it still needed to be said. He waited a minute or two, then took a deep breath and excused himself.

Using a hand lantern, he carefully picked his way past makeshift buildings and through scattered equipment and rubble. He knew where her tent was located outside a warren of sheds and tents that housed men, tools, and archeological equipment. The lamplight briefly revealed empty fuel barrels, tarps, tables, screens, an artifact bath, and other items assembled over years of working in the valley and cave complex.

The night air smelled of wood smoke, while sodden lichen covered limestone clung to the sides and lip of the small cenote south of the camp. Brooding thunderheads streaked with dancing lightning moved over the western highlands, buffeting them with an occasional brisk breeze laden with moisture that promised to sanitize the air. It would rain soon, and it was best to speak to Karen as quickly as possible.

Balaam told Marcos to go to the excavation site, straighten out his messy affair with the *gringa* archeologist, and insist the priest come to Taniperlas to meet the Bone Man in person. The latter was not an option. The priest would come willingly or not.

Marcos estimated it would take an entire day. They would spend at least four hours negotiating the jungle, then several more on four-wheeled Kawasakis before arriving in Calvario, where they would spend the night before meeting his father in Taniperlas the next day.

There was more. The Bone Man told his son to learn as much as he could about Father Lopez—his beliefs, family, his intentions regarding the Catholic Church, and whether he was committed and capable of enduring hardship. Was he a leader? Would he be willing to live like an outcast from society for his beliefs?

After nearly ten years of demanding and mostly unrewarding effort, Marcos wished his father would tell him the whole picture so he'd know what was at stake, but the old *curandero* remained as cryptic as always when issuing instructions and expecting absolute obedience from those around him. Marcos had little doubt that the men chosen to accompany him on the mission were also under instructions from the old shaman to tell him what Marcos said and how he handled his duties.

Time was wasting. Dr. Wolf remained in jail. How Balaam thought he could help the professor was a mystery to Marcos, but he was a good soldier, and the Zapatista elders in the villages, and his father in particular, did a good job of managing the difficult, complex arrangements of running a part-time war with the state of Mexico while still planting and harvesting crops.

* * *

"It's going to rain, Marcos," Karen said without looking at him as he stood silently at her side, collecting his thoughts. "Look at the lightning. Lots of energy in that storm."

She waited for him outside her tent. She didn't want him inside. She sat sideways in a hammock strung between two trees. She felt no urgency to explain Salvador or to argue—just the opposite. Marcos always arrived and left unexpectedly, a man moved by the whims of his superiors and at the mercy of a capricious conflict that, while probably unwinnable, remained symbolically important to the Maya Indians. She knew he was pursued by a gaggle of young Zapatista women, and he bedded more than a few in the many years since she took up with him. She decided to let him lead. Perhaps he would show some maturity and make the situation easier for both of them.

"Karen, Balaam sent me to…."

"You're here because he sent you?" She despised his father. Her experiences ten years earlier, when she came to Mexico searching for missing Maya books only to be kidnapped, nearly raped, and bludgeoned by government troops moving drugs through Chiapas, permanently soured her on the grizzled old Indian. He was rude, condescending, and downright weird. She had trouble believing he was one of the masterminds behind the Zapatista rebellion.

"I…came to tell you that I'm getting married. Balaam wants your new friend, this priest, to meet him in Taniperlas."

A rush of adrenalin made her want to stand and insult or challenge Marcos.

Silence hung like the distant thunderheads. Karen looked sideways, seeing the silhouette of her former lover backlit by the distant flickering bonfire. Although tired from the day's journey and mellow from her time in the cave with Sally, she was surprised by her conflicted emotions. Shouldn't she be relieved that Marcos wasn't going to be a problem?

"I…I don't know what to say. I'm surprise, I guess. I didn't think you were the marrying type."

"I didn't want to hurt you, Karen. I have met, have known a woman in Lacanja for many years. I have come to love her and decided to marry her."

Karen decided she felt insulted. "I wish her luck."

"What does that mean?"

"It means that you're like most men. You always follow your dick to the next watering hole to replenish an inflated ego. Does she have any idea what you're really like?"

His anger flared. "Keep my dick out of this. I hoped we could talk without fighting. I'm not here to…."

"They're really very silly looking things, you know?"

"What?"

"A man's penis. They're silly looking to be the entire basis of a man's psychology."

"Karen, what the hell? Why are you saying…?"

"Get out, Marcos." She jumped down from the hammock and faced him. "You can stay the night, but I want you gone in the morning. Whether Sally goes with you is up to him. I won't let you force him. I'm sick to death of your Zapatista intrigue and womanizing and showing up just long enough to fuck me a few times before heading off to another war or another woman's bed."

"I didn't want it to end like this, Karen, but you…."

"Getting married!" She walked away into the darkness. In a few moments, her breathing returned to normal. *Good God,* she thought. *Who can understand men? These things always end ugly, don't they?*

She brushed tears from her eyes. First the bad news, then the blame game, followed by name-calling and recriminations. She didn't want him anymore, but he still made her cry and planned to take Sally. She knew he'd go, too.

Sometimes, she wished she could be as callous and uncaring as a man. Her life was a mess. She was in the middle of the Lacandon Jungle; a place few people knew existed, having lost a relationship with a Zapatista guerilla and about to lose one with a renegade priest. Neither man had a future.

Sighing, she blocked it out, putting the problem in the back of her mind, turning to watch the storm move across the mountains and dip into the valley. Brisk gusts of wind woke the forest canopy from its slumber. Rain sprinkled down, but she didn't go inside. When heavy rain arrived, she withstood it, daring the lightning to strike and the wind to accost her.

The raucous sound of men fleeing the downpour caught her attention, and she turned to watch them scatter from the campfire toward their tents. One man approached, walking slightly stooped and holding something over his head to ward off the rain. His gait revealed Salvador moving quickly to her side.

"Why are you standing in the rain, Karen? Are you OK?"

Her head was tipped back so she could catch the rain in her face. "I've been soiled, Sally. I'm getting the dirt off."

"What dirt? You mean the cave? Why don't you come inside?"

The rain became heavier, propelled by gusting winds. Lightning crackled, and thunder echoed through the mountain peaks of the jungle-covered sierras. Karen turned to face him, moving a clump of sodden hair from her face behind her ear.

"Sally, would you hold me and help me feel better?"

"Always."

"Good. I don't feel much loved right now, and something tells me you're leaving soon."

* * *

After Karen and Salvador made love in her tent during the storm, they lay quietly entwined in each other's arms. Their encounter was different. It felt strong but distant, filled with melancholy. Each sensed something was ending, and such occasions were always sad. There was no anger or recriminations, just acceptance of the inevitable.

Karen disengaged herself from his arms and turned on her side, facing away. He softly trailed his index finger from her neck to the bottom of her spine, then softly cupped her butt. "Don't," she said.

"I care for you very much, Karen."

"We need to end it, Sally. You can't stay here. It won't work."

"Did Marcos say something?"

"It's over. You have your life's work, whatever that will be. You should leave with Marcos in the morning."

The gusting wind that accompanied the storm became a gentle breeze, and fresh, moisture-laden air wafted into the tent. As Sally considered what to do, he heard the forest waking up. First one cicada called, then others answered. The distant cry of a howler monkey from the canopy farther down the vale echoed through the valley. The forest was a neighborhood of ancient denizens, each with its own abode and niche.

He felt out of place, his entire life out of synch. It was an awkward situation, and he didn't want to hurt Karen, but he had absolutely no experience with that sort of thing. He sat up, looking around in the gloom.

"I'm going to dress and see what the campground looks like at night," he said.

She didn't reply. He dressed in the dark, nearly falling when he tripped over the edge of a bedroll.

"Careful." She rolled over to face him before covering herself with a thin cotton shawl. "Be cautious. The paths are muddy. Take a lantern with you. If you want to talk to someone, I'm sure

Marcos will accommodate you. The man never sleeps."

CHAPTER TWENTY-TWO

Even though the rectory at the diocese in Tuxtla was quite comfortable, Father Gregory slept restlessly before rising early to assist with six-o'clock mass. The bishop went out of his way to ensure his guest was well-tended and had access to telephones and a computer. Father Gregory was impressed. Having easy access to an Ethernet connection wasn't something he expected to find at the diocese.

The bishop explained they were also building microwave towers in the mountains, and that Tuxtla Gutierrez would soon have what it needed for the new cell phones that appeared in the United States and Europe. The bishop heard the phones were expensive and often lost connections. He couldn't imagine why anyone would want one.

Father Gregory smiled without replying. He loved the new technologies and brought his cell phone to Mexico. Unfortunately, European systems weren't compatible with those in Mexico.

The papal inquisitor relaxed on a large, overstuffed couch and sipped strong, Chiapan coffee. He liked the room. The paintings were well-known copies of originals hanging on the walls of the Vatican Museum. The colorful curtains were open, and an ebullient sun shone through louvered windows on the east walls. Dust motes glided across bars of sunlight. Although a screen was in place, the sliding glass door to the marble floored patio was open to allow fresh air into the house. Birds fussed and chirped as they flicked their wings around the central fountain, splashing water and cleaning themselves. The bougainvillea grew even brighter as the sun shone directly above, warming and drawing the flowering buds of red and purple to open wider and reveal expansive bouquets.

Father Gregory felt comfortable as part of a church that had changed little since Vatican II, and before that virtually not at all. However, the populace it served had changed greatly. Europe, once the focus of the Church's entire being and resources, lost importance. Italy and many of its neighbors were Catholic in name only, and many of the citizens didn't attend mass. Italy was at zero population growth, and, if it weren't for immigration from poor Muslim nations, its population would be in decline.

Much of Europe mirrored Italy's situation. The new global economy and sophisticated communications revolution changed the world in only a few years.

The growth of the Catholic Church, however, was among the poor in low-income countries worldwide. In 1800, there were an estimated one billion people on the planet. Currently that number was seven billion. Islam captured most of Indonesia, a prize of 230 million souls. Muslims controlled all of North Africa and parts of West and East Africa, leaving the Catholics and Protestants in a race to divide the rest, which was unquestionably the poorest continent on Earth.

Most of South America and Mexico had been Catholic since the conquest 500 years earlier, but various Protestant sects, especially the Assembly of God, the Seventh Day Adventists, and the Mormons gained converts in the Church's backyard in areas that also happened to be some of the poorest, most poverty-stricken regions of the New World.

With extreme poverty came credulity and ignorance. Religion had long been the salve of the poor, because it created hope and gave purpose to desperate lives. Miracles proliferated. It was extremely important that home and purpose be based on valid church teachings and verified miracles. Father Gregory's job was important.

Although he was in Mexico only five days, he already felt homesick for the clean streets and sonorous bells of the many old churches in and around Vatican City and Rome. The previous day was quite taxing. Father Sanchez from the Tuxtla diocese and Inspector Leyeva accompanied him to facilitate his inquiries. Mexico was an interesting nation. Like most Third World countries, everything visiting dignitaries did and said was reported to someone else. He was surprised at the number of people interested in his activities. Was it just a way for them to earn a few dollars in a country of bitterly poor people?

So far, the investigation was taxing and unproductive. The missing priest, Father Salvador Lopez, reported to Father Sanchez that he saw Mormon missionaries at the site of the ruined church several times. Perhaps they knew something about the missing body. A call to the Mormon Temple produced nothing. Officials claimed they had no knowledge of anyone visiting the tomb.

Without informing anyone of their intentions, Father Sanchez, Inspector Leyeva, and Farther Gregory went to the Mission House to check for themselves. The place was in an uproar. The Mission director and another young man were missing. An elder of the church named John came by to assure them all was well. He promised to send another staff person to run the house and organize activities sometime within the week after he returned to Salt Lake City.

After getting a description of Elder John, Inspector Leyeva was positive it was the same man he interrogated two days earlier regarding a very dead, decomposing body that was mauled by a wild animal. There was more to learn about that situation. He warned the man not to leave the area until his investigation was complete. The elder had no good explanation for why a member of his staff would carry a handgun in Mexico, nor had he given a good reason for his own trip to Chiapas.

After being questioned, the elder immediately returned to Tuxtla, checked out of his hotel, and disappeared. Had he bolted and left the country? No one, including the area's Mormon authorities, had called to claim the body. Did the young man's family in the United States know he was dead? That was suspicious behavior, but did it have anything to do with Father Gregory's quest?

The lying, know-it-all Professor Wolf remained in the San Cristobal jail. Hopefully, he would see life from a different perspective and was adjusting his mind to be more cooperative. Although he was a well-respected archeologist in Mexico, in Father Gregory's mind, the man was no better than a grave robber. David Wolf snatched the books and lied about how many he had. He undoubtedly knew more about the missing body than he said. Even if he didn't know where the body was, his contacts should.

It was unfortunate the matter was taking so long, and Father Gregory imagined the corpse was more than likely a bloated, stinking mess by then. Quite probably, it was already buried. Still, he must complete his mission. His main reason for coming to Mexico was to investigate the mysterious being. Finding old manuscripts in conjunction with an uncorrupting body was the sort of thing he investigated. The fact that David Wolf already used his contacts to have several of the books translated was alarming, and the translations were shocking.

Much was at stake. Father Gregory must move quickly to protect the Church from such a fraudulent attack. He must secure the Church's property. The Mormons, academics, and archeologist had better move aside, because Father Gregory was committed to returning everything to its rightful home in the Vatican.

David Wolf's brother-in-law, a minor diplomat, was pressing hard for David's release. Father Gregory didn't know how much longer the authorities in Guadalajara would be willing to keep the professor jailed. Time was running out. He had no intention of pressing charges against the man. The papal inquisitor would visit him that day. Father Gregory needed something good to happen. He must have a break in the stalled investigation that would lead him to the remaining books and the body.

He must also encourage Inspector Leyeva to spread the word among the ne'er-do-wells and snitches he undoubtedly knew that Father Gregory would pay well for information leading to the body.

The housekeeper, knocking twice, opened the study door. "Inspector Leyeva is here to see you, Father."

"Thank you, Maria. Send him in." He glanced at his wristwatch. The man was forty-five minutes early, and he wondered if something new had occurred.

He glanced outside once more at the birds, finished his coffee, and stood to greet his assistant. Leyeva appeared in the doorway carrying an umbrella and a small satchel.

"Come in, Inspector. I'm not quite ready yet. Breakfast will be served in half an hour. Will you join us?"

"Sorry I'm early. Frankly, I've been up all night. I have news, and something I'm sure you will like."

Father Gregory was taken aback by the man's disheveled appearance. His face sagged with fatigue, and crow's feet radiated from the corners of his eyes. "We have news? Good news?"

"And something you'll like." He held up a manuscript cylinder unmistakably like the others.

Father Gregory's breath caught, and he made the sign of the cross, while a smile spread across his face. "Praise the Lord. Where'd you find it, my good man?" He walked forward to accept the cylinder.

"Our missing friend, Mormon Elder John from BYU, had it in his hotel room."

Father Gregory fiddled with the cylinder and saw the wax seal was broken, which meant the container had already been opened. He hoped the contents weren't damaged. *The Lord provides,* he thought.

There was no doubt God's hand was guiding him to a successful completion of the matter, and He wanted to see the manuscripts and the body returned to His church in Rome.

"You're very resourceful, Inspector. I knew you'd find him. I have lots of questions for him now. He was obviously lying and is in this affair up to his neck. The other young Mormon who was mauled by an animal must have been working for the man.

Elder John will tell me the truth this time, or I'll have him locked up, too."

"That will be impossible."

"How so?" Pausing, he gazed at Leyeva's face.

"He's dead, murdered in his hotel room last night. He was shot several times in the chest and head. It's a strange one, Father. It's clear he wasn't robbed. The cylinder lay on a nightstand beside the bed. He was also behaving in a very un-Mormon-like manner. He was watching porn on his computer and was reported to drink alcohol at the bar last night."

"Murdered? Why? If he wasn't robbed, and they didn't want this manuscript," he shook it for emphasis, "then why?"

"Unknown, at least for now, Father." He looked around the room as if feeling out of place at the diocesan headquarters. "Nice place." He walked to view the patio through the screen door.

Backlit in the sunlight, the man looked extremely fatigued. He'd been up all night, and Father Gregory had work to do that day. Would the inspector be up to it?

The housekeeper appeared at the door with a pump thermos of coffee and two mugs. "Will he be staying for breakfast, Father?"

"Yes. We'll eat on the patio, please, Maria." He glanced at the inspector to see if he declined. Instead, he smiled.

"Maria, we'll be leaving immediately afterward," he added. "If the bishop hasn't returned from his meeting, please tell him I went to San Cristobal today. I'll see him this evening."

The housekeeper hurried to the kitchen, and Father Gregory guided Inspector Leyeva onto the patio. They sat in the shade under the alcove of the east wing, sipping coffee while watching birds flap and fuss in the birdbath.

"We're making progress, Father Gregory." The detective eyed the birds before switching his gaze to the heavily laden avocado and lime trees on either side.

"Yes, thanks to your efforts and dedication to this investigation, inspector. I'm not positive, but I think our little atheist bird in San Cristobal will be ready to sing a song for us today." He raised his mug in tribute, and the inspector copied him.

"God's work, Inspector."

"God's work, Father Gregory."

CHAPTER TWENTY-THREE

Dr. Bin Saud watched with irritation as the guard at the San Cristobal jail pawed through his briefcase. The guard frowned, seeing the items were written in foreign languages—English and Arabic—and pursed his lips in indecision. Alexandra accompanied Yusuf to translate on his behalf, knowing he wouldn't be allowed to visit David without her intervention.

"It's just some academic stuff," she said, "translations of my husband's writings. We aren't sneaking in guns or money. Dr. Bin Saud is from the University of Beirut and is consulting with my husband regarding a book they're translating. Why would that be a problem?"

The guard continued to frown, looking first at the stack of papers he couldn't read, then at the two visitors. When the man's jaw set, Alexandra said, "Just a moment, *Señor*." She placed her purse on the countertop. "I believe your wife asked me to give you this list, so you could pick up a few things before coming home tonight."

She handed him a blank envelope from a stack held together with a rubber band. He quickly folded it and slipped it into his pants pocket.

"Of course. Thank you, *señora*. She promised to give me the list before I left this morning."

He replaced Dr. Bin Saud's briefcase contents. The academic looked at Alexandra, then the guard, aware he witnessed a bribe being offered and accepted in a transaction that went smoothly and without any argument or negotiation. He gave her an appreciative look. Such things happened often in his own country. It was important to learn the customs of the nation he visited so he wouldn't offend and end up in jail as a resident, not a visitor.

Alexandra instructed Yusuf to tell David she would return to visit in the afternoon. She would bring him clean underwear and a shirt, and he should maintain his personal hygiene. She bid him good-bye and swept briskly through the jail's rotating glass doors into San Cristobal.

She planned to go to the consulate to visit Joaquin. She had more questions for him and a possible plan, and she didn't want to wait until later in the day. She just started her car and pulled away from the curb when she remembered she forgot the envelope the old Indian David called the Bone Man gave her early that morning.

She didn't know what to think of the old *curandero*. David was alternately amused and disgusted by him. Lately, he'd been unhappy, because he believed the old man allowed Protestant militia groups into the area of the Xibalba cave site to interfere with operations. The Bone Man seemed impatient and annoyed with women, though she could tell he tried to be polite around her.

He was very adamant she get the message to David, but she left it on the kitchen counter when she got her car keys and purse. She really didn't want to bother David with Zapatista intrigue or issues at the excavation, but she promised.

She glanced at the dashboard clock. It was only five minutes on the highway back to their *rancho,* and Joaquin wouldn't likely arrive until ten o'clock. She turned left, exited the *zocalo* area, and drove through narrow cobblestone streets lined with high curbs and stucco buildings.

Reaching the highway within minutes, she drove north toward the *rancho.* She really needed to get organized. The business with David and the Church was very distressing. She was becoming forgetful and procrastinating, which were totally uncharacteristic of her.

* * *

Yusuf was directed into the jail's inner chambers. The administrative offices in front were clean and in good repair. The odor was better than he expected in a jail. In his country, they smelled of body odor, vomit, rotting food, tobacco smoke, strong coffee, and eastern spices. He placed his briefcase firmly under his arm and allowed himself to be led down a hallway and into an elevator into the bowels of despair, where the enemies of the state and his friend David sat, despondently contemplating their misery.

* * *

David sat on the edge of his bunk stewing in a miasma of ill feelings and the odors of sanitized vomit and cigarette smoke. Two other prisoners occupied the cell block, one a petty thief and the other a drunk. David's desk, a few shelves attached to the wall, beckoned, but he was in no mood to write. A stainless steel commode and sink were firmly entrenched in the concrete floor and wall at the end of the cell. A bucket of water was filled for him every morning to pour into the commode and flush the toilet.

It's convenient having the sink so near the toilet, he supposed, *especially if I were ill. You can poop and puke simultaneously. Judging by the smell, people have done that.*

Had someone told him he'd be spending time in jail at the age of sixty, he would have laughed. It was difficult to concentrate on anything. One unresolved issue after another danced through his consciousness, demanding attention.

When is Alexandra coming? Did Yusuf Bin Saud arrive safely? Has Joaquin found a way to get me out of here? Did Alexandra call

222

Ocosingo? If so, how long before Sally and Karen return? Salvador left the ruins with me and returned to San Cristobal, where he spent the week with Karen. Do they know anything about the mystery body? Who would steal the body and box, and why?

Father Gregory really bothered him. He was accustomed to getting his way and had resources far beyond anything David encountered before. He claimed to be an archeologist, yet he worked for a religious system that David saw as serving only the rich and powerful. As a scientific agnostic, David rejected magic, ridiculous beliefs, and the take-it-on-faith approach most people routinely used to navigate through life with religion as their operating system. To him, religions served the state and appeased the poor and suffering by justifying the status quo of the rich and powerful. Religion told people how they got to earth, what they should do while there, and what happened after they died. Religious systems were vague enough for everyone and provided the expectations of behavior and belief, whether it was in a hunter-gatherer society or the high-tech, high-income countries of the world. All anthropologists knew that—except Father Gregory.

David stood to retrieve one of the books Alexandra left with him the previous day, but instead walked to the cell door and gripped the bars firmly. Being behind bars meant one thing—he was classified as a deviant, a lawbreaker, and he'd been removed from the mainstream to protect the rest of society.

My God, he thought.

Such perspectives became more meaningful when he experienced the visceral reality first hand.

A key rattled in the cell block door, and the handle turned. There, with a briefcase under his arm, was his friend, Yusuf Bin Saud, the man he sent the faxed documents to in Lebanon.

David slid his arm through the bars and offered a weak wave in greeting.

"Welcome to San Cristobal de las Casas, Yusuf. Sorry about the accommodations, but this isn't the Sheraton in Washington,

DC, my friend."

* * *

Yusuf listened carefully to his friend's tale of woe, taking notes as David explained the sequence of events leading to his imprisonment. Although the Lebanese scholar was tempted to interject questions, he held his tongue to better understand the circumstances. David was focused on getting out of jail. In the short term, only producing the missing books and body would suffice.

David's story was incredible—an uncorrupting body, a burial box with a winding feathered serpent, and glyphs on the wall of the burial vault over which a Catholic church had been built 400 years earlier. It sounded like romantic fiction, but Dr. Bin Saud wasn't writing fiction. More than anything, he wanted to see the objects that caused so much trouble. What if, against all odds, they were real and verifiable?

"David, can we talk about the manuscripts you faxed to me?"

"I don't have them. Father Gregory took them. I imagine they're already on their way to Rome by now. It's too bad you came all this way for nothing."

"Yes. So you say." Yusuf felt betrayed by circumstances. His one-in-a-lifetime chance to share in the discovery of material of such implausible, extraordinary importance to Western civilization seemed to be disappearing down a Vatican rabbit hole. Although the Vatican occasionally allowed scholars to look at some of their earliest documents,

224

they reserved many for their own study. Their contents were unknown to scholars and were never made available to the general public.

David seemed content to let the subject of the books die, but Yusuf refused. Perhaps if he could link the subject of the books to his friend's release from jail….

"David, do you think there's any way you could bargain for your release?"

The professor's head shot upward. "How so? Bargain with what? What do you mean?"

"Knowledge is power, David. They can't remove from your mind what you know after the discovery in the tomb. I have copies of the translations I made of the three books you sent. The original translations are locked in a document vault at American University in Beirut. Even though they're only photographs, they will be examined and published. It will also become known they are only a few items from a treasure trove appropriated by the Catholic Church with the complicity of the Mexican government. The demand for their release and for more information will be insistent and long-lasting. You can be a principal player in this matter if you play your cards right."

"How should I play them, Yusuf?" He spread his arms wide. "Our system of justice in Mexico is very old and is called Napoleonic Law. I'm guilty unless I can prove myself innocent. I have very few rights, my friend."

"In many ways, this discovery and your situation are just the beginning of what could become a long, interesting story, but you must make sure you know the entire story."

"The books? All we can know is what you translated."

"We can guess and infer based on what we have."

"What if it's a fraud?"

"That, too, will become a big story, and the Vatican will gain a black eye for their heavy-handed response."

David scratched at his two-day's growth of beard and shrugged. "It isn't much, but you could be right. This thing is a long way from being over. OK. What's the story? What can you infer from what we have?"

Dr. Bin Saud crossed his arms on his chest. "Are you familiar with the early days of Christianity, the difficulty of forming the

Church, and the problem with heresies?"

"More or less. Probably more than the average guy walking the street. It's fascinating stuff."

"Indeed. What's really fascinating is what we don't know. Most of the hundred-year period after Jesus' crucifixion is a mystery. The Roman destruction of Jerusalem in 70 AD is well documented, but it was also during that time that many different traditions of Christianity sprung up around the

Mediterranean."

"The Gnostics?"

"Along with the Ebionites and Marcionites. There were many, David. One of the documents you recovered appears to be a first-century manuscript of the Gnostic Gospel of Thomas. It's even written in Aramaic, the language of Palestine at the time of Jesus. If it's not a fraud, it will likely be proved to be the oldest existing copy of this mythical text."

"Incredible. How could such documents have come to Mexico? It's just not possible. There are thousands of miles between the two continents. Who…? How…?"

"The author of one of these documents claims to be the Apostle Thomas, who traveled the same paths Jesus took as a young man. In his book, he records going to Persia, Egypt, and even India. He speaks of a time living among the Jewish

Essene community in the desert outside Jerusalem. That's where the Dead Sea scrolls were found."

"I read that, or part of it, before Father Gregory took it. I must say that such an audacious claim shocked me."

"Exactly. The New Testament provides no information on Jesus' life after his emergence in the Temple at age twelve until twenty years later, when he was around the age of thirty-two. Then he surfaces preaching a well-developed philosophy and ideology."

"Do you think it's possible that Jesus traveled and studied so widely?"

"Yes, but it's apocryphal. A group of Christians in India claim to be descended from peasants who were proselytized and recruited by Thomas. Then there are other things. See if you remember this story.

"According to a legend, a mother has a dream in which she learns she'll give birth to a son who will be proclaimed a great religious leader by the elders. As a young man, he disappeared into the wilderness and contemplated the nature of existence and was tempted by the devil. He resisted the devil's entreaties and began his ministry after finding a few followers who he convinced to give up all belongings in order to accompany him. He traveled about, healing the sick. Many people who observed him thought he was a god. When he died, his followers and fans believed he would return someday."

David frowned. "That's the story of Jesus, Yusuf. What's your point?"

"No, my friend. It's the story of Siddhartha."

"The Buddha? He lived five hundred years before Christ!"

"Exactly. You can see the influence of eastern religions, not just in the manuscript you sent but in Jesus' teachings in general. Many stories in the Vedas, the oldest Hindu scriptures, are similar to ones Jesus told. Christ's Sermon on the Mount, the Beatitudes, and all that other stuff isn't original material. It's been traced to the Essenes and their Teacher of Righteousness."

"I read that."

"It's well-known today, but did you know that a Russian journalist named Notovitch discovered a saying attributed to Jesus in a Himalayan monastery in northern India? It appears very possible that Jesus went to India as a young man, probably along the Silk Road like other travelers. After returning to Russia, Notovich published news of his discovery. The Orthodox clergy in Russia condemned and pilloried him for publishing it. Soon afterward, the evidence of his find disappeared from the monastery."

"Fascinating. Just a minute, Yusuf. I could use a drink." He reached under his bed for a bottle of brandy, unscrewed the cap, and placed two paper cups on the desk.

Yusuf became alarmed. "They let you have alcohol in here?"

David turned to him. "I know you're Muslim, but I remember you sharing a drink with us in Amsterdam."

"Yes, and yes, but they let you drink alcohol in here?"

"Yes, if you've made arrangements."

"Arrangements?"

"In Mexico, you can…. I'm not proud of it, but the level of service you have in a Mexican jail depends on what you can afford to buy. Frankly, the only thing I can't buy is my freedom.

That apparently has no price."

He handed one paper cup to Yusuf and raised his cup for a toast. "To friends."

"To friends." Yusuf supped and grimaced. "This is very good brandy, is it?"

"The best." He sniffed the rim of his cup for the aroma. "I'm drinking too much now that I'm in here, but there isn't much else to do. I need to have Alexandra bring me another bottle." He sat on the bunk, facing his friend.

"What's an Ebionite? Father Gregory alluded to them the other day as he locked me up, and now you mention them. Do they have something to do with your translations?"

"Not directly, but there are several other manuscripts in his possession. We don't know the contents, but it would be reasonable to speculate, assuming the whole business isn't a hoax, that they're all from the same era just after Christ's crucifixion. Our manuscript, the one supposedly authored by Thomas, mentions a trip to France where he meets with Joseph of Arimathea, Marta, and Mary Magdalene."

"You're kidding. Isn't there a Catholic Church somewhere in southern France that claims to have her bones?"

"Yes. It's St. Maximin la Ste-Baume, in southern France. It has a skull on display believed to be that of Mary Magdalene. When it was discovered in the thirteenth century, they gilded it with gold. She supposedly spent the last thirty years of her life meditating and praying in a cave there. The area in France later became a hotbed of heresy.

"The Cathars are from that area, and Knights of Templar treasure stories abound. The first really big Christian heresy sprang up there. That's the Albigensian Heresy. The Catholics built a chapel in the cavern and claim to have other relics from Mary Magdalene." He chuckled.

David swirled brandy in his cup. "The Catholic Church has always done things like that. Items that have been in contact with other things share a relationship. It's a type of contagious magic found throughout the world, very common among primitive people, though the Church doesn't think of it that way. There are bones from saints and shards from the cross on which Jesus was crucified in dozens of churches throughout the Middle East and Europe."

"Agreed. That's well known." He hesitated, then blurted, "The manuscript you sent also says that Mary Magdalene had a daughter named Sarah."

David choked on his brandy. He sputtered, wheezed, and groaned. "Damn it, Yusuf. You need to better prepare me before saying things like that."

"The implications are enormous."

"Does Thomas say who the father was?"

"Not as far as I can tell, but the implications are huge."

"You just said that."

"The manuscript also says that Thomas planned to go west to a mythical land."

"Mythical land?" David rubbed a sleeve over his mouth and pinched his nose to stop the burning. "Is there a word in Aramaic for mythical land?"

"Not to my knowledge. It appears to be a derivative of a Greek word, something similar to Atlantis."

David snorted. "There goes your authenticity, Yusuf. No offense, my friend, but I can predict the reception your translation will receive." He finished the remainder of his brandy.

"None taken, David. The book says what it says. This particular manuscript is the most poorly worded of the three you sent." Yusuf extended his cup through the bars.

"And that means?"

"Unknown, but I'm sure it's significant in some way. Maybe it was written hastily before he sailed for Atlantis."

"It's probably a fraud." David frowned but rose to accept the cup.

"Maybe. Maybe not."

"I remember the Gnostics, but what's an Ebionite?"

Yusuf understood why his friend didn't want to argue about the legend of Atlantis. He hadn't been happy to read that word, either, and he tried unsuccessfully to find an alternative interpretation.

"It's interesting that your papal inquisitor mentioned them. There were several traditions of Christianity after Christ's death and Resurrection. All the writings of the Ebionites were condemned by many of the more-orthodox bishops around the Mediterranean and destroyed. However, Bishop Irenaeus of Gaul wrote a five-volume work called *Against Heresies* in the second century, and so did Epiphanius, a well-known Biblical scholar on the early fourth century. They quote Ebionite texts."

"Maybe the Vatican has some of their writings. If so, they probably aren't telling anyone."

"Exactly. Maybe these books, if they're from the first century like the others you sent, could shed light on this era and this heresy."

"What was the heresy?"

"Pretty bland stuff for that time, though it would be considered radical now. The Ebionites believed that you had to become a Jew to be a Christian, and that Jesus was born a man, not a god. He became divine when He was adopted by God after being baptized. He had to fulfill the Jewish tradition's expectations of the messiah by dying for their sins, then God rewarded Him by resurrecting him from death."

"The Marcionites?"

"They were a little more radical. They believed in two gods, the Old-Testament God of the Jews and the God of the New Testament. They were very anti-Semitic. The Old-Testament God was seen as harsh, mean, and vindictive, as opposed to the God of love in the New Testament. The Marcionites didn't appear until the early second century, so it's unlikely manuscripts reflecting that heresy would be in this group."

"If your hypothesis is correct."

"My hypothesis?"

"Yes, that all the books in that burial box were first-century documents, because the three you translated are written in Aramaic and appear to be from that era."

Dr. Bin Saud hesitated. "Yes, it's possible, if…."

David held up his cup again. "Let's drink to your big if."

"You go ahead. I'll pass. If I must drink, I prefer red wine."

The door handle on the cell block entrance rattled. The jailer, wearing a gray uniform with wide, black belt and holstered automatic pistol, sauntered down the hall toward their cell.

"Will he make me leave?" Yusuf asked.

"I don't think so. I have…purchased special privileges. It must be something else."

"Your wife's here to see you, Dr. Wolf." The jailer looked bored. "If you'd come with me, I'll take you to the meeting room."

David finished his cup and set it on the shelf before turning to Yusuf. "Women can't come into the cell block, or at least they aren't supposed to. Perhaps with enough money anything is possible. Why don't you come along?"

"I don't wish to intrude."

"Witnessing a man receiving clean underwear from his wife while he's in jail isn't an intrusion. Embarrassing, maybe, but not an intrusion."

* * *

Alexandra stood in the meeting room when they arrived. She wore a colorful print dress of orchids with a cloth belt at her waist and a small purse in her hand. She looked stressed and fatigued, and her eyes were bloodshot from crying. The guard maintained his usual bored expression as he waved at a small camera placed high in one corner before taking his position near the door. He glanced at his watch, sighed, and pretended to ignore the greetings and affection shown between prisoner and wife.

Alexandra chattered nervously. "David, sorry to interrupt your meeting with Yusuf, but I think you should see this. I'm sorry. I opened it a moment ago, because I didn't think it was important and didn't want to bother you." She waved an envelope.

"That Balaam character, that Indian friend of yours, came by this morning. I forgot to bring this with me. I promised to give it to you today."

He took it from her.

"He seemed to think it was important. I opened it, and....

My goodness, David, is it good or bad?"

David frowned. *The Bone Man came to see me and left a note? He can't read or write.* David extracted the note while recalling just two weeks earlier, he was very short with Balaam. The Bone Man was a top general in the very loosely knit Zapatista military and agreed to maintain security around the area of the excavation, which was far from roads, police, and civilization. David suspected that Protestant militias were

233

running drugs near the Xibalba cave, and he wanted something done about it.

Ahua, David,

Mi nieto in Ocosingo write this me. I hear you in jail because priest and nasty *gringa* at Xibalba cave. This no make *sentido*, but then *nada* of white people do make *sentido*. I find body of the ancient man family Reyes two weeks *pasado*. Holy Man dead box be robbed and no clothes.

I come tell you Holy Man and tell you I find bag and old books in Holy Man box. You no home. I leave books in shed your house. I have Holy Man. What I do with him? You want Holy Man? Holy Man help you with *policia?*

You me give message at *farmacia* in Ocosingo. *Mi nieto* work there.

David gasped in astonishment. That was how the books got into his shed. That flea-infested shaman! That Zapatista meddler! David wanted to put both hands on the old man's neck and squeeze until his tongue turned purple.

"He's got the body," David said, handing the sheet to Yusuf.

"He's the one who took it, that damn meddling Indian."

"What language is this?" Yusuf asked.

"David, settle down." Alexandra patted his shoulder. "This is important, isn't it? Is this the body everyone's been looking for?"

"That miserable Zapatista shaman, always screwing up something! He can't even keep that kid Marcos under control. Always meddling, always running all over the countryside getting into other people's business...."

"Here are your cards, David," Dr. Bin Saud said.

"What cards?"

"The cards you need to play to get released. He's got the body. This *is* the body, yes?"

"Probably. It sounds like it."

Yusuf spread his hands wide. "Now you can deal with the Vatican's man. He wants the body and the books. He already has the books, and you can get him the body."

"Maybe."

"Maybe?"

"I've never worked with Balaam, this Indian shaman. The Maya call him the Bone Man, because he's a *curandero.* He's also involved with the Zapatistas."

"The Indian rebels?"

"The same. He's hard to locate when you need him and even more difficult to nail down to an agreement."

"But he said you could call his nephew at the *farmacia* in Ocosingo," Alexandra said, "If you can get the body for Father Gregory, I'm sure he would release you."

"I wouldn't bet on it," David said sourly. "It's probably rotting and stinking up his house by now. I'd want to get rid of it, too."

CHAPTER TWENTY-FOUR

Alexandra left temporarily to call and leave a message at the *farmacia* in Ocosingo for the Bone Man. It was imperative that the old shaman turn the body over to Father Gregory immediately.

Why did Balaam remove it from the ruins at the old church? David wondered. *Why is he willing to return it now? I'd bet another week in jail it must stink to high heaven. Whatever was done to preserve it must have worn off. The Bone Man wants to find it another home rather than keep it himself. That proves the body's condition can't be attributed to miraculous or supernatural intervention.*

David and Yusuf returned to his cell, where they discussed strategy to secure David's release. The deal would be tenuous at best. The priest, depending on how difficult he wanted to be, could insist on having physical control of the body before releasing David, and that could take days.

David knew the Bone Man well. He felt confident the old man would refuse to transport the body back to San Cristobal. The papal inquisitor and his minions would have to go wherever Balaam could make good on his promise without risking anything, such as being arrested. Besides, it was unlikely Father Gregory had the authority to grant such a request.

In many ways, the situation was very predictable. The papal inquisitor, who was more foot soldier than top general, would turn the manuscripts and body over to the Vatican hierarchy. Vatican specialists would study the materials for years before considering making them accessible to the public. Meanwhile, David must notify the Vatican's man that he had valuable information and would reveal it if Father Gregory could guarantee his immediate release from jail. Yusuf understood his journey to Mexico wouldn't be the scholastic windfall and life-changing discovery he hoped. Without access to the original scrolls, they could not be dated or authenticated. The Muslim academic had translations of the three manuscripts Dave sent before his arrest, but there was no way to prove they weren't frauds. He felt in his heart they contained stunningly unique, vital information that would help clarify apocryphal, word-of-mouth history that had been transmitted orally for 2,000 years.

The fact that they were written in first-century Aramaic, as well as their content, proved a Christian chronology that was much more problematic and less orthodox than heretofore believed. It made him sick that such astonishing documents would be held by the Vatican. He wasn't optimistic that he or anyone else would be part of any review.

The cellblock door rattled, and Yusuf and David looked down the hall. It was only fifteen minutes since Alexandra left, and David wondered if something went wrong. Was she unable to make the call?

He stood and walked anxiously to the cell door bars and looked down the hallway.

"Who is it, David?" Yusuf asked.

He took a deep breath and glanced at his friend. "Speak of the devil," he muttered sourly. "And he's smiling." "Eh?" Yusuf walked up to join him.

* * *

Accompanied by the jailer, the papal inquisitor and Inspector Leyeva, looking neither right nor left, strode purposefully down the hallway to David's cell.

"Why don't you introduce me to your guest, Professor Wolf?" Father Gregory appraised the balding, middle-aged man at David's right.

"I was just leaving," Yusuf said. "I think I have everything I need for now." He shot a pleading glance at the jailer, who ignored him.

When David didn't make introductions, Father Gregory asked, "Who are you, Sir, and what are you doing here with *our* prisoner?"

Dr. Bin Saud hesitated before saying in a strong voice, "I'm Dr. Yusuf Bin Saud, a friend of Dr. Wolf's."

"Of course you are. I recognize the name from the fax cover sheet. You're the man David involved in our business without permission. Too bad. How ironic and convenient you're both in the same cell. I have half a mind to make the situation permanent if I don't get some answers this morning."

"I've done nothing wrong," Yusuf protested weakly. "I've broken no laws in this country."

Father Gregory, waving off the protestations, turned his attention to David. "Dr. Wolf, there have been positive developments since I saw you two days. I managed to recover another of the missing manuscripts. It's too bad you can't recall how many were in the burial box. It would certainly improve your situation."

"Nice to see you so cheerful," David replied. "Please don't spoil the mood by threatening my friend."

"All decisions have consequences, Professor, especially those involving greed and taking things that don't belong to you." He turned to face the Middle-Eastern academic. "I personally have nothing against our misguided Muslim brothers, but there are those with whom I work who see them as the ignorant, pretentious spawn of the devil that follow the teachings of a cave dwelling-schizophrenic and are the primary perpetrators of hate and political instability in the world."

"There's no need to be insulting, Father Gregory," David said, clenching his jaw.

"I just wanted to clear the air so everyone knows where I stand. If Dr. Bin Saud has anything positive to add to this situation, I'd be glad to hear it."

Realizing how much was at stake, Yusuf pretended not to take offense. "We all have our opinions, Father Gregory. I'd welcome the opportunity to discuss your purpose in Mexico before you leave."

"You're mistaken, Sir. I'm not leaving without having what I came for."

David interjected, trying to defuse the inevitable, unproductive argument. "I think I know where the body is."

"Do you now?" Inspector Leyeva smiled and turned to Father Gregory. "You were right."

Father Gregory nodded without speaking, looking first at Yusuf, then David, aware they'd been talking and scheming. "I'm listening, Professor."

"I want out of here." Gripping the bars, he stared into the inquisitor's eyes.

"I want a private conversation with you before leaving Mexico," Yusuf added.

The papal inquisitor hesitated. "I'm a man of my word, Gentlemen. I negotiate in good faith. Be sure you do the same." "Can we return to the meeting room to talk?" David asked.

Father Gregory looked at the jailer, who shrugged indifferently.

"Sure. Why not? I suppose you want your friend to attend?"

"Yes. My wife will return at any moment."

"I see. She has knowledge of this matter?"

"She should, if the telephone call went through."

"And if it didn't?"

"I can still get to the body. I think I know who took it."

The priest hesitated. "I hope so for your sake, Professor. My patience is nearing its end." He turned to the jailer. "Take these two conspirators to the meeting room. Inspector Leyeva and I will be along soon. We'll greet Professor Wolf's wife in the lobby and visit with her before the meeting. It's very important she understand what's at stake."

* * *

The clang of pans and the shouts of camp workers contested with birdsong, as the wafting odor of cooking beans and tortillas rode morning thermals through the camp. Sunlight leaked through the tent's bottom edge and entry flaps, and Salvador judged it must be eight in the morning. Day followed darkness, and his mind buzzed with the promise of hope and a solution to the worry of a long night.

That morning was the first in years to bring a sense of purpose, and it became increasingly clear as he lay in his hammock in a mosquito net in a tent that stank of fuel oil, molding canvas, and rotting humus. Palpable excitement buoyed and focused his thoughts.

Father Lopez and Marcos talked until almost five o'clock in the morning, pausing only to toss more logs on the fire as their conversation grew longer and more involved. Sally was astounded at the breadth of the Zapatista leader's knowledge. They discussed the history of Mexico since the revolution and the consequences of those events. They spoke of present-day

Mexico and agreed the revolution had been short-circuited. The rich and powerful, as they did in all countries and revolutions, took all the land and wealth and left nothing for those the revolution intended to help—the Indians and the poor.

Marcos, Sally learned, had studied Liberation theology and worked among the Indians in Nicaragua and El Salvador while still a callow youth on the swim team in preparatory school. He understood and agreed that present-day Christian values were divorced from the scriptures and teachings of Jesus. He concurred that Jesus hadn't said anything terribly complicated. It might be revolutionary, but it wasn't difficult to understand. Jesus said people must love and help the poor, women, and children unconditionally.

That wasn't what the Christians or their churches did, at least not enough to have a noticeable impact. The poor would be utterly destroyed in the face of corporate and individual greed unless they organized and fought back. Few men of conscience were willing to provide informed leadership.

"What we need," Marcos said, "is a man like you, trained as a priest and with the conscience and benevolent spirit of Christ, who is willing to go against the inflexible, hierarchical nonsense and laws of the church to bring about real change."

That was a role he could play, perhaps the most-significant role possible, if he was up to the challenge.

Father Lopez felt as if he'd been offered a great gift, one he sought since his schooling in Rome. He asked questions and became excited by the answers, then he thanked his new friend. With much to consider, he rose and excused himself when he heard crows chattering.

The first robin stirred and sang in the gloaming as he sought his hammock. Salvador planned to sleep a few hours, but instead, he ruminated on the previous day's extraordinary events. He traversed through the Lacandon jungle, made love to Karen, and had a long conversation with Marcos. It was God's grace that the past twenty-four hours had been a catharsis of emotion and purpose he sought upon abandoning his vocation in Tuxtla.

Now he could begin. He was committed. Personal redemption, he realized, was incremental, not total. It was achieved through faith and good works, not belief and passive acceptance of the status quo. His role would be to provide not just spiritual guidance and the salve of the sacraments but counsel and instruction on political and secular affairs.

It was truly God's work, to empower the poor to overcome society's prejudice and state tyranny. That work and mission was the essence of Jesus' teachings. He could no longer obey a bishop or church that operated in opposition to the core themes Christ insisted all aspire to. He must completely change his lifestyle. He would no longer be recognized as a priest by the Church and would have to endure the condemnation of the state. He was also ready to endure personal privation and poverty.

He lay in his hammock, praying, while tears of joy streamed from his eyes, thanking God for such a great task and asking for His help and guidance.

* * *

While David Wolf and his Muslim friend from Lebanon were being brought to the jail's visitation room. Father Gregory sat and reviewed what he must say. After talking with Alexandra, he understood the so-called miraculous body that didn't decompose was apparently in the possession of a shaman. To retrieve it, the Maya Indian called the Bone Man insisted that the papal inquisitor travel to a remote place on the periphery of the Lacandon jungle near a large park reserve.

It was a Zapatista hot spot where the Mexican government handed over control to the Mayan rebels who demanded local autonomy to make decisions free of state and federal interference. The Zapatista conflict was in a lull at the moment, primarily due to the government's concession, and the powers-that-be in Mexico City didn't want to stir up the situation.

Inspector Leyeva couldn't go into the area without permission from the Indians, and Father Gregory's request for assistance in the matter was unexpectedly rebuffed. Mexico was a very mixed-up country.

The only solution was to enlist David's aid. He would secure the body and get it out of the hands of those who had absolutely no idea what they had or why they wanted it. Father Gregory was certain Dr. Wolf had knowledge of the politics and the people, and he also knew the shaman who snatched the body.

The papal inquisitor would endure David's assistance by making it a condition of his release from jail. Reneging on an agreement bothered Father Gregory, because he was a man of his word, but the unusual conditions required he sacrifice his personal integrity for the mission's success. It was God's work, and he was just a servant.

Moments later, the jailer held open the door as David Wolf and his Arab friend entered. They stood and stared at Father Gregory with blank faces, unsure what would happen. He motioned them to chairs across the table, where they sat down.

"After conferring with Colonel Leyeva, I have decided to release you, Professor Wolf. No, don't smile. The situation has changed. I must make your release contingent on performing a task for me."

"There were no contingencies in our agreement," David said, "only that I set up a meeting with Balaam in Taniperlas for you to pick up the body."

"As I said, things have changed."

"You gave your word."

"I misunderstood my own limitations in the matter. Apparently, the body is in a place in the highlands that your government has granted local autonomy. State and federal officials can't go unless invited by the Indians."

The archeologist glared at him, then looked at his Lebanese friend before saying, "I can't believe this crap."

"Neither can I, Professor," Father Gregory said, "but I can tell by your response that you know what I say is true. I know little or nothing about the conflict with the Indians, and it appears I have no alternative but to enlist your help."

"And if I refuse?"

"Then you can return to your cell and think it over." He pointed toward the door. "Take all the time you want."

David, groaning, lowered his head to his hands. When he looked up, he seemed resigned. "What do you want?"

"I want you to leave in the next hour. You can even take your friend along." He waved his hand at Yusuf. "I rented a pickup truck for you. I checked a map with Inspector Leyeva, and he assures me you know the area very well. He says you can easily be in Ocosingo by this evening, so kiss your wife good-bye and get on the road.

"Spend the night and relax. Have a couple drinks with Dr. Bin Saud and do some serious Catholic bashing. Talk about what a liar I am and how the Catholic Church is the root of all evil and that sort of nonsense. I don't care. Just get there.

"Tomorrow morning, go to Taniperlas or Calvario and meet this Indian troublemaker friend of yours and ensure that everything will be ready when *I* arrive the next day in Ocosingo. I don't want *any* problems. I want to pick up the body and leave.

"Inspector Leyeva will accompany me. I also want to meet this priest friend of yours, Father Salvador Lopez, who created this whole mess. I have questions for him and a message from the bishop in Tuxtla concerning Church business."

David hesitated, looking at the other two men. "What if Balaam refuses to bring the body to Ocosingo?"

Father Gregory shrugged. "Then you go back to jail, and maybe your friend here, too."

"You have no right...." Yusuf began.

"I finished reading another of your translations last night, Dr. Saud. You know the one that talks about a young girl named Sarah? I'm sure your translation is incorrect, but then, I wouldn't expect a Muslim to represent such a sensitive matter in the proper light."

"My faith and beliefs have nothing to do with my academic pursuits."

"Of course not," Father Gregory said sarcastically. "I'm sure Professor Wolf would say the same." He waved off further protests and raised his hand. "Listen, both of you. Get this thing done and make it work without any problems. I want this transfer to go like clockwork. Believe me when I say that I'll have you both in jail unless I get that body. The true Christian Church must have its belongings returned."

As he stood to leave, Father Gregory tossed a set of car keys to David. "It's the blue Toyota parked out front. Looks brand new and has an Alamo rental sticker on the window. Try not to wreck it, OK?"

The priest turned to the jailer. "Tell Superintendent Diego that I said it's OK to release Dr. Wolf."

He addressed David again. "I have many things to do before

I can leave tomorrow. There's an index card in the glove box with two telephone numbers on it. The first is the church rectory in Tuxtla Gutierrez, and the second is Colonel Leyeva's. Call me when you arrive in Ocosingo tonight. I may have news or instructions for you."

After giving them a thin smile, he walked around the table and opened the door to leave. As he walked down the hall, he said loudly, "Get to work, Gentlemen. It's never too late to do God's work."

CHAPTER TWENTY-FIVE

Cryptic lightning lit clouds in the distance, threatening a deluge of Biblical proportions as the dark, jumbled thunderheads of an early morning thunderstorm moved resolutely over the forested mountains, casting a pall over the highland valley in the distance. David and Yusuf walked into the dead gray streets of predawn Ocosingo. A sulfurous glow emanated from a handful of streetlights leading south to the main highway that wound through, around, and down into the lowland Lacandon jungle east of the sierras.

Although it was a little after five o'clock in the morning, people were already stirring and going to work. It was Saturday, and Chol and Tzeltzal Indians filtered in from a warren of villages strung throughout the highlands, bringing their homemade goods to town for sale. Soon the sidewalks would be packed with Mayan women in traditional dress, carrying small children, vying for space in the *zocalo,* the central park in every town.

"We can eat breakfast later," David told Yusuf, but he didn't reply, dutifully falling in behind the professor as he walked toward the rental car. "Yusuf, you really don't need to come along if you're worried. I know this is asking too much."

"No, I'm fine. I'm OK, David." He sounded tentative, tossing his overnight bag behind the seat. "It's just that this is a big adventure for me. I had no idea I'd be traipsing off into the jungle with you when I arrived. Now that I'm here, I wouldn't dream of missing this. I know the Vatican's man has put you in a very difficult position, but I trust your judgment. If you say we'll be fine, then I believe you. Besides, I've never seen an Indian shaman or a Zapatista, nor a miraculous body that doesn't corrupt. A man ought to witness at least one miracle in his life."

"Yeah, well, I'm pretty sure you'll be disappointed in that respect. However, there are a lot of Indians and Zapatistas where we're going."

"How long before we arrive?"

"With luck, four to six hours, depending on the roads. Once we're off the blacktop, there's no way of knowing the road conditions. It's a good thing we have this." He patted the Toyota's steering wheel. "It sits high off the ground and can handle rough terrain. We'll see some today."

Finally, they left. The storm with its black thunderheads seemed to stall on the western range, gathering strength before sweeping across the verdant valley to release its fury.

As the sun rose behind the clouds, David drove cautiously, his eyes on the narrow road as he navigated the perilous, serpentine asphalt highway up and over the Sierras and down into the lowlands.

They talked about the big task ahead, choosing not to think of jail or threats or mysterious bodies and manuscripts. When David inquired about Yusuf's children and wife, then the university in Beirut, they had a companionable chat that lasted nearly an hour.

The sky darkened, and the wind gusted, creating a dangerous driving situation. When the storm arrived, David quickly found the nearest clearing along the roadside to stop and wait it out. It was the rainy season, and storms during the day were often heavy but brief. It was too dangerous to drive a road like that in such rain. They had to wait until it was safe to continue.

The window fogged over, and it became impossible to see out. The small pickup swayed occasionally when it was buffeted by powerful winds. Thunder cracked and echoed through the mountainsides.

After a few minutes of benign talk, Dr. Saud sighed and looked at David. "My friend, we've never really talked about some things. If you don't mind sharing with me, what do you believe?"

The question startled David. "What do you mean, *believe?*"

"Religion and belief. What do you think? What's it all about?" He lifted his hands at his sides, palms outward.

David smiled at him. "This is one of those, 'I'll show you mine if you'll show me yours' moments?"

"If you please. I'm not easily offended. I mean, I'm a practicing Muslim, but that doesn't meant I stopped thinking."

David hesitated and cleared his throat. "This could take some time."

Yusuf grinned and gestured to the windows. "I hope so. It looks like we'll be here awhile."

"Let me begin by saying this, my friend—I don't believe in miracles or magic, and I don't know if God exists. My intellect tells me that man and society invented God, but my emotional intuitive center, that part of me that can't be found in an anatomy textbook, isn't so sure. If God exists, I strongly suspect we're so insignificant that He either doesn't care about us, or He's very disappointed in how we behave."

The conversation continued, as they shared their personal understanding of how life and the universe was ordered. Comfortable silence ensued. There was no disagreement, just a companionable pause with no urgency to continue, as the storm exhausted itself.

They rolled down the windows to air out the car. The air was spectacularly cool, fresh, and moist at that altitude. Both got out to stretch their legs and peer over the edge of the highway, a plummeting, sheer cliff face that descended into verdant, dense foliage several thousand feet below.

David judged the road to be relatively clear of water, so he restarted the Toyota and carefully navigated the slick asphalt into a lowland valley before driving toward the gravel road heading south to Taniperlas and Calvario, Tzeltzal Indian communities that were hotbeds of Zapatista activity near the controversial national park and bio preserve.

He estimated they had another four hours of difficult roads to travel once they left the blacktop. A small town lay downhill in the valley, so they drove carefully along the highway, both men craving a stout cup of coffee and breakfast. The meaning of life had to wait. That was a conversation that never ended, always available to start anew.

CHAPTER TWENTY-SIX

The odor of *chorizo*, beans, and tortillas rose from the campfire as Sally ate breakfast. Intense sunlight reflected on puddles left from the previous night's storm. The camp was muted, as workers hovered near fires or barrel lids staked for support over fires to cook tortillas. Salvador, Marcos, and his companions got a late start, because a blustering morning storm swept the area with more fury than the previous night's. During the unpredictable rainy season, sometimes clouds threatened but delivered nothing, while at other times, the storms arrived in series and inundated everything.

Sally, anxious to leave, knew the day's meeting with Balaam was more important than a meeting with a bishop. He heard David discuss Balaam several times. While David admired the old *curandero,* the tone of the conversation wasn't always complimentary. Marcos, however, left no doubt that Balaam was a person of extraordinary ability who was revered throughout the Lacandon and Guatemala. His knowledge as a shaman and *curandero* was legendary, and his leadership among the Zapatistas was respected and rarely questioned.

Marcos told him not to worry. If Balaam said he would support and assist Salvador in his mission to bring the true spirit of God to the Maya and help them find their voice so they spoke as one people again, that's what he would do.

The errant priest, glancing at his backpack, went through his mental checklist again. He recalled leaving a pair of socks on the line to dry overnight, so he chuckled as he went to retrieve them. They'd be soaked.

He found them on the ground under the polyester clothesline strung between two trees. He picked them up and wrung water from them before placing them in a plastic sandwich bag. He hoped they weren't moldy before he had time to rinse and air them out again. Socks would be at a premium where he was headed, so there was no need to be careless.

As he returned to the campfire and put his baggie of soaked socks into his backpack, he saw Marcos in his green, military issue beret and pack, heading toward a group of followers who stood patiently around a campfire and barrel lid, roasting tortilla shells. Sally hefted his pack and joined them. He didn't want to be the one who held up such an experienced group of woodsmen and guerillas.

The man carried only backpacks and rifles. The Indians nodded respectfully to him, though they had lean, serious expressions. Fit and muscular, they looked as if they belonged in the jungle. Short, stocky, black-haired, with hands calloused from years of field work, they wore cotton pants and T-shirts. Two wore worn tennis shoes, while the others wore heavy leather sandals with tire-tread soles. All had black armbands, the sign of the Zapatistas, and they looked in their twenties except for one middle-aged man to whom the others deferred. Sally spoke and smiled to them, but only the middle-aged Zapatista replied.

"They probably understand you, Father, but they don't speak Spanish well. These men grew up in *Los Altos*, the highlands, and they've never been around Mexican people much. I can translate if you say something they don't understand."

"Marcos?"

"*El Commandante* speaks all the Mayan dialects and several other languages. He's a very educated man."

Sally nodded. "So I gathered." He shook hands with, Balthazar, the middle-aged Zapatista leader, and took another look at the forested valley and mountainsides. Everything seemed sharp and clean after the storm. Crooked, broken limestone stained with black lichen lay tumbled in piles, and broken flagstones littered the ruin. The valley looked larger than before, and he felt a passing whim to spend more time exploring the ruins.

Instead, he turned and craned his neck to track the trail far above on which they must return. It was as steep and narrow as he remembered. The descent was exhilarating, but they had to climb that winding path several hundred meters along a sheer, narrow cliff face before turning back into the rocky wall to follow the fissure through which the valley stream flowed. It would be another hard slog through the Montes Azules biopreserve and into humid forests with biting insects, ants, mosquitoes, angry howler monkeys, and the ever-present danger of lurking jaguars.

Marcos looked at his men, nodded toward the campground, and said something in dialect, making them laugh. Balthazar glanced at Sally in embarrassment, but he chuckled, too. No doubt Marcos made a comment about women, so he offered a brief smile. He knew enough about women to know, like most men, he knew nothing about them at all.

Marcos turned to appraise Salvador, noting his clothing, pack, and shoes. He spoke to his men in dialect again, then said, "You look as if you're ready, my friend."

Salvador scrutinized the man to see if he was being ridiculed and decided he wasn't. "I'm anxious to meet your father, the healer you say can help me help the Indians."

"Balaam has very powerful medicine. Everyone throughout the Lacandon and Guatemala highlands knows that. We need a different kind of weapon in our war against the greedy *ladinos* and the Mexican Army—men like you, a true believer who can motivate the people to organize and retake that which God gave us thousands of years before the Spaniards stole it. If you want your life to mean something, if you want to accomplish what armies and money and fast-talking diplomats can't, you'll join us. There is very much to do. By this time next week, you'll have the life you said you wanted last night, and you have my guarantee and the word of Balaam Reyes that we will protect you."

"I'm ready. I'll give you my best."

Marcos slapped his back. "Welcome to the *Ejercito Zapatista de Liberacion Nacional*, Father Lopez. You are now a soldier in the Zapatista Army, a very special soldier who fights by bringing the graces of God to those whom the world has forgotten and cast aside, a people who have had everything stolen from them. Poor people can't fight solely with anger. They must know their battle is righteous and just, and that God has their backs."

"Jesus made it clear that God loves the poor, women, and children above all people."

"Yes, well, we'll talk as we go, Father." He motioned, and two of the six men jogged to the trail's head and moved quickly up the path to scout ahead.

"I am not so sure what God said or didn't say," Marcos added, "but I know that everyone, especially these people," he swept his arm to indicate the campground workers, "will be successful only if they think God is on their side."

He accepted a rifle from Balthazar and said something in dialect. Balthazar barked an order at the remaining soldiers, who turned toward the trail head, followed by Marcos and Father Lopez. Balthazar brought up the rear after turning to wave at the camp workers, who shouted encouragement.

Sally followed Marcos, who wore light cotton pants and shirt but heavy boots with rubber soles, moving like he could walk uphill for days. In only an hour, Sally was exhausted. His eye constantly noted the automatic pistol at Marcos' hip. He did his best to quash the wish that his spirit was one with Christ in Heaven instead of here in his body in a terrestrial hell that would test the limits of his endurance.

Father Lopez decided that God's work couldn't be performed from the comfort of a pulpit. It could be accomplished only among the poor who eked out a living in the jungles and warrens of forgotten villages that lay anonymous and hidden, where the damned were sentenced to lives of misery and neglect. That was his future, he realized, and, for the first time since returning from Rome, the joy of purpose gave him hope of true redemption.

CHAPTER TWENTY-SEVEN

"I understand, Cardinal Nizzi. Yes. Thank you, Sir. Yes. I promise to be careful. You're too kind, Cardinal," Father Gregory said politely almost embarrassed by the effusive praise.

What originally seemed an unimportant case requiring little investigation or explanation took a dramatic turn upon Father Gregory's arrival. The implications of his unexpected discoveries resulted in several very-important people in the Church's upper hierarchy being made aware of his quest. Securing the body and books resulted in a surreal, almost circus-like atmosphere among the few who knew of his mission. He suspected his colleagues in the secretive Congregation for the Protection of the Faith were nearly jumping out of their skins in discussions behind closed doors at the Vatican, while Father Gregory attempted to recover the body and books.

When he faxed the Muslim academic's translation of the three manuscripts to Cardinal Nizzi, he was unprepared for their impact. Father Gregory was suddenly required to report twice a day, and, on two occasions, his sleep was interrupted by nervous officials requiring an update. Extra help was offered. Did he need anything? Money? Assistants? More *policia?* Perhaps they should send a delegation to help.

Father Gregory declined it all, saying the task would likely be completed before help arrived, and, in his opinion, it was imperative not to draw unwanted attention to the mission. He would stay in touch. If matters took a sudden change for the worse, he would accept their offer of help. Meanwhile, they should pray for the mission's success.

He thanked the cardinal again for his praise before hanging up. Father Gregory called Inspector Leyeva to tell him he was ready to be picked up.

He rented a second Toyota pickup, as he planned to place the body and burial box in the truck bed. That would be especially important if the body stank, which he firmly believed would be the case. They would drive from Tuxtla Gutierrez over the forested mountains of the highland Lacandon jungle to Ocosingo and wait for Professor Wolf's call so they could agree to a time and place to pick up the miraculous or putrefying corpse, whichever it was.

Cardinal Nizzi insisted the corpse, no matter its condition, be transported to Rome. All artifacts should be returned to the Vatican. Their own experts would perform tests and make assessments that Father Gregory couldn't do in such a primitive location.

Father Gregory inspected his valise one last time, checking his passport, money, and official documents to ensure his passage anywhere in the country. With those items and Inspector Leyeva's badge, they should be able to forestall the efforts of anyone inclined to thwart them, even the Mexican Army, which set up roadblocks every day all over the state to capture gun runners and drug mules.

Placing the valise under his arm, he stepped into the courtyard for fresh air, walking without purpose to admire the gardener's skill. He paused at the far end of the patio to view a koi pond covered with broad lilies. Spotted red-orange and black koi with wet, sucking mouths wallowed and rolled, exposing yellow bellies near the bank. Their activity became more urgent when they saw him, and they fought to push toward shore, poking gaping mouths above the water as they grunted.

He suspected it was near feeding time, reminding him of the hungry mouths and hungry souls around the world, deprived of life-giving food and spiritual nourishment. God's work was difficult and sometimes lonely, but it was the only goal in life worth pursuing.

He glanced at his watch. It was best to be in the parlor waiting when Colonel Leyeva arrived. Preparation and execution were the keys to success, and the papal inquisitor was ready to bring his task to completion.

* * *

David and Yusuf drove through the mountains following the Perla River south on winding, gravel roads. They went through a succession of small Indian villages—Placido, Flores, Monte Libano, El Censo, and they were finally arriving at Taniperlas, the Tzeltzal Mayan village of 1,300 inhabitants straddling the Perla River.

"This is fascinating, David, but I'm ready to get out and stretch. Can we stop for a soft drink?"

David slowed, looking for a place to stop. "I planned on it. We have to buy gas here. There probably isn't another service station between here and Calvario."

"This town looks pretty prosperous compared to the others. It's difficult to see how these people make a living."

As they entered the town, Yusuf saw rows of stucco houses, most in poor repair. Many had corrugated sheet-metal roofs. Some had paintings of Emiliano Zapata on them, and Zapata graffiti was everywhere. The few more-prosperous homes had walls and gated driveways behind which the owners locked their vehicles.

Small garden patches abounded, as did enclaves of pigs and chickens. Streets stretched randomly, without plan. The community wasn't laid out in the traditional geometric pattern around a central square with its hubbub of activity so common elsewhere in Mexico.

David and Yusuf passed an occasional horse and rider, but most people walked. The women wore black skirts and white blouses heavy with colored embroidery in traditional Indian designs. The men wore dark or off-white cotton pants or jeans and collared shirts with either cowboy boots or sandals.

"This place has a different feel to it, David."

"It's an Indian community, as well as one of the central locations where the Zapatista uprising happened."

"Look. There are soldiers." Yusuf pointed at a roadblock ahead, just like the four through which they passed earlier.

"There's lots of new activity. The government's building a big military base near here. When the rebellion began in 1994, the Maya tried to force all government officials out. In 1998, the Indians painted a mural along the entire wall of their municipal building to celebrate their autonomy from the government. It was beautiful. I saw it before it was completed."

"It depicted various Tzeltzal themes, village life, and the birthday of Zapata on April tenth. The next day, the Mexican government decided to squash the rebellion here and sent soldiers to deface and destroy the mural. A friend of mine from the Metropolitan National University, Sergio Valdez, directed the entire painting process. The military detained him and put him in Cerro Hueco prison for his efforts."

Silence fell, as each collected his thoughts on the matter.

"That's a very bad story, David," Yusuf said finally.

"There's much worse, my friend."

"Why here? What started the rebellion? Was it the regular things, like an insensitive government, or the Maya not wanting to be part of Mexico?"

"It's much more complicated than that. There's so much history, I can't tell it all in a day. The Indians have been marginalized since the Conquest. There are almost a million of them here in Chiapas and on the other side in Guatemala. They don't have legal title to any land. It was given away in the various revolutions to people who didn't deserve it.

"As the Indian population grows, they need more small farms. When they move into areas with unused land, powerful people object. The Indians are desperate and have moved into parts of the national park nearby, El Parque Natural de Montes Azules. It's a huge bio-preserve that belonged to them before the government confiscated it. It's mostly jungle and marsh in the lowland Lacandon Jungle, but with areas the Maya can make a living.

"Rich people, who believe they own the land, are in secret agreement with the Mexican government. They finance their own militias to expel the Tzeltzal and others like them. Most but not all of these militias are Protestants who attack the Catholic Indians who moved into areas in the bio-preserve. The Indians never have anyone who can represent them in the government in Mexico City of Guatemala City. There have been major flareups, a few massacres, and some Protestant militias have become active in running drugs and weapons. It's a damn mess."

"Politics is complicated, David. We have Hezbollah, the Syrians, and the Marionite Christian militias fighting in Lebanon. Hate and mistrust have destroyed any hope of resolution. Your story about the mural is sad."

They stopped talking as they approached the roadblock, where they were questioned at length, and Yusuf's passport was perused carefully. What was a Muslim doing in Mexico?

None of the men had seen a Muslim before, but they were certain they didn't like them.

David produced the letter from the *Federale Policia* Father Gregory placed in the glove box. The letter was passed around, read, frowned over, and discussed. Eventually someone made a call on a portable telephone while Dr. Wolf and Dr. Bin Saud waited nervously.

Finally, the letter and passports were returned, and they were on their way again, averaging thirty-five to forty miles per hour on the ragged stretch of highway. The road quickly deteriorated once they left town.

They stopped at the last Pemex to refill the gas tank and buy soft drinks, then they drove on. David estimated it was another two hours before they arrived in Calvario in late afternoon. He hoped there was no trouble with the Bone Man. Other than checking in at the local *abaceria*, grocery store, to make inquiries, David had no plan.

Since the entire area was a Zapatista hotbed, he knew Balaam would hear of their arrival within fifteen minutes. He and Yusuf would get a cold drink and snack while waiting to be contacted.

Then the real adventure would begin—dealing with the old shaman's inevitable demands and quirky personality. The archeologist glanced at his friend, realizing Yusuf was in for an unusual experience. David would bet a year's salary that retrieving the body for Father Gregory would become complicated in ways no one predicted.

* * *

The Bone Man stared in avid wonder at the vision. Colorful clouds above the Sierras leaked brilliant hues onto terraced valley walls where corn stalks stood erect, their tassels shifting in the breeze. It was hot and humid, difficult to find a breath of air that wasn't warmer than the previous.

It was unfortunate that *Ahua* David arrived too early. The shaman promised to perform a healing ceremony for the daughter of a trusted adjutant. The girl had problems with her moon cycles, and the local midwife hadn't been able to provide relief. The girl was erratic, tearful, and frequently upset, so the mother was upset, too. If the mother was unhappy, no one was happy.

After much pleading from the father and seeking the permission of the midwife to help the girl, Balaam agreed to a full intervention, which entailed communing with the spirits to ascertain the cause of her dysfunction.

As far as he could tell, the child's problem was caused by blockage of her menstrual blood by the winds. His intricate curing ceremony required concentration. Having a white man present, even if it was *Ahua* David, was vexing and distracting.

White men were completely out of sync with the universe, and the *curandero* didn't have time to babysit them. Maybe he should send them away.

He ate the narcotic water lilies and began.

* * *

"So, Balaam, when can we pick up the body?" David asked. "I can tell you're busy and don't have time for us. We don't want to interfere. I know what you're doing."

"You already interfere, *ahua.*"

David saw the Bone Man attempting to ignore his vision and gain a foothold in what he called the *always world*. He shifted his gaze to Yusuf, and Balaam's eyes, wide and glazed from hallucinogens, narrowed to slits.

"Why you bring this *ladino* with you? It's hard talk with spirits when white people here. Spirits no can find you, because your souls are corrupted with greed and stained with noise."

Stained with noise? David looked to Yusuf and held up a hand, cautioning him against speaking, but he saw that was unnecessary.

Yusuf gawked about, keenly focused on his surroundings. They were in a small hamlet two kilometers east of Calvario, a Tzeltzal Indian community of about 300 Indians. The people were very poor. Though a few chickens ran about, there were no fields, only small gardens adjacent to one-room adobe buildings with thatched roofs. One home had ears of corn drying on the corrugated metal roof and a fenced pen with a small child tending a hog. None of the Indians spoke Spanish, and David and Yusuf had trouble following the Bone Man's discourse as he alternated between dialect and Spanish.

Balaam raised his head, trying to give David a withering stare. That was difficult in his current mental state. "I don't know what body you talk about, *ahua*. You mistaken. Go back town or shut up and stay out of the way. Today, I help *Señor* Jacobo's daughter."

He gave them a dreamy look and turned away, ignoring the intruders. Smiling, he spoke calmly to the child's mother, who was confused at seeing the two foreigners.

Shit, David thought. *Damn, damn, damn!* He wanted to wring the wiry, raisin-faced old shaman's neck. Though he always spoke to David using the polite, respectful form of Mayan address, Balaam was rude and abrupt by nature, especially with white people, which meant anyone who wasn't an Indian.

They had no choice but to wait. The old *curandero* was stoned on water lilies and who knew what else, perhaps mushrooms, and wouldn't deign to interact with David until after the ceremony.

David motioned to Yusuf, and they walked slowly away from the group.

"I see what you mean," Yusuf said. "Is he always like this?"

"No. He's usually worse. I don't know why I put up with him."

That wasn't true. David knew that the old shaman was probably the most widely respected Indian he ever met, and he had the most-extensive contacts among the native Maya of Chiapas and Guatemala David ever found. Balaam's knowledge of herbs and traditional healing was unsurpassed, and he always seemed in control of an item or have knowledge of something David needed. The *curandero* spent seventy years spinning a web of influence and favors that became the Mayan Indian version of a modern-day *Godfather*.

"Have a seat." David pointed at the ground. "Watch and try to be quiet. You'll find this as interesting as anything you ever saw."

The Bone Man built a small fire beside the family's hut. The girl, looking very unhappy, required constant reassurance from her mother. The father, a stout muscular man with skin baked dark brown from toiling in the sun, stood awkwardly, unsure of himself but ready to assist.

As fragrant copal incense rose from the coals and wafted through the air on summer thermals, Balaam removed a small green stone from his bag. It looked like jade, and David knew it was the man's *satsun,* a stone or crystal employed by healers to communicate with the spirit world.

While grasping the stone, the Bone Man extracted several bundles of grass, called smudge sticks, from his tote sack. One at a time, he placed the ends of each in the fire to make them smolder and smoke. David witnessed the smudging ceremony many times during his years as an anthropologist. It was the preamble to a more-involved sequence of actions.

The afflicted person first needed to be ritually cleansed of negative energies and spirits by bathing him in the smoke of sacred plants or resins. Balaam took each bundle one at a time and slowly waved it back and forth from the child's feet to her head, pausing momentarily at her abdomen. The pleasing aroma of cedar grew stronger.

When he finished with that herb, he followed it by the sweet redolence of sage as he moved the bundled grass over her body like a wand. When the girl was purified, Balaam tossed more copal incense onto the coals to carry prayers to God.

Cacao beans, corn, and chili peppers were placed on a small altar nearby. Balaam motioned, and the mother appeared from the hut with a nervous chicken. Its wings were trapped, but its legs pumped rapidly as if riding a bicycle, and it squawked in protest. In one practiced motion, the Bone Man slit the bird's neck and allowed the blood to drip over the sobbing child's hair and shoulders. He returned the dead chicken to the mother, who gave it to another woman standing nearby. It would become that night's dinner. While the others watched, the shaman prepared a cup of liquid and herbs to drink.

Oh, no, David thought. *This can't be good.*

Balaam handed the cup to the mother, who passed it to her daughter, coaxing the girl to drink. She frowned, refused, and set it aside. The mother grasped the cup and held it to the child's lips, insisting she drink it all. Weeping, she choked it down.

A moment later, the girl vomited. Balaam tossed a large handful of herbs onto the coals, creating a billowing cloud of lavender-scented smoke. He began an incantation in dialect. The girl sobbed with each stomach contraction, puking and emptying herself repeatedly until she produced nothing but bile and mucous.

David was nearly sick, too, watching the child's tearful retching. He glanced at Yusuf, but the Lebanese academic seemed enthralled. He occasionally caught David's eye but said nothing.

Several minutes later, the child ceased crying and retching, and the mother helped her stand. She swooned and nearly fell, but her mother kept her upright. The girl's eyes were wide, and her pupils glowed like black obsidian. David realized she'd been given hallucinogens, probably datura or peyote. She'd be in the spirit world for hours.

The girl's mother led her into their house, and the Bone Man followed, rolling his *sastun* in his palm, muttering in a whisper. He would stay with the girl for an hour or more, chanting and besieging the spirits to restore the child's equilibrium.

The girl's father appeared holding two plastic cups of brew for David and Yusuf. The Indian spoke only dialect, so it was an awkward situation. Yusuf seemed reluctant to imbibe, so David tasted the offering. He recognized it as *balche*, fermented from the sap of the balche tree. He smacked his lips.

Not bad, he thought. *It's not as sour as some I've tasted.* He motioned Yusuf to try it.

"This isn't the stuff the girl drank, is it?" Yusuf frowned, peering into the disposable cup for floating debris.

David smiled. "It's an acquired taste, but you'll be surprised at how well it goes down. I've had worse."

Yusuf sighed and tipped the cup to wet his lips, licking them to get the flavor before taking a sip. "Smells funny," he said benignly.

"So does some of that fermented goat crap you drink in the Middle East." David motioned with his cup toward the hut where the Bone Man disappeared. "This could take a while. We might as well get comfortable."

* * *

Late afternoon became evening. The Indians brought them tortillas and beans with more *balche.* Much to his surprise, David relaxed and was able to enjoy himself. He just spent a week in jail. Alexandra had been tearful when he told her he must leave immediately.

After a hurried trip over the mountains, he and Yusuf arrived in Calvario to pick up the body only to find the old shaman pretended not to know anything about it. All David could do was sit and wait, as he participated in whatever happened around him.

It touched his anthropologist's soul. Although he felt certain Balaam was deliberately jerking him around, he decided to savor the time of peace and contentment. He wouldn't let Balaam vex him. Yusuf did OK, trying to talk to a few of the Indians who drank *balche* with them. They smiled at his questions.

David realized day was becoming night when he saw the sun become red-orange and slump toward the terraced hillsides along the valley. It was time to make up his mind. He could return to the Toyota and wait for the Bone Man to finish and seek them at his leisure, or they could hang around until dark, when mosquitoes came out to devour every living thing. Neither was a good choice.

The tasty *balche* made David slightly tipsy. Darkness cloaked the mountainsides in grim shadows, reducing visibility to 100 meters.

As he stood to walk toward the Toyota, someone called out. He saw Balaam leaving the hut, followed by the girl's parents. They chatted briefly, then each of them gave the irascible, smiling shaman a hug.

Whew, David thought. *Perfect timing.* He stretched, joints stiff from sitting on the ground. Yusuf joined him as the shaman left the couple and shambled toward David.

"Will he shake my hand if I offer it?" Yusuf joked.

"Not likely. Follow my lead. He's hard to predict."

Balaam approached, and six men carrying rifles suddenly appeared from the woods. David and Yusuf hadn't known they were being observed, but David wasn't surprised. He learned years earlier the Bone Man rarely went anywhere without protection. He controlled a network of couriers who shuttled messages through the jungles. There probably wasn't a town in Chiapas that didn't have Zapatista sympathizers and skilled woodsmen eager to maintain and be part of the network.

Radio and telephone might be faster, but there were places in the Lacandon Jungle where neither was accessible. Although a few Indians were tech savvy, most of the uneducated Indians, suspicious of technology, felt it had betrayed them. It was better to use people than risk the white man's methods.

As Balaam approached, he stared first at David, then at Yusuf. He peered back into the forest, then turned and asked a question of one of the gun-toting Zapatistas. They conversed briefly, and the shaman nodded.

He turned his attention to the professor, and David saw his pupils were still enlarged, and the effects of the hallucinogens he ingested were still visible. However, his words weren't slurred or slow.

"I no see *musulman* before."

"Muslims are just like everyone else, Balaam." David felt uneasy. Why was the shaman suddenly concerned about Muslims?

"My son, Marcos, tell me *musulmans* like to kill all Christians. He say they enemy of Christians."

Damn you, Marcos, David cursed. "Not all Muslims are the same, Balaam, just like not all Mayas are Zapatistas. You know?"

The statement seemed to mollify the Bone Man, who turned and looked directly into Yusuf's eyes. He held his stare until the Lebanese academic felt uncomfortable and looked away.

Balaam returned his gaze to David. "I hear black robe from pope country put you in the jail, *Ahua.* My contact in the San Cristobal tell me black robe accuse you steal from a church. That doesn't make sense to me, so I have Marcos me get the truth me.

He bring you friend the priest me."

"Sally's here?" David pointed at the ground.

"Father Salvador Lopez come yesterday. I talk him all night, and he go back jungle. He want work with people." Balaam waved his hand. "You know…. Help talk them their religion and politics?"

Help to talk to them their religion and politics? David wondered. *Is this a good thing? What's the conniving shaman up to now?*

"I really need to talk with him, Balaam. The bishop in Tuxtla has a message for him, and the papal inquisitor wants to ask him some questions. I really wish that you...."

"He doesn't want work bishops and church now, *Ahua*. He is real Christian now and wants work Indians."

David caught Yusuf's eye, but neither spoke.

"I find box with *El Hombre Sagrado*. I find holy man that belong Reyes family many years. A bad man take the body. He rob body and leave in jungle. I find body. I check burial box and find things, like old books you tell me about. I put books in you shed, because you not want talk me. You still mad me because of damn Protestants from Ocosingo that want land back from Tzeltzal Indians. I know black robe think you steal books and put in your shed."

"Thanks for the apology, Balaam."

"I am not apologize. I not no wrong thing. I not want to give you *El Hombre Sagrado,* but I think maybe I can no care for him now Reyes family gone. Reyes family know all about holy man, and they dead, gone. If I give you *El Hombre Sagrado* for black robes in pope country, you me promise that musulmans not have, *Ahua?"*

"You're worried the Muslims might get the body?" David chuckled and smiled at his sometime friend. "Yusuf doesn't want the body, Balaam. Nobody wants a stinking, decomposing body."

Balaam's eyes narrowed, and his small chest and shoulders swelled. *"El Hombre Sagrado* not stink, *Ahua!* He not stink any more than white man, *musulman,* or shit-fuck pig-breath Mexican solider!"

Whoa! David stepped back. The Zapatista guerrillas frowned, and their expression grew hard. David raised his hands and spread his fingers. "OK, Balaam, my friend. Look,

I'm sorry. I didn't mean to offend you. We're just tired. I…. It was poor choice of words."

"You and *musulman* go, *Ahua.* You take *El Hombre Sagrado* to pope man. You not lose him, OK? I have follow you my men make sure you OK. You not worry about Father Salvador Lopez. He is not work church now. He is work Maya now. Marcos and Zapatista help him. We his family now. He tell me tell you *adios.* He like you. Maybe see you sometime else, but I don't think so. No." He turned to walk away.

"What about the body, Balaam? When can I get it? We have to…."

"Body in your truck, *Ahua.* You go tonight before big rain come. My men follow you."

What the hell? The body's been in the back of the Toyota all this time? He wanted to wring the rude little shit's neck.

Frowning, David turned to Yusuf. "Let's go."

"Great idea, David. My comfort level just fell to zero."

As they started the short trek downhill toward their vehicle, Yusuf asked, "Does he always talk like that?"

"He's stoned on mushrooms or water lilies or something. I've seen him so bad he can't even mumble. The effects of whatever he took for the curing ceremony are starting to wear off, or he wouldn't be able to talk at all."

The Zapatistas melted away, some into the forest, others following the Bone Man, who wasn't walking toward town.

David and Yusuf went only a few meters toward a copse of trees near the road when the Bone Man called after them. "*Ahua!* You tell dirt digger gringa with big *chi chis*, tits, that she not to bother Father Salvador. He going have new woman, Zapatista woman." He waggled his finger at them.

David frowned and waved the old shaman off. "Sure, Balaam. I'll tell her." He turned back to Yusuf. "I'm so sick of

271

this. I can't wait to return to Ocosingo and get rid of the body. I have never in my life been involved with something so stupid. I hope the body rots all over Father Gregory and stinks up his house, and that those pious, pathetic dipshits in Rome suffer the embarrassment they deserve."

"Easy, David. I see what you mean. That old man is—what's the English saying?—a piece of work."

"He's a rude, insensitive, overbearing bully who has caused me more trouble than I can count."

"He gave you the body." Yusuf pointed to the truck when it came into view. The box was clearly visible in the bed, and three Indians, two carrying rifles, guarded it.

As they approached, David stopped and turned to Yusuf. "We should have brought nose plugs for the stink and some lime to toss on the corpse. I think we've got napkins in the glove box we can wad and stuff into our noses."

He waved toward the truck. "Let's move before it's dark. Check the glove box and make sure we have all the paperwork Father Gregory sent to help us. We don't want any problems transporting the body."

David greeted the soldiers, but only one acknowledged him. He was surprised to find them standing so close to the truck. The holy man, as Balaam called him, should reek by now.

David stopped at the truck bed while Yusuf entered the passenger side and looked for the paperwork Father Gregory provided. Though it was too dark to discern details, David saw the coffin lid was intact, secured with heavy strapping tape. Even in the near darkness, he saw the outline of Kulkulkan wrapped sinuously around the body.

It looked very familiar. It occurred to him he never had the chance to examine the box in daylight. The lighting in the ruined church was poor, and in the jungle at night there was no light at all. He sniffed the air but didn't smell anything. If the body stank, it was contained by a good seal. There was no way he would open the lid just to view a decomposing corpse.

"I think this is it." Yusuf held aloft a set of papers. "It's hard to tell in this light." He stooped inside the cab to use the dome light.

"Great. Let's go before that nasty man changes his mind." He turned to the Indians. "We're off, Guys. We're leaving now." They didn't reply.

He nodded at them, circled the truck bed, and got behind the wheel. Glancing at the guards once more, he started the engine, and mouthed, *"Adios."*

With a curt wave, he turned the Toyota off the apron of road and onto the rutted dirt path leading to Calvario.

* * *

Fifteen minutes later, they bid Calvario and its one streetlight good-bye. A quick glance in the rearview mirror revealed only dim shadows of small adobe houses with corrugated steel roofs. It would probably take three hours or more to drive back through the same string of small towns.

David yawned and stretched, looking at Yusuf, who read sheaves of paper from the glove box. David's good mood was replaced by ill humor. He wanted to be quit of the whole affair. He wished Father Gregory, the books, and the decomposing body were already on their way to Rome, while David sipped brandy and worked on a crossword puzzle with his wife at the ranch.

Speaking of which, he shouldn't have had so many cups of *balche*. He shouldn't have argued with him. He certainly shouldn't have been involved in the whole mess.

How had the situation spun so badly out of control? Yawning again, he looked at his odometer, calculating distance. The drive would take longer than he thought.

He glanced through the door window, but the darkness revealed little. Fleeting shadows and vaporous wraiths fled by as he drove. Tall trees of ceiba, mahogany, and pine stood like silent sentinels near the roadway. Brush and exuberant plants encroached the road's edge, trying to reclaim what was theirs before the highway was built. That area of Chiapas had been impossible to travel through before the rebellion of 1994. That would change with the new military base under construction near Taniperlas and an asphalt road nearly finished in the north.

David and Yusuf traveled an insignificant valley trail in the middle of the mountainous Lacandon jungle to a poorly maintained gravel road. Fortunately, he had a new truck. Having vehicle trouble out here would be a disaster.

He looked at his speedometer and slowed a bit. There was no reason to push their luck. He took a deep breath and sighed, trying to expel his fatigue. They had several long hours ahead, but, with some good luck, he'd be home in his bed the following night, and Dr. Bin Saud would be on a plane to Lebanon.

CHAPTER TWENTY-EIGHT

Father Salvador Lopez, lying in his bedroll inside a polyester tent, closed his eyes, listening to the cries and chirps of jungle birds. The odor of beans, tortillas, and overripe fruit tantalized him. Hungry, he was ready to embrace the new day, anxious to begin his new life among the poor Indians of Chiapas and Guatemala.

Perhaps he should say mass. He hadn't said mass in over two weeks, and the thought of engaging the sacred ritual given by Jesus to mankind created an inner glow and brought a smile to his face.

The previous day, he met an unusual man named Balaam Reyes, while Marcos huddled with other Indian leaders. Balaam had been kind, earnest, and spoke with passion of the Indians' plight. Poverty, ignorance, and disease were their inheritance after 500 years of occupation by the white men. They owned nothing and were prevented from having a voice in their own affairs. Their culture changed little in several hundred years. They were guided by tradition and custom, but their way of life was threatened. Rapacious loggers, powerful landowners, and duplicitous politicians threatened the Indians' existence.

Multinational corporations wanted the incredibly rich resources of Chiapas, and technology and communications brought drugs, strange music, and obscene clothing to traditional, remote villages, encouraging the young people to feel ashamed of their families and to worship those false gods.

Upon listening to such heartfelt thought, Father Lopez knew he made the right decision. Balaam promised unquestioning support and security, including food, clothing, or anything else he needed. Salvador was a priest, and the Maya respected holy men. Father Lopez must help the Indians and encourage them to organize and oppose the powerful thieves in Mexico City and Guatemala City. The Maya must reclaim their land.

Father Lopez must demonstrate to them that this action was blessed by God, reminding them that Jesus spoke directly to people like them. The shaman talked for nearly thirty minutes without stopping while Father Lopez listened, wishing he could deliver such a sincere, moving ceremony. Then he realized he would have the chance soon. He agreed with Balaam's message. He wanted the mission. It was God's work as explained by Jesus in the New Testament.

Before taking his leave to meet with Marcos, the Bone Man reached into the canvas sack he always carried and took out a cup.

"Here, Father Lopez." He offered Salvador a rudely wrought ceramic. "I know you know *El Hombre Sagrado,* holy man family Reyes. This his cup. You remember snake man on burial box with cup in hand give people? This cup belonged that man. He painted onto walls old cities Maya. He at Yaxchilan and Bonompak. He on wall Xibalba cave your friend *Ahua* David.

"This be holy cup, old cup used by powerful priest a thousand years past when God like people Maya the first. That man a priest and a king. My people call him Kulkulkan, the Feathered Serpent. Family Reyes take good care *El Hombre Sagrado* many generations, but they dead now. I giving you this cup, because I want you know holy man and because you must know that holy man had great power."

Father Lopez accepted the cup. He needed a cup for mass and hadn't brought his mass kit from Tuxtla Gutierrez, just a small Bible. He didn't care if the cup wasn't gold and shiny. If it made Balaam happy to entrust a relic into his care, Salvador was willing to accommodate.

He had to rise and go into the world, imbued with joy and a sense of expectation absent since his ordination ten years earlier. He rose from his bedroll, yawned, and stretched. A howler monkey issued the first challenging cry of the morning, warning others that he claimed his territory.

Sally stepped into the daylight to be greeted by three women cooking and joking with the Zapatista men who milled about. Marcos wasn't there, and his bedroll was vacant.

What better way to begin his mission than by celebrating God's gift to mankind? A short mass would be the best-possible start to a day, any day. He borrowed a tortilla from the ladies, who fussed and made much of such a simple request. He thanked them and went to the side near his tent, where a small aluminum stand supported a gas lantern.

He cleared it, placed a canteen of water, the tortilla, and his small Bible on the small table's top. He prayed quickly, intoning the liturgy and ritual from memory. It seemed a specially blessed day, and he was so taken with the moment that he failed to see everyone—soldiers, cooks, and workers—stopped what they did to watch or participate.

Looking up, he felt a thrill run through him at their earnestness. Mass was meant to be shared. That was its purpose. He had only canteen water and one tortilla, but that didn't matter. He would break it into small pieces as Jesus did with the loaves and fishes. Size was meaningless. God didn't care if the poor didn't have wine.

He filled the cup with water and quietly intoned the familiar prayer over the water and tortilla, asking God to share His spiritual essence with all present. He partook first, then he offered the cup and a small piece of tortilla to each worker. They fell in line quickly, eager to participate. Usually sacred wine wasn't offered to those who attended mass, just the sacred wafer as the body of Christ. The additional sharing of the cup felt right and good.

The sharing lasted only two minutes, during which time Father Salvador felt cloaked in a shroud of peace and healing. He felt as if he were leading mass for the first time among those whom he wished to celebrate it most. He would always remember that moment, and he thanked God for the gift and those people. He prayed, completed his ablutions, and blessed all present, thanking them for sharing with him.

Five minutes later, he was in the midst of plain, delicious food, hot coffee, and smiling people. A few of the Zapatista men came over to try out their Spanish. He understood most and encouraged them to continue, realizing he crossed a barrier. He acquired a level of respect among them, and they demonstrated their trust and acceptance. It was a humbling moment, and he felt very grateful.

The morning passed with Sally doing little but attempting to converse and become acquainted with the people among whom he would travel and share his life.

* * *

Marcos, appearing from the forest at midday, hailed Father Lopez from a distance. He stopped to talk when mobbed by the soldiers and camp followers. A quiet but intense conversation ensued, dominated by the women and one of the older Zapatista soldiers.

One woman pointed at Father Lopez. Marcos listened, looked intently at Salvador before asking questions. Two of the women buried their heads in their hands, and the man seemed on the verge of tears.

Salvador became worried. Had he unknowingly breached a custom or offended one of the young women?

After a few minutes, Marcos walked away from the group, leaving the three women and the man smiling.

Oh, well, Sally thought. Though they were obviously talking about him, he felt no trepidation. They treated him well all morning, and he was more curious than worried. Most of the Indians spoke no Spanish, so Salvador imagined they were sharing details of the morning in dialect with Marcos.

The dark-faced, strong man walked toward Father Lopez and removed his hat before approaching. "I see you've made a big impression already." He extended his hand in greeting and smiled as they shook.

"Really? Through incompetence or my miserable efforts to try to speak their language?"

"Father Lopez…." He turned and pointed at the group.

"That family is from the shaking village."

"The what?"

"The shaking village—Benediciones, a small Indian community near Realidad. Many of the people there have the shaking disease. You know, palsy? They tremble uncontrollably. Corporations and the Mexican government used the upstream area as a chemical dump for almost fifty years, and the people in the village are sick. They have lots of cancer and birth defects.

The mother and daughter come from that village."

"How sad." Salvador was upset. "That's exactly the kind of behavior we must fight. We have to stop that sort of thing. We must organize them to fight the government and businesses that do it. It's called environmental racism, and it's responsible for…."

Marcos stopped the angry diatribe with a raised hand. "Yes and no, Father. You don't understand. That mother and daughter and those people I just spoke to," he pointed at them, "they say they are cured. They don't have the shakes anymore. They were cured after receiving the body and blood of Jesus Christ from you this morning."

* * *

Father Gregory hung up the phone. It was evening in Rome, but his call was expected, even greatly anticipated. He knew his return was quietly being heralded among the movers and shakers in the Holly See, perhaps even by the Holy Father himself.

Mexico wasn't so backward after all. He was treated very well and given access to every available resource. The telephone service was good, and his beds were comfortable. He couldn't say that about many of the places to which he was sent to investigate miracles. The conditions and technology in many

African and South American countries was best described as primitive. With the exception of having to deal with that wretched atheist, David Wolf, and his posturing brother-in-law, Father Gregory enjoyed his stay in Mexico.

It was the big day. Dr. Wolf called late last night from headquarters at the Ocosingo *Policia* to notify him that the body was in the Toyota truck, which was safely lodged at the *policia's* garage.

Father Gregory glanced at his watch. It was time to pick up Inspector Leyeva at the Hotel Palenque. They would meet Dr. Wolf and his Muslim friend at the garage to view the box and body.

Father Gregory, nearly overcome with anticipation, would transport the body and books back over the jungle-clad

Lacandon Sierras to San Cristobal, then on to the Tuxtla Gutierrez airport, where he would catch a nine o'clock evening flight to Rome. He already said good-bye to Bishop Alvarez in Tuxtla and extended the gratitude of several very-important people in the Vatican to the bishop.

Inside his valise on the coffee table were the books and necklace sporting a Star of David and a shepherd's crook. The necklace was purportedly on the body when Wolf last saw it at the ruin. The papal inquisitor felt an intuition that the corpse would prove as unique as the papyrus books, decomposed or not. Regardless, they were all part of the same investigation. He must view the evidence and the setting in which the events take place in their entirely, not focus on individual aspects.

* * *

Half an hour later, they stood in the *policia* garage near the Toyota truck. David and Yusuf arrived, looking tired and disgruntled. The professor's hair was uncombed, and it had more gray than before. Bags showed under his swollen, dark eyes. No doubt he was ready to return to San Cristobal before the usual series of thunderstorms passed through the sierras in late afternoon.

Inspector Leyeva removed the heavy strapping tape that held the cover of the box, which sat on the floor. Father Gregory walked around the mahogany rectangle, admiring the handcarved art and painted coiling snakes and glyphs. As a trained anthropologist, he decided immediately that the snake was Quetzalcoatl, the feathered serpent of Mexican Indian lore. In this particular case, it would be Kulkulkan, the Mayan version of the same creature.

According to legend, Quetzalcoatl was a very well-known Toltec king who unfortunately shamed himself by getting drunk and having sex with his sister. To atone for that evil, he abdicated his throne, left his people, and went east over the great water, promising to return someday in triumph. The legend was so important and pervasive in Mexico that the overly religious ruler of the Aztecs, Moctezuma, mistakenly believed that the conquistador Cortez was the returning Quetzalcoatl. Rather than destroy him and his small army, the Aztec king welcomed the Spaniard and his soldiers into Tenochtitlan—a very big mistake.

"Look familiar, Professor?" he asked.

"It's Kulkulkan," Dr. Wolf said. "You're an archeologist. You know what it is." He circled the box, too, pursing his lips. He stopped to trace the snake's coils with his hand, then paused and touched the outline of the creature's body before it wound around the box.

Father Gregory thought it odd that he detected no odor, but he and the others readily accepted handkerchiefs sprinkled with disinfectants from Inspector Leyeva. The papal inquisitor smiled grimly, holding his handkerchief to his nose as did David and Yusuf, watching Colonel Leyeva lift the lid and place it beside the coffin.

In the light of the flickering fluorescent bulb overhead, they saw a body clad in white pants, crude sandals, and the cotton work shirt of a typical Mayan Indian. A black arm band, the sign of the Zapatista, was tied around his left arm.

In silence, they eyed the corpse's condition.

Finally, Father Gregory looked at David. "He looks too good to me, Professor. He looks like…."

"…he just died an hour ago. This is truly amazing. It is…."

"…a miracle." The papal inquisitor trembled at the importance of the knowledge. "You're positive this is the

282

same body you saw in the ruined church over two weeks ago?"

David looked from Father Gregory to Yusuf. "Yes, I'm sure. The clothes are different, but I always remember faces. I can't explain its condition, but yes, this is the body."

Yusuf's breath caught, and he held a hand to his mouth, staring at the body as if mesmerized.

Colonel Leyeva slumped and dropped to his knees, crossing himself. Father Gregory knelt beside him, placing an arm over the *federale's* shoulders as he began a whispered prayer. David and Yusuf watched awkwardly, knowing they were in the presence of something extraordinary but not knowing how to react.

David shifted his weight to the other foot, glanced again at Yusuf, and looked into the box.

"Time for you to go, Professor." Father Gregory rose from his knees and helped the colonel stand. "You and I are done. You and your Muslim friend should return to San Cristobal immediately. Leave the Toyota at the Alamo rental return. It's been paid for."

He looked at Yusuf. "I've been instructed to ask that you not attempt to publish your translations. You know they can't be examined for accuracy without the original documents being available. You would bring embarrassment and shame to yourself and your career if you tried."

"I really think you should reconsider, Father Gregory," Yusuf replied. "These documents belong to all of us. Hiding them in a Vatican archive is unethical and sinful."

"Unethical? Sinful? You lecture me on ethics and sin? One of you is an atheist, the other a Muslim. Please, Gentlemen, get out." He pointed at the gaping garage door. "Get in that truck and go. I'm sorry we must part in this manner, but I have no time to argue with scientists."

"Science is the way of God," David said angrily.

"No, Professor. Science can't explain the ultimate causation, and you know it. It can explain proximate cause and effect, but it can never satisfactorily explain how the universe came into being. The Big Bang, which all scientists believe, tells us nothing of the original material from which the universe came. The basic laws of physics tell us that something can't come from nothing. Matter and energy came together to form the universe, and matter can't be created or destroyed. It just changes form. Only the First Physicist, God, can explain the universe."

"You don't really understand how science works, Father Gregory."

"And you don't understand that science is just another kind of faith, an inadequate and erroneous one, I might add."

"He said to go, and I want you to go, too," Colonel Leyeva said, moving his jacket aside to expose his firearm. "Neither of you is welcome here. Return the truck and go home, especially you." He pointed at Yusuf. "God has more patience with Muslims than I do."

* * *

David and Yusuf talked a long time as they drove up and over the lush, green mountains and forest toward San Cristobal. It was clouding up again, and wind gusted. The stormy mountain breezes were difficult to predict, because they were capricious and gusted strongly without warning. Although David drove that road countless times, he knew he couldn't relax when behind the wheel. It was a steep, winding, very dangerous highway. One lane hugged the mountainside, and the other sometimes went for miles without any safety railing.

The view over the edge was breathtaking but distracting. A careless driver could easily slide off and plunge several thousand feet to his death. Concentration was imperative if someone wanted to reach his destination. If was unlikely anyone would find a missing car and driver for a long time.

Yusuf didn't know if he should attempt to publish. Perhaps he could contact the Vatican and request an audience with someone in authority who understood the importance of the books. David nodded encouragingly at the idea, but he knew it wasn't likely. The papal inquisitor made it clear that no one would take Yusuf seriously. Though David had photographs of the three scrolls, someone would immediately claim they were frauds.

Both men were tired, and their fatigued minds found no solutions. Perhaps an idea would come to them later.

They speculated how the body remained in such perfect condition, because they certainly didn't believe in miracles.

"There must be a reasonable explanation," David said.

"I agree."

Still, nothing satisfactory occurred to them.

Finally, with nothing more left to discuss, they fell silent. Yusuf thought of his family in Lebanon, while David thought of Alexandra and his home in San Cristobal. He wondered how Karen was doing at the Xibalba site and whatever happened to Sally.

What's he up to now? David wondered. *Why didn't he meet me in Calvario?*

Though he hoped all was well with Sally, he strongly suspected he'd been drawn into the Bone Man's web of intrigue and endless plotting. Balaam warned everyone had to leave the priest alone, including Karen. He mentioned something about Sally finding a good Zapatista woman.

That certainly conjured interesting images. David couldn't imagine what kind of agreement the Bone Man used to entice Father Lopez. Finally, he tired of speculating. He had no way to contact Salvador. Unless the priest decided to leave the jungle and his misguided mission, there was little anyone could do to help him.

Maybe he didn't need help. David had enough problems without becoming more involved with the Bone Man's schemes.

Good luck, Sally, David thought. *I hope it's what you were looking for.*

* * *

"It's been a long day, Father Gregory." Colonel Leyeva sighed and relaxed slightly. They were exiting the steepest part of the mountain range, moving rapidly down the highway into San Cristobal de las Casas. Dark clouds with bulbous, roiling pouches of moisture hung heavily, threatening a huge thunderstorm approaching from the west. "It's too bad we got a late start, but I'll get you there in plenty of time."

"I'm confident you will. It doesn't matter if I'm a little late. I just want to make sure we have ample time to load the box and have everything taken care of. There's much at stake."

"I called the office in Tuxtla before we left Ocosingo. I've been assured that we're expected, and there will be no problems with Customs. You'll be in Rome in time for breakfast, Father."

"Thank you. Your help has been invaluable. I'll be writing a letter to your supervisor commending you for your help. I couldn't have done this without you. You're a good man and a good Christian."

The *federale* smiled his appreciation but didn't reply. The storm looked twenty kilometers away, with forked lightning lashing out from the backlit, tumbling, gray-black mass that moved inexorably toward the mountain range they spent the last three hours negotiating.

"Are you sure you don't mind riding in the rain, Father? Do you want to pull over for a while in San Cristobal?"

"Not unless you insist, Colonel. I trust you. You know the roads and weather. Just drive carefully. I really can't miss my flight." Glancing at the valise in his lap, he pulled it tightly against his chest. "It's strange. Now that I finally have everything I came for, I'm worried I might lose it."

"Not a chance."

"I know. It was just a thought. Let's drive through San Cristobal without stopping. I've seen all of David Wolf's town I want to see for this lifetime."

They drove on, circling the old colonial city and heading down the mountain toward the lowlands where Tuxtla

Gutierrez lay. The sheer cliff face dropped several thousand feet in places, and the winding road was as treacherous as the one they just traveled. Guardrails were absent. They were in the outside lane, the one nearest the cliffs only a few feet away.

The storm arrived sooner than expected, whipping the road with gusting winds and sheets of driving rain. Lightning cracked, and thunder roared, shaking the mountain and nudging the Toyota. At such a high altitude, they felt as if they were drifting into the bowels of the tempest. Visibility was almost zero.

"This is terrible. Maybe we should stop." Father Gregory's voice cracked.

"I'd like to, Father, but this isn't a good place. We need to find a safe spot up ahead to pull off."

Rounding the next curve, they found a stalled truck in their lane. Driving to the side, they stopped momentarily. Father Gregory rolled down his window, so the *federale* could speak to the truck driver.

The driver couldn't move his vehicle. The rain caused a rockslide to cover the highway, and he struck a small boulder, which cracked his oil pan and leaked oil all over the road. The weather was impossible, anyway, and there was little that could be done.

Colonel Leyeva and Father Gregory were in danger of arriving late, so they drove carefully around the truck and down the road to the next curve. The narrow highway was very steep, and the Toyota slid and wallowed, having difficulty finding traction. The sky grew darker as the center of the storm arrived.

Father Gregory gripped his valise in one hand and held onto the dashboard. He glanced hurriedly at the inspector.

"It's the oil on the highway, Father," Leyeva apologized. "We'll be OK. I just need to get around the next curve, and I can pull off on the other side."

Just as they negotiated the curve, a large Dina truck rounded the corner with its high beams on. The truck was lit up like a Christmas tree, with colorful outside lights on the cab and grille, which featured a large picture of the Virgin of Guadalupe.

It occupied the middle of the road, almost forcing the Toyota to the edge of the cliff. Both men cried out in alarm, and Colonel Leyeva cursed, jerking the wheel right and quickly left to stabilize the skidding Toyota.

The truck missed them by a hair, but they slid in oil from the stalled truck above. As they neared the next curve, Colonel Leyeva turned the wheel left to cross the opposite lane and park on the inside shoulder.

Just as he crossed the centerline, a black Ford Expedition with nothing but its fog lights on barreled around the corner and hit them. The Toyota spun completely around, throwing the box from the truck bed before stopping with its front end teetering over the cliff face. It stalled there for a moment, the dropped nose first, plummeting 2,000 feet to the canyon bottom and exploding in a ball of fire.

* * *

"Jesus Malverde," Luis muttered, jumping from his car and attempting to jog back down the road to where he struck the small pickup. The road was unnaturally slick, and he could barely see or stand, as wind and rain buffeted him nearly to the road's edge.

It was crazy. What the hell was that truck doing crossing the road in the middle of a storm? He steeled himself, bent over with his hand shielding his face from the rain, and carefully moved toward the roadside.

"*Chingada!* Fuck!" he cursed. "Only *cabrones* and fools drive this road in the rain."

A small fire blazed far below at the base of the cliff.

Damn it, anyway, he thought.

Looking around, he saw nothing. A few headlights were visible down below as drivers inched up the mountain road. There was nothing he could do. He carried a load of meth in a false floor under the Ford Expedition's back seats. He had places to go and people to meet. It was clear whoever was driving that truck was dead.

He walked uphill to his car and got in, reaching for a hand towel he kept in the glove box to dry his face. *"Chingada.* What bad luck I have."

The sicario stroked the Santa Muerte on his muscular forearm and Jesus Malverde on the other. Starting the engine, he looked once in his rearview mirror and slowly pulled back onto the road, driving more slowly.

Luis cursed thunderstorms, wind, and stupid drivers. He would drop off his load of crystal meth in San Cristobal and head back down the highway to Tuxtla Gutierrez. Cuca was singing that night at the club. He needed a drink after this day's work.

EPILOGUE

One Month Later

A month passed after David's unwanted adventure with Father Salvador Lopez, the Bone Man, Dr. Bin Saud, and Father Gregory, the Vatican's papal inquisitor. He was back at work, though memories of the ordeal lingered.

He was stunned to learn that Father Gregory and his *federal* confederate met their deaths in a storm driving down the old mountain road from San Cristobal to Tuxtla Gutierrez. David hated that dangerous ribbon of highway and barely escaped disaster several times when confronted by trucks or buses driven by aggressive, macho men. A new, safer four-lane was under construction but wasn't yet finished.

Although he had no love for the papal inquisitor and his methods, the priest's death was a tragedy. Someone somewhere would miss him badly. The loss of the body and box, and, most assuredly, the ancient manuscripts, was a catastrophe.

Yusuf, completely distraught over the whole affair, boarded a plane to return to Lebanon two days after the accident. The night before he left, he proposed that the body could be the remains of the Apostle Thomas, citing the papyrus manuscripts and their contents, the body's original clothing, and the accompanying artifacts as proof. No one would ever know, because so much was lost in that terrible accident.

David returned to Xibalba to assist Karen. He spent the second day at the site photographing the southern wall in the cave's main room where the altar, skulls, and much evidence of ritual activity for hundreds of years had been unearthed. Many of the paintings and glyphs were marred and blurred by natural cave processes, but he took a closer look and realized the Kulkulkan painting wasn't as he remembered. Perhaps he saw too many representations of the god over the years, but he suddenly saw that the men in front of that particular Feathered Serpent weren't fearful captives. Instead, they knelt with their eyes reverently cast down, waiting to receive something from Kulkulkan.

He realized that the Feathered Serpent's hands didn't hold a scepter of office or a sword. They held a cup extended in offering to the kneeling Mayans. That wasn't a typical scene commemorating warfare or human sacrifice. The image demonstrated distinct, familiar religious symbolism and was hauntingly similar to that on *El Hombre Sagrado's* coffin.

Although the old man was under the influence of hallucinogens at the time, David recalled that the Bone Man said he gave Sally a cup that the shaman found in the coffin. No one had been able to contact or find the priest, because he was being protected by the Indians, primarily the Zapatistas. The governments of both countries were alarmed at the unusual turn of events, but they were helpless when trying to locate a mysterious religious figure who performed miracles and incited the Indians to demand their rights and the return of their lands.

So far, all efforts to find and capture the radical religious figure failed. The close-mouthed Indians refused to provide information concerning his whereabouts. They were protecting him. He was theirs, a religious man who performed miracles, a modern-day Feathered Serpent, the Holy Man returned from the east as promised to heal and unite the Maya.

After a week on the site, David began hearing stories from the Indian workers. He listened to tales of religious services resembling Catholic masses being held in the jungle on both sides of the Usumacinta River that were attended by thousands of Indians. Whole villages hidden in the sierras and jungles in nearly impossible-to-reach locations were moving, seeking the Holy Man in the jungle, who was perhaps a renegade priest and who held a magic cup that healed the sick.

It was disturbing, and David felt very strongly that Sally was the mysterious religious figure, and the cup might be the source of the miracle healings. That meant Sally had fallen under the influence of that damnable Balaam Reyes, who enticed him with promises of the perfect religious vocation, working among those who were most in need.

At night on the dig, David lay in his tent and speculated. *Was Yusuf right?* he wondered. *Was the incorruptible body that of St. Thomas? Were the paintings and glyphs of the Feathered Serpent in the cave and on* El Hombre Sagrado's *burial box accurate records of events that occurred 2,000 years ago in Mexico? How and why had St. Thomas traversed an ocean to get here?*

Perhaps the most-outrageous question of all concerned the cup. Was the cup taken from the burial box by the Bone Man and given to Father Lopez the Holy Grail, the mythical cup of the Last Supper? Would anyone ever know?

David lost his faith many years earlier as a student of anthropology. He quietly but resolutely lived his life in the best manner he knew, recognizing that all people benefitted from the moral laws and expectations of the Bible.

He didn't believe in the magic and miracles ascribed to the main players, though. Like most anthropologists, he saw those as credentials that were added to provide validity and proof of someone's divinity. All the world's great religions required its followers to suspend the evidence of their senses in lieu of faith. Virgin births, magical healings, and messages from visions were indistinguishable from hallucinations and were standard fare for all religions. All students of anthropology and archeology knew it. It was all academic, wasn't it?

Or was it? It was vexing enough to turn a man's liver yellow and send him to his knees.

* * *

Cardinal Nizzi sat alone in an overstuffed chair in the curia, pondering his next move. The unexpected death of his friend and colleague shook him to the core. He hunkered down in his chair. No platitude could contain his despair in the face of the catastrophic events. Like many rooms in the Vatican, that one contained old, ornate artifacts the Catholic Church acquired over 2,000 years. On an ancient Oriental carpet in front of him lay the shattered remains of the box from Mexico.

It was late morning, and he had a lot to do that day, yet he found himself sitting and staring at the coffin. He decided it was beautiful but primitive. Perhaps it was the home of the blessed Saint Thomas, before he was flung over a cliff and immolated in an ignominious, fiery blaze. It was a tragedy for Father Gregory and the Catholic Church. How could an event that promised to be such a source of celebration and triumph turn to defeat and disaster? Had evil triumphed over good? Why had God not intervened to ensure the success of His church and its mission? Was it the books and their content?

Cardinal Nizzi read the manuscripts faxed by Father Gregory from the parish in Tuxtla Gutierrez and found them as surprising as they were enticing. He knew some would view those contents as a dire threat and demand they be destroyed or withheld from the public forever.

What of the other texts, the five or six remaining books that vanished in that shocking accident? Was it part of a divine plan that the books be lost in such an appalling event? Will I ever know the rest of the story, or will I merely remain tantalized by the knowledge that it had been written? Why is this particular fate so personal and devastating? Is the Church being punished or protected?

It was very humbling. He had to contact the Muslim academic, Yusuf Bin Saud, and try to reach an agreement with him. With the destruction of the originals, Cardinal Nizzi was reduced to bargaining with a Muslim and an atheist. The Mexican archeologist, Professor David Wolf, of whom Father Gregory spoke so poorly, reportedly had photographs of the three manuscripts he faxed to Dr. Saud. Father Gregory jailed and punished Dr. Wolf for his involvement in the affair. Could he be convinced to share his information?

Even more disturbing were the reports from Guatemala and southern Mexico. One of their own priests had gone rogue and taken up with radical elements in the Zapatista conflict. According to the bishop, Father Lopez deserted his vocation for a woman's bed, an archeologist employed by the same Dr. Wolf who had photographs of the manuscripts.

Then Father Lopez deserted the woman and disappeared into the mountainous jungles of Latin America. The errant priest's behavior would normally be a diocesan issue, not necessarily so rare. What was troubling, though, were the stories emerging from that inaccessible place into which the priest disappeared. All told of miracles and a magic cup that healed all who drank from it. Miracles were the business of the Congregation for the Protection of the Faith, Cardinal

Nizzi's office, and he would be asked to investigate the matter.

As he pondered the matter at length, he decided the reports of miracles were simply an extension of the unresolved issue regarding the body and books. The miracle of St. Thomas alone, if it were true, would have shaken the Vatican to its foundation. Suddenly, a miraculous cup that healed was added to the mix. If the cup could be traced to the incorruptible body and burial box, the implications were astounding.

Although the task hadn't yet been assigned to him, he wondered if the cup could be the Holy Grail, the long-lost vessel Jesus used at the Last Supper to teach his disciples how all could share in the body and blood of Christ.

It couldn't be true! It defied comprehension.

Journeying into a primitive area of virtually uncharted jungle and mountains spanning two countries to find someone who didn't want to be found would be the most-difficult task his office had ever undertaken, and the most important. He couldn't afford to fail.

Cardinal Nizzi stood to leave. He would go to the Pauline Chapel, his personal favorite in the Vatican. Its beautiful, marbled walls with large paintings of Biblical scenes extending beyond the altar under a spectacular lattice of white marble, with a domed ceiling featuring scenes of the Resurrection, always brought respite from the stress of his duties.

He walked down the aisle and knelt in a wood pew under a large painting of Jesus being nailed to the cross as someone dug the hole in which the cross would be placed. Cardinal Nizzi needed guidance and thought the scene to be particularly suitable to his state of mind.

He began with a prayer of penitence, then out of habit, he reached for his rosary and began reciting the first decade of prayers.

"Hail Mary full of Grace…the Lord is with…."

* * *

"Quickly. Hurry!" The Bone Man pointed up the hill to a cave opening that was cleared of brush and rubble. Dark thunderheads boiled in a leaden sky, and the wind gusted strongly, whipping and bending the forest canopy.

His crew of six Zapatista Indians labored mightily to carry a body up the rubble-strewn hillside without dropping it. Balaam hadn't visited the place in twenty years, but he remembered the spacious, dry interior of the ancient tomb. In nearly pristine condition, beautifully colored glyphs and pictures of great rulers and warriors lined the walls.

One day, he knew, white men would find that place, but not until long after he died. *El Parque Natural de Monte Azules* was a huge wildlife reserve with few roads. Much of it was still unexplored, the big expanses nearly inaccessible. It was a special place known only to a handful of Lacandon Indians who lived in the lowlands east of the great mountain range. As a young man, Balaam's mentor guided him to it.

Thirty minutes later, he shooed his men from the cave, keeping a torch for himself to take one last look around. A stone altar of grinning skulls, some with missing jawbones, lay to his right. Below them were empty bottles of liquor, indigestible remains of food packages, and scattered streaks and ridges of gray ash, the remnants of copal incense burned to send prayers into the spiritual ether of the supernatural.

The burden of the ages weighed heavily on his shoulders, but it was a comfortable fit. The Bone Man felt at ease in the ancient tomb, surrounded by the remains of great kings and leaders. He knew the souls of great men and women never left their home, and he felt their presence here and in the forest when he passed through the area.

He took a final look at *El Hombre Sagrado* where he'd been placed on a rock ledge near the altar. Dressed as an Indian peasant and still sporting a black armband, he appeared serene and lifelike, unperturbed and uncaring, his spirit dormant and waiting for purpose in being.

"You nothing but trouble," the old shaman chastised. "You not help nothing now. But you fine here. These men your friend. I give your cup to good black robe. Priest man with soul who know the spirit is need good works and belief in poor people. He be new *Hombre Sagrado*. Your time much passed. You be happy with him. He help good people of the forest."

He turned to go, then hesitated and said, "I be back soon. We need talk of cup. I think pope man send others steal back cup. Cup not for fancy black-robe priests. It for poor and sick."

* * *

Father Salvador Lopez knelt by a small, portable altar in his tent somewhere in the Lacandon jungle. He rehearsed the themes of the upcoming sermon he must deliver soon, but his mind kept slipping to thoughts of *Life just keeps getting better.*

It was very humbling. He did little to deserve the wonderful circumstance in which he found himself. Gone was his fixation on the conflict between faith in God and analytic reasoning. He felt deep in his bones that the three burning questions everyone faced, *How did I get here? What am I supposed to do while I'm here?* and *What happens to me after I die?* had been answered.

298

The answer was to keep the mind calm and allow the spirit to soar. It was so effortless these days. God's love was a font of spiritual fire that buoyed the spirit and strengthened the will. It gave purpose to neglect and intensity to resolve. It allowed clear thinking and empowered courageous acts of will. It allowed anyone to surmount life's disappointments and to vanquish the outrages of the powerful who exploited everyone else.

The past two months were a whirlwind of activity, moving from one location to another. He went where directed by his Zapatista handlers. He trusted them implicitly to protect and care for him while leading him to those most in need. He'd been steered into the mountainous jungles of Guatemala on three different occasions and held at least two masses a week in remote areas of the highland Lacandon Jungle.

The crowds grew as word of the cup's healing power was whispered among the faithful, spreading like fire through a parched forest in need of respite. The power of faith remained triumphant. Belief nourished the soul, and prayer fueled the engine of God. The cup was a vessel that expressed God's love, a gift to those who needed it most. Salvador remained astonished that he was chosen to assist in this great work. He knew that the momentous events and miraculous healings that occurred at each mass gathering had little or nothing to do with him. He was just a purveyor of God's graces.

Marcos told him earlier that today's mass would be the largest gathering of Indians in the Lacandon since ancient times. Word of the impending religious service spread through hamlets and villages in the mountainous jungle like a fierce wind stoked by God's breath. How they would accommodate so many was worrisome, but Salvador let those concerns pass, trusting in God and the efforts of his Zapatista brothers to ensure all went well.

A larger worry simmered in the back of his mind. He pieced together the story of *El Hombre Sagrado*, the miraculous body that remained uncorrupted for hundreds, perhaps thousands, of years. The ancient manuscripts and cup came from the Holy

Man, who Sally believed was the Apostle Thomas. He also felt the cup was the Holy Grail of lore and literature, the most coveted artifact in the Christian world.

It was unbelievable that the story of the cup and its many miracles would find unsympathetic ears in places far and near, in Houses of Parliament and in Vatican councils. Dismay and outrage would be voiced. All would covet the cup, but especially those who found fault with the one who possessed it, believing it should be taken from undeserving Indians who couldn't understand its true value.

The cup would be feared by those who didn't have it, and its worth would be denied. They would say it was being misused or defiled, that it could only be protected and wielded by those strong and spiritually worthy who possessed true knowledge and wisdom. A common, renegade Catholic priest didn't fit those criteria.

That, he knew, was why they moved constantly, usually at night and always to remote areas without road access, reached only by jungle paths known to the Indians who traversed the area of southern Mexico and Guatemala for thousands of years.

They must accomplish much in a short time before the battle for control of the cup began. The Catholic Church would see his teachings as heresy, while the state would call them seditious. It was likely he would lose his life in the coming conflict, but he was resolved to see his mission through to the end, whatever that end might be. He believed all things and events had purpose, and he was part of such a purpose.

Meanwhile, it was time to go to work. He reached for the shoulder strap of the plain, gray woolen sack that held the cup and his Bible. Placing it on his shoulder, he walked from his tent toward the open valley floor deep within the forest that shielded him from the masses. His attendant, the young girl who was healed by the cup at his first mass at the Xibalba site, smiled a greeting and took his hand. She was pregnant with his child, and that knowledge brought him greater joy than he could express. She was always with him, unselfishly serving and caring for him in ways he never dreamed possible.

They were joined by an entourage of ten more Zapatistas who formed a wedge to part the crowd. As he became visible, the raucous din of loud voices and crying children dropped to a murmur, then a whisper. People craned their necks to see *El Hombre Sagrado,* bearer of the holy cup. His pulpit would be a hill in the midst of the valley. The sick and infirm had already been led there, and they lay about the area, tended by others.

Not all would be healed, but everyone would be offered an opportunity to partake of the Holy Blood of Christ.

Father Lopez smiled and stood on his earthen pulpit, surveying the valley floor that extended 200 meters north and south, an area with a stream running through a normally sere, rocky landscape like a gash in the forested mountainsides surrounding the valley. He had no idea where it was on a map, but that didn't matter. It was the rainy season, and all streams and rivers ran strong and clear through the Lacandon, where they eventually joined the wide Usumacinta River that wound east to the Gulf of Mexico. Dark cumulus clouds hung heavy and oppressive over the valley and surrounding sierras, and the smoke from hundreds of campfires rode capricious thermals high above.

In a strong, clear voice, Salvador thanked everyone for enduring the difficulties of travel to such a remote area to share in God's Grace. He told them he felt sure they would be rewarded. He asked them to join him in prayer and bowed his head, giving thanks for life and health, asking His strength to demand from the rich and greedy that which had been stolen from the Maya.

He paused, taking a deep breath before beginning his sermon. Suddenly, a glory hole opened in the clouds, and a beacon of sunlight burst onto the valley floor in a blaze of righteous splendor. The crowd gasped and moaned in near religious ecstasy, as pent tension escaped the lips of thousands.

Father Lopez stood awed, watching the marvelous sunbeam expand and bathe the entire valley in its brilliant evanescence. *Thank You, God,* he prayed, then looked down at his smiling partner who cupped her pregnant belly protectively while holding prayer beads in her other hand.

Taking a deep breath, he began his sermon, paraphrasing a talk Christ delivered in his famous Sermon on the Mount, a parable that was already 400 years old before He spoke it. The message had been delivered to the Essenes by their Teacher of Righteousness, a leader of a monastic community that hid the Dead Sea scrolls in caves above the monastery, where Bedouin shepherds found them almost 2,000 years later.

"Blessed are the meek, for they shall inherit the earth," he said, choosing his favorite beatitude to begin.

He spoke simply and passionately, telling the Indians that Jesus spoke directly to poor people just like them 2,000 years

302

earlier, and His message was as powerful and meaningful as it had been then. Their land was stolen and must be returned. He praised their resilience in the face of extreme poverty and their unbroken spirit, and he swore God was on their side.

He ended his talk minutes later by asking that everyone present examine their heart to see the truth of his words, which were the same as those Christ spoke many years ago. He paused to survey the immense expanse of humanity that traveled so far for days, most of them on foot. It could take hours, but what else had he to do but offer the cup to whoever wanted to partake?

First, he would offer it to those most in need, the sick and crippled, who were brought forward by family members for healing.

Father Lopez extracted a canteen from the woolen bag at his feet and poured spring water into the cup, then he recapped the canteen and set it aside. No more water would be needed. Regardless of how many partook, God always provided.

Head bowed, he held the cup in both hands and prayed, not a priestly prayer of transubstantiation that converted water and wine to the Blood of Christ, but a simple prayer of gratitude for the myriad gifts of God. No traditional prayers or incantations were needed, only sincere thanks. That he learned by doing.

The sun shone strong, and fresh air gusted through the valley, lifting the spirits of all and promising a renewal of faith. With his Zapatista bodyguard clearing a path, Salvador turned and walked down the hill to the sick and dying who lay at its foot. People of every imaginable age and condition sat on the ground, lay on their backs, or leaned on crutches. Some were held upright by relatives.

He bent, offering the cup to a gnarled, stinking, rheumy eyed old woman covered with sores. She was a beggar with no family and appeared to be nothing more than a hank of hair and a bag of bones, but he smiled as he placed the cup to her lips.

"Bless you, Mother. Please remember that Jesus loves you and that this land belongs to you."

The End

Author's Final Note

Gospel of the Feathered Serpent is a story of my own creation and all errors are mine. Although some may be offended at the notion of the Holy Grail in Latin America, I would like to say that it's no more ridiculous than following the adventures of the Arthurian Knights of the Round Table doing the same in England around 500 A.D. I have long been fascinated with the early years of Christianity. Many anthropologists and religious historians believe that the seminal ideas of Islam, Christianity, Judaism, and Zoroastrianism are ultimately traced back 5-7,000 years to early Babylon, Acadia, Egypt, and Persia - the Fertile Crescent where civilizations first took root. History instructs us that all the major religions of the world contested with established religions and began as cults before becoming mainstream pillars of religious thought in today's societies. The little known history and processes that resulted in Christianity and today's Bible is a fascinating story that can only be inferred and may never be known in its entirety.

In the year 1800 there were 1 billion people on the planet. Today, only 200 years later, over 7.5 billion people, most of them poor beyond our imagination, are searching for a home, employment, food, education and health care. As a handful of high income nations have launched themselves into the 21st century where religious orthodoxy wrestles uncomfortably with science, billions of poor around the world have no access to the economic and social mainstream of society. They also have little or no access to what we take for granted: food, the Internet, technology, communication, equality for women, health care, personal safety and freedom from capricious, corrupt, totalitarian governments. Ideologies, religious and political, continue to place us in extreme opposition to each other while multi-national corporations become the ascendant socioeconomic, political institutions of our time. The complexity of the problem is mind boggling. I always discuss these issues with my students in class, but we ultimately agree that there are no easy solutions, or certainly none that won't offend the rich and powerful.

Although my effort may be inadequate, I wrote *Gospel of the Feathered Serpent* to entertain, while bring attention to the plight of the poor and illustrating what a potentially powerful aid or encumbrance religion can be to society. I have always envied those who are firm in their faith, whether it be science or religion. I'm 69 and the more I study, the more I realize I don't know. My generation and those previous have not done a good job with these matters. Young people today, more so than at any time in mankind's history, live in interesting times.

www.ingramcontent.com/pod-product-compliance
Lightning Source LLC
Chambersburg PA
CBHW071106250626

47159CB00002B/622